ONE NIGHT FORSAKEN

LAKE LAVENDER SERIES

USA TODAY BESTSELLING AUTHOR
PERSEPHONE AUTUMN

BETWEEN WORDS PUBLISHING LLC

ONE NIGHT FORSAKEN

LAKE LAVENDER SERIES

USA TODAY BESTSELLING AUTHOR
PERSEPHONE AUTUMN

BETWEEN WORDS PUBLISHING LLC

One Night Forsaken

Copyright © 2022 by Persephone Autumn

www.persephoneautumn.com

ISBN: 978-1-951477-63-9 (Ebook)

ISBN: 978-1-951477-64-6 (Paperback)

ISBN: (Hardcover)

Editor: Ellie McLove | My Brother's Editor

Proofreader: Rosa Sharon | My Brother's Editor

Cover Design: Abigail Davies | Pink Elephant Designs

BOOKS BY PERSEPHONE AUTUMN

To all the women that bust ass, kick ass, and manage to keep going when you're exhausted. I'm right beside you, cheering you on!

PROLOGUE
ALESSANDRA

Nothing like whirling around in speedy, dizzying circles for two minutes then stumbling to walk in a straight line. The cherry on top… I am not alone in my alcohol-free wobbly walk. Dozens of others walk on unsteady legs with their arms outstretched as they try to find balance. All in the name of fun.

How often do we have festivals in Lake Lavender? At least one per season, if not two. But after this centennial celebration, it wouldn't surprise me if smaller carnivals or jamborees pop up.

I trail behind a couple and warm as I watch them. The way he laces his fingers with hers and strokes her thumb with his. The sporadic giggles as he leans in and kisses beneath her ear or nips at her earlobe. Their obvious love is coveted and adorable.

Deep in my bones, part of me wishes for romance. A love story of my own. For sweet kisses and morning cuddles. Someone to hold my hand and heart. To be my greatest cheerleader but also the one who picks me up when I fall.

In the same breath, I can't picture it. Can't fit these pieces into the busy puzzle I call my life. Love doesn't seem to be in the stars for me. And over time, I have accepted this fact. Or so I keep telling myself.

No romance. Just fun.

Shifting my gaze from the couple, I steer toward the next form of amusement. And for the next fifteen minutes, I wander—and get lost—in the house of mirrors. Exiting, I peer over my shoulder at the tiny building and wonder how the hell I got disoriented in such a confined area. Maybe the inside is bigger than it appears.

After a handful of rides, I aim my feet toward my favorite part of the entire festival. The food tents and trucks. Not only am I eager to try one of everything, but I'm also excited at what ideas the fair foods will give me for Java and Teas Me.

I tug my jacket tighter as I peruse the onslaught of menus. Fried pickles, several types of flavored pretzels, chocolate-covered bacon, fried macaroni and cheese bites, corn fritters, kettle corn, every type of dessert imaginable—deep fried to perfection—and more.

Gah! I want to try one of everything. *Damn, I should've brought a bag.* If I had a bag, I'd fill it then take everything home to gorge in privacy.

As I survey the lines at the nearby tents, I spy a man at the fresh-made churro tent passing out bags to the customers after purchase. "First stop, the churro tent," I mutter to myself as I shuffle toward the line.

I read the long list of flavors as the line inches forward. By the time I reach the vendor, I order three specialty churros. For myself. Although they'd taste best fresh out of the fryer, I plan to do my taste test at home.

Is it weird that I ask the vendor for an extra bag? He cocks a brow, subliminally asking why I need two large paper bags for three churros—which barely take up space in a single bag. I give a sheepish grin and he concedes with a shrug. Maybe he knows the method to my madness.

By the time I reach the last tent—number twenty, hence my need for an extra bag—my arms are weighed down with countless sweet and savory confections. A mountain of fried deliciousness. Enough to last more than a week and make me sick to my stomach just as long.

I couldn't be happier.

When I reach the front of the line, I order the batter-fried corn on the cob and an octopus dog (basically, french fries stuck to a battered hot dog and deep-fried). I shimmy off to the side so others can order while I wait. But when the woman behind the table goes to hand me my order, life shifts into slow motion.

The bag in my hand slips. I lunge forward in the hopes of rescuing it while trying to simultaneously secure my order. It all happens so quick. As I watch the bag fall, the backs of my eyes sting. *What a waste*, I think as I witness this fried food catastrophe. On the cusp of tears, I prepare myself to break down in front of hundreds of festival attendees.

But my tears vanish when I glimpse him. The man crouched inches in front of me, rescuing my bag from certain death.

"Got it," he states as he rights the bag and rises to his full height. His eyes widen as he peers into the sack. "Wow. Did you buy one of everything?" he asks as he hands over my goodies.

"Thank you." I take the bag and add my recent order. "And no. I did order from each tent, though," I add. Heat spreads across my chest and crawls up my neck. I clutch the bags closer, hoping to conceal my flush.

He steps to the side with me, smiling as I fumble to reorganize my bags. As I tuck the corn cob between the fried s'mores and Mexican street tacos, a thought pops in my head.

Should I offer him one of my confections as a thank-you? He did prevent tears. Plus, he lost his spot in line.

"Want to share my octopus dog and fried corn?"

The right side of his mouth kicks up in a half smile. The brow on the same side mimics the action. Heat flushes my skin as my eyes roam his expression. As his brow inches above his black-framed glasses, I notice he has a scar above his eye.

Cute.

"Sure. But maybe we should sit," he suggests then points to a cluster of picnic tables nearby.

He takes one of the bags and we wander toward the table. Every other step, I spy him peeking in the bag and inventorying the goods. He remains quiet, a soft smile tugging at his lips, and follows in my wake.

With the bags on the table, I open the packages from the last tent and inhale. No way any of this is heart healthy. Right now, I don't care. I only eat like this during special occasions—birthdays, milestones, anniversaries, and town celebrations. And there is no shame in eating what you love.

Sharing the hot dog turns out simple after an uneven tear down the middle. The deep-fried corn cob, on the other hand, not so much. Inevitably, we take turns nibbling rows. It's offbeat to be so intimate with a stranger, to feel the whirl of thrill beneath my diaphragm.

And when he looks away, I ogle him more than is appropriate.

"Haven't seen you around town before. Do you live in

Lake Lavender?" The town isn't the smallest of small towns, so it is possible to not know everyone.

He shakes his head and swallows his bite. "No. Just in town for the festival. I live in Seattle."

Out-of-towner and easy on the eyes. *Perfect*.

"They mentioned our small town festival in Seattle?"

"Not sure. I'm a journalist for Washington's Hidden Gems magazine. We're always searching for something new to publish. Fun events and places to see."

Out-of-towner, easy on the eyes, and he travels. Even better. The likelihood of us bumping into each other again is slim. If he is only here for the festival, his chances of returning are minimal.

"Well, I hope you get lots of juicy tidbits while you're here."

He eyes me for a beat and I get lost in the carnival lights reflecting on his lenses. No, not the lights. It's more than the lights. Behind his lenses, I spot something else. Something magnetic and captivating. A hint of his amber irises. Swallowing, I blink a few times and focus on *him*.

"So far, tonight has been the best yet."

Is it the best because of the festival? Or is there another reason? Like me.

Knowing my luck, I misinterpreted him. In general, I read people well. Pick up on words left unsaid. In this instance, my hormones may override my foresight. Just because *I* feel something doesn't mean he does too. Only one way to find out.

"Yeah. Big carnival junkie?"

He subtly shakes his head. "Not so much. Honestly, heights and I aren't the best of friends." He points to the scar hidden behind his glasses.

"What's made it so great then?"

He cocks that right brow again as if I'm being daft. "Maybe it's this blonde I spotted near that tent." He points to the tent where I almost lost my precious fried foods. "She has a killer smile and offered to share her food as repayment for saving her twenty pounds of carnival delights."

When was the last time a man flirted with me? Truly flirted. Most just let on to what they want and the deed gets done. But this man, his flirting... a flush spreads across my skin. I fight to disguise the quiver of my body.

"Yeah, think I saw her. What a klutz. You like her smile?"

He clamps down on his lips, fighting a smile, and nods subtly. "Caught my eye."

"Hmm."

Minutes pass with nothing more than silence and smiles. We finish eating and he tosses the trash in the bin nearby. When he returns, I hoist one of the bags on my hip like a toddler as I reach for the other.

He jogs up and takes the second bag. "Here, let me."

"Thank you."

We head for the car lot and I *feel* his gaze on my backside. Heat rolls up my spine and spreads to my limbs. All without a single touch or word spoken. Our walk is blanketed in silence, but his proximity speaks volumes. Calls out to and beckons me closer.

At the car, I stow the bags in the passenger seat—half tempted to buckle them in—then close the door. I spin to face him and stop short, my breath caught in my chest. I swallow but don't dare move otherwise. Not with his lips right there, mere inches away. They are all I see—that and his tongue as it darts out to moisten his lips.

I want to taste them too.

I push up on my toes and lean into him. Feel the heat of his breath dance over my skin. Smell the sweetness of honey as it spills from his lips. Hear the slight hiccup as he watches me stare at his lips.

Without hesitation, he presses his lips to mine. Soft yet intense. Gentle. Needy. Hungry. His lips caress mine in an all-too-familiar dance. It isn't until a moment later, when his hands grip my hips and drag me closer, that I lose all sense of gravity.

His lips leave mine and trail along my jaw. Nibble my ear. Suck the lobe. Make me gasp as my legs become jelly. My legs give out and he catches me. Pins me to the car and continues tasting my skin.

His lips trail down the column of my throat as I hear giggles nearby. Pressing a hand to his chest, I push back and stop him.

"Maybe we should take this somewhere else?"

I don't know this man. Don't know if his thoughts have veered down the same path as my own. But if they have, sex in the parking lot of the centennial festival is far from appropriate. Not that I am opposed to parking lot sex. Been there, done that.

But there are too many eyes here. With half the Lake Lavender police force here, the likelihood of getting caught is high. Not to mention the possibility of having our photo taken —semi-naked and gasping—and splashed across the internet.

Wouldn't that be great for business. No. No, it wouldn't.

He inches back, his eyes darting between mine. "If you're okay with that." His voice is filled with uncertainty. Not at the idea of more, but at the invitation I handed him.

I don't know him, but I have no reservations. I hold his gaze and nod. "Did you drive here?" He nods. "Follow me."

He jogs off, jumps in his car and follows me out of the lot.

Every other minute, I peek up at my rearview mirror to make sure this isn't a dream. That I didn't just imagine meeting him. That I didn't dream up this irresistible, sweet guy who is now following me. To my home. For a one-night stand.

No romance. Just fun.

The motto jingles in my head as I park the car and exit. He helps me haul the bags up the stairs and inside. Once they hit the counter, the night turns into a lust-hazed blur. One I will never forget.

CHAPTER 1

BRAYDON

"Son, I need more of your magic."

I peer over the top of my computer as Dad enters, his large frame taking up what little space my office has left. The forty-nine square foot room is swallowed by the massive oak desk and credenza Dad insisted I needed. Half the drawers sit empty, while a quarter house old issues of Washington's Hidden Gems. And let us not forget, I barely have room to walk around either side of the desk to get to the door.

But the small space houses everything I need to do my job, so I guess that counts for something.

"My magic?"

He narrows his eyes but can't disguise the smirk on his lips.

Edward Harris. My father. Owner and founder of Washington's Hidden Gems magazine. Not a great user of words, but always good with people. And one of the best people in my life.

"Yes, son. Magic." For emphasis, he lifts his hands in front of his face then parts them to shape a rainbow. "Or whatever you want to call it. Whatever magic you found in Lake Lavender; you need to conjure more. That piece has us selling more copies than any previous issue."

At the mention of Lake Lavender, my body heats. Tingles wrap around my spine... and lower. Flashes of one of the best nights of my life resurface. The Lake Lavender Centennial Town Festival. And her... the striking blonde with a smile I will never forget. Or the night I spent between her sheets.

Quickly as the memory appears, I squash it down.

It was one night. Six months ago. I never got her name. She never got mine. And that is how it will stay.

"Dad, I didn't conjure up anything," I say, chuckling. "The town has its own magic. Not me. I just took pictures and wrote a story. Nothing more."

He plops down in the chair on the opposite side of the desk. The only other chair in my office because the door won't close without a fight if I add another. For a beat, he studies me. Presses a finger to his lips and stares with narrowed eyes. Keeps his lips sealed.

But I know this tactic all too well. I grew up under this tactic. The one where he waits for me to crack under pressure and spill facts left unsaid. *Good luck.* I've had years to master not word vomiting truths to my father. Not because we keep secrets from one another. If it is important, Dad knows. But everyone should have a secret or two. Something no one ever knows about them.

What happened in Lake Lavender... is one secret I refuse to share. With Dad or anyone else.

"Really?"

The single word has an edge. A sharpness that tells me he knows something happened during my journalism trip to the small town a little more than an hour south of Seattle. And the fact I am unwilling to share has him more curious.

"Really," I answer with a nod.

A wide smile slowly stretches his face. His eyes on mine shine as if he knows something I don't. I swallow past the expanding nervousness in my throat. My knuckles bleach as I squeeze the chair arms.

This cannot be good.

"Alright then." He rises from the chair and walks way too leisurely to the door. A door less than three feet away. I exhale as one foot steps past the threshold but hold a new breath when he spins to face me again. "Well, since there was no magic, yet you wrote the best article of your career"—he pauses and I cringe at what is undoubtedly coming next—"I'm sending you back. Different season, different perspective on the town, different story."

How did I not see this coming? Hell, I set the trap. He knows I intentionally omitted something. So by sending me back, he assumes I will confess my secrets.

Wrong. Better luck next time, old man.

"Sure, I'll go back," I tell him with a smug smile on my face. "What should I write about?"

He shrugs. "Last time, it was the start of fall. The time of year for pumpkins and sweaters and outdoor fires. Now, people are shedding their sweaters for short sleeves and sandals. Show me what happens in Lake Lavender this time of year. Maybe they have spring or summer festivals. Meet the townspeople. Make nice with the shop owners. Give me a feel-good story."

"A feel-good story?"

"Yes. Something that will make Washingtonians eager to visit."

"And when do you *suggest* I make this visit?"

He glances down at his watch as if it has a calendar instead of an analog face and studies it too hard to be checking the time. "The sooner, the better. Have dinner with us tonight and take tomorrow to book your stay. Two weeks should be a sufficient amount of time to get another whirlwind of a story."

"Two weeks?" I all but squeak out.

The corner of his mouth tugs up. "Yes, two weeks. Not like you don't have the time." That well-known fact twists a knife in my heart. "And the weekend doesn't count, but spend it there anyway."

Why does it feel as if I'm in grade school all over again and Dad is sending me to summer camp?

I remember those days. When summer camp included weeklong camping excursions. Just the group of us, coolers of food, tents and sleeping bags, and nature. I didn't want to go, but Dad swore I would enjoy it, that being with my peers in the woods is an adventure every child should enjoy.

Though I love the outdoors now, I remember coming home from the trip with itchy red rashes on my skin from the poison ivy I trekked through unknowingly. Let's just say I memorized the "leaves at three, let it be" phrase really quick.

"Anything else?" I ask with a hint of sarcasm.

He spins on his heel and all but skips away from my office. "No. See you at dinner."

Everything looks greener. Brighter. More abundant.

On my previous drive along this highway, I remember more buildings through the thinning trees. Signs to lure passersby to mouth-watering restaurants, fun tourist traps, and quirky shops. Vendors on the side of smaller roads selling farm-fresh produce. Easygoing residents with friendly smiles. The air thickly scented by the rich earth and piney evergreens.

In the city, the view is filled with tall buildings. The streets packed with cars. The distant skyline a mix of tall trees and mountains. The air a blend of salt and pine and exhaust.

Taking the next exit, I steer the SUV east and drive toward Lake Lavender. With each passing mile, the forestry grows thicker, lusher. Tall mountain hemlock trees line either side of the road, partially shading the street from the early afternoon sun. I roll down the window, inhale deeply, and sag into the seat as the crisp, piney air fills my lungs.

In no time, I have grown addicted to the air outside the city. How each breath smells better than the previous. How each pass of the breeze feels on my skin; cool and invigorating and full of promise. Every now and again, I question why I still live in Seattle. Question why I haven't moved away from the noise.

My eyes rove the forestry as my wheels eat up the miles, and it isn't long before the town welcome sign comes into view.

Welcome to Lake Lavender, Washington. Established 1919.

Lake Lavender is a populous town but not clouded by racket and congestion. Life is simpler. Residents travel on foot or by bicycle often. Strolling down the sidewalk and peering in shop windows. Pedaling in the bicycle lane on the main road, head bopping as they listen to music through earbuds.

Everyone here is just… happy.

I drive down Main Street until I reach Lavandula Lane, then turn right. Half a mile down the street, I steer into the lot of the Lake Lavender Bed and Breakfast.

Most B&Bs I've lodged at are small and quaint. A handful of guest rooms with one or two communal areas.

Not the Lake Lavender Bed and Breakfast. This place is huge. Closer to a resort than what most people call a bed-and-breakfast. In this small town, I suppose they need space for more than five to ten visitors, considering it is the only place for guests to stay.

Perhaps this posh bed-and-breakfast existed on a smaller scale in the early days. Perhaps I should add its history to my list of places to research for my story.

I wind through the lot in search of a place to park, finding a spot on the third row. I cut the engine, hop out, and stretch my limbs. Ambling to the rear, I open the hatch and fetch my suitcase, pop up the handle, and shoulder my camera bag. After a press of the fob, I head for the B&B entrance with the suitcase gliding at my side.

Everything looks identical to my last visit, only brighter. Same tall gable roof. Same cream-painted wooden shake siding, cobblestone, and plastered exterior. And so many windows. Trees line the sidewalk, the drive, and the back of the property—which butts against the town-named lake.

It all looks the same but doesn't.

The change isn't seasonal. Not the brilliant greenery on the lush spruce trees nor the colorful blossoms on the flowering shrubs. Not the picturesque blue sky nor the lively chirps of nearby birds. And not the scents of the season; cherry blossoms in the distance and blooming lavender much closer.

Rather, it's more like a new perspective. Seeing the town with new eyes. As more than another story. Which is odd since a story is why I am here. Again.

Nervous energy builds in my chest. Swirls and expands. Like when I was a child and I went too high on the swings.

The excitement of defying gravity for a second here and there, followed by the anxiety of falling.

The last time I felt this familiar buzz in my chest, it didn't end well. Hell, it broke me. Made me see most people as dishonest and artificial. Devious. And I refuse to go down that road again. Not for anyone.

Wheeling my suitcase through the lobby, I approach the reception desk.

"Welcome to the Lake Lavender Bed and Breakfast. How may I help you?" the man asks, a glowing smile on his face.

"Checking in." I dig in my back pocket for my wallet and hand him my identification. "Braydon Harris."

Tapping fills the momentary silence as he looks up my reservation. Tucking my license back in my wallet, I sign for my stay and he hands me the key to my room. I stare down at the key card hooked to a blue-and-white tag, the bed-and-breakfast name and a sprig of lavender etched in the metal. And for two breaths, memories from my last visit flit through my mind.

Shake it off, Harris.

"Take the stairs to the second level"—he points to the staircase—"turn right at the top and follow the hall. Your room is three doors down."

Before I step away, he gives me the rundown on meal times and hours of the pool area, circling them in a brochure before handing it over. I thank him, wrap my fingers around the suitcase handle, and head for the stairs. Several stairs and lengthy strides later, I locate my room.

The lock beeps after a swipe of the key card. I open the door, cross the threshold and come to a stop. My eyes widen as I survey the room. One look and my last stay here dwarfs in comparison. During my fall visit, the better rooms were obviously unavailable. This room is easily the size of my bedroom and living room combined—maybe bigger—not including the bathroom. A definite upgrade.

Bold blues, creams, and subtle earthy tones draw you in. A cobblestone fireplace at one end of the room with a television mounted above. The king bed and pillows dressed in white-and-blue linens, a bold blue floral print quilt at the foot and matching decorative pillows at the head. Opposite the bed, a wall of windows with white wood plantation shutters brightens the room and grants the perfect view of the lake and forestry. Beneath the window ledge is a six-drawer dresser, a vase of dried lavender sprigs in the center and a television remote beside it. Nightstands sit on either side of the bed with glass-based lamps topped with a cream shade.

Two wingback wicker chairs with matching footstools sit near the fireplace, a small wooden side table between them. At the far end of the room, on one side of the fireplace, is a small nook with a desk. On it, a coffee maker, landline phone, lamp, and guides for the area. A small fridge and microwave hidden on the right wall. On the opposite side of the fireplace is the entry to the bathroom and closet—which seems far too large for a nonpermanent residence.

I wheel my suitcase to the bed, toss it on top, and start unpacking my things. Seeing as I will be here two weeks, it's best I don't spend my days living out of my suitcase. Until I return to Seattle, this is my temporary home.

Once my clothes are stowed and toiletries added to the posh bathroom, I pluck the guide from the desk and start surfing the list of things to do in this quaint town. Lake Lavender may be small in comparison to Seattle, but it has plenty of options to keep tourists and residents busy.

According to the guide, gatherings or festivals happen each

month. Some are themed by the time of year or holiday, while others are just for fun. Parades and food contests and several annual fundraisers for local schools and food banks. Summer barbeques, fall bonfires, winter snowmen, and spring walks through lavender fields. Music concerts and film fests and local beer and wine tastings. Not a single month is vacant.

From the desk, I grab the bed-and-breakfast logoed pad of paper and pen. After perusing the guide a little longer, I jot down several sites, shops, and restaurants I want to visit during my stay. I strategize my time in Lake Lavender with all the places listed, noting I should just wander the town with no agenda for a day or two. Observe the residents and tourists. Get a true feel for the town.

Perhaps today, I meander the streets. Just me, my camera, and pen and paper. With the sun still high, I should get some great day shots of Main Street. And as the sun sets, shots near the lake will be gorgeous.

I tear the paper from the pad, shove it in my pocket, and snag my camera from the closet. Donning a hoodie, I loop the camera strap over my head. I forgo the pad of paper and simply take a few extra sheets and the pen, stuffing them in my front hoodie pocket.

Double-checking I have my room key, I exit and head for the stairs. Less than ten strides after I hit the bottom floor, I step through the front door of the bed-and-breakfast, out into the spring sunshine, and walk down Lavandula Lane the way I came.

Not sure what it is about this place, but a frenetic energy exists in the air. Stirs me to life. Revitalizes the blood in my veins. And for the first time in almost four years, I breathe easily.

CHAPTER 2

ALESSANDRA

I always recognize the start of the season. The small shift from quieter days to more boisterous ones. It isn't the warmer air or the longer hours of daylight. Nor the sweet fragrance that drifts from the lavender fields near the lake and blankets our town each year. Or the sight of residents wandering down Main Street with frozen treats or bubblier smiles.

It's when my *season is here* radar beeps as I see random new faces in the café. One today, followed by another a couple days later. For weeks, they trickle in. Then all of a sudden, the line for the café is out the door. Every seat in the house is full. More new faces than familiar ones step up to the counter.

It is a madhouse, but I wouldn't want it any other way.

Our small town doesn't *need* tourism to survive, but it helps the residents and small businesses thrive. Aside from the tourists, residents from sister towns visit often. Enough that we consider them fellow townies and vice versa. We may not need them, but it is nice to see them. The uptick in business doesn't hurt either. Every drink and food item sold gets me one step closer to the remodel.

"Welcome to Java and Teas Me," I say as an unfamiliar woman enters.

Like most patrons who've yet to step into the café, she hangs back to study the menu. A menu with enough options to make someone dizzy.

Over the years, I questioned if minimizing the menu was smart. Staring at the board, I see how easy it is to get over-whelmed. But every time I give the idea merit, every time I sit down with the printed menu and a pen, ready to cross items off, the pen never touches the paper.

There isn't one thing listed I don't sell.

Most regulars order the same thing every visit. On occasion, they like to throw me for a loop. Order tea instead of coffee. Biscuits and gravy instead of a bagel. It keeps me on my toes but also keeps me from making changes.

As with most stores and restaurants, weekends are busier. Today is no exception. The current lull after the early risers is a mini breather until the real crowd enters. Which is why I stand front and center alongside Mandi to take orders.

The woman steps up to the counter, still a bit hesitant. She blinks a few times before meeting my gaze.

"What can I get started for you today?"

"Uh…" She nibbles on her upper lip. "An iced Heavy Hitter and the Sunny Day on a blueberry bagel."

I enter her order. "Regular ice or coffee cubes?"

"Coffee, please."

Once she pays for the order, I hand her a numbered table tent and tell her it will be out shortly. Mandi and I ring in a few more orders before the line ends.

"I should go tidy the tables," I tell Mandi. "You good here while I straighten up?"

Mandi nods and tosses me a thumbs-up. "All good."

By no means is Mandi new to the job. But manning the counter can go from dull to unbearable in minutes. Crunching numbers and signing checks aren't my only jobs as the owner. It's also my responsibility to make sure everyone is happy and as stress-free as possible. The café runs smoothly because we are a team, a family, and I aim to keep it that way.

I grab a cleaning towel and dunk it in the sanitizer tub, then wring out the excess. Weaving between tables, I toss out any debris left behind, wipe down tabletops, and straighten askew chairs. The tables with patrons, I approach with a smile, asking if there is anything I can get them and how their food and/or beverage tastes.

Owning a restaurant is no simple feat. It isn't just taking orders and fulfilling them. Although Java and Teas Me is only open from six in the morning to two in the afternoon—three on weekends and during the season—I spend twelve-plus hours a day here. The hours come with the job.

During the first year, I clocked more than a hundred hours each week with no days off. Back then, it was me, August in the kitchen, and Mandi out front. I worked wherever I was needed. Whenever they had time, Mags and Lena pitched in. I saved every penny possible until profits allowed me to bring on more staff. It took a lot of blood, sweat, tears, and time, but Java and Teas Me became a staple in the community.

In a small town, where a healthy chunk of your income comes from regular patrons, becoming a prominent, vital business is quintessential. Not a day goes by when I don't thank the business gods.

Java and Teas Me had been a dream for years before I got it off the ground.

When we were kids, Mom and Dad took me and Anderson —my baby brother—on annual vacations. Each quirky coffee shop and unique restaurant we set foot in, I fell in love more with the idea of having my own place one day.

Each place had its own personality, unlike the chains. Fun themes or art on the walls. Eccentric names for the menu items or crazy upbeat employees. Bopworthy music or tableside entertainment such as checkers and wooden pegboard games. I took bits and pieces from each one and made my own version for Java and Teas Me.

Anyone who enters the town of Lake Lavender knows or learns of Java and Teas Me. And I am damn proud of that fact.

First off, the name of the café grabs everyone's attention. How could it not? Past patrons always recommend it as a must-see location in town. And that form of advertising tops any paid marketing I have done.

The exterior is far from flashy. It matches the same brick and wood exterior as most of the storefronts along Main Street. The town is adamant about maintaining the small-town vibe. Merchants may tweak the exterior of their shops, but the end result must stay within town guidelines. All exterior changes must get preapproved by the town council, which I am a proud member of.

But the interior... I have free rein.

Vibrant and eye-catching artwork fill the cream-painted walls. Oils and watercolor; pastels and charcoals; canvas coated with colorful patches of newspaper, intricately placed to form portraits. Enough art clings to the walls to hide most of the paint. Each piece created by a local artist and available for purchase.

Hardwood flooring spans the entire space; the rich mocha a nice accent to the lighter and brighter colors.

Opposite the entrance and outdoor seating, the service counter spans twenty feet with three order stations, a seven-foot bakery case, and a pickup area for drinks and to-go orders. Behind it, a wall of brewers, coolers, an iced drink mixing station, and industrial toaster ovens, as well as the entrance to the kitchen, make up the service alley.

The café comfortably seats two hundred, including the outdoor patio. Lightly stained wood tables with colorful chairs occupy most of the indoor dining area. Off to the side is a cute study nook with smaller tables and simple seating. It's the perfect spot for professionals or students that need somewhere to sit, sip a beverage, and work away from distractions. The covered patio is the perfect place to have brunch and read a book or catch up with friends.

Originally, when I sat down with Mags and Lena to discuss my business venture, I flashed them a horribly drawn concept sketch. Talked animatedly about every idea I'd come up with and why I thought it would work. Between my business and culinary degrees and the passion vibrating in my soul, I had every confidence Java and Teas Me would be a success. I refused to believe otherwise.

Thank goodness, my best friends thought the same and signed on as my business partners. Java and Teas Me wouldn't be what it is today without the two of them at my side. They are my glue as much as I am theirs.

I wipe down a table then organize the condiment station in the center. Once the sweetener packets and shaker jars are tidy, I inspect the vacant indoor tables before heading to the patio.

The spring air warms my skin as I greet patrons. I clear and wipe down a vacated table. Setting the dishes in the tub near the garbage bin, I survey the patio one last time. As my eyes roam the tables closest to the street, I stop breathing when a man comes into view.

No way. Not possible. My eyes must be playing tricks.

He *cannot* be here.

I blink several times as if I am having some sort of episode. *I wish. I'd rather have a fit than deal with this.*

My eyelids cramp, so I stop blinking. Stepping back, I try to blend into the wall. Make myself a chameleon against the brick —which is downright impossible. As best I can, I make myself small. I should go inside, but my legs refuse to budge.

On the sidewalk across the street, peering through the window of For The Love of Paws, he stands there with a gentle smile on his lips. Lips I have kissed.

Without thinking, I lift a hand and press fingers to my lips, remembering the bruising kisses those lips once delivered. Memorable kisses. On my lips and skin and...

I drop my hand and shake off the memory.

Get it together, Lessa. No romance, just fun. Remember?

"Ugh," I groan and wander back inside.

When I step behind the service counter and deposit the towel in the bucket, I tell Mandi, "If you need me, I'll be in the office."

She nods. "Cool."

Not that I have an abundance of tasks to do in the office at the moment—every single detail of this business gets detailed and broken down into days and time slots. Right now would not be one of my typical office times.

Regardless, I will find something to do. Even if that means reorganizing the paper clips and sticky notes. Sharpening pencils and filling the business card holder I purchased months ago. Surfing the web for new menu ideas.

Could always start the next stock order list. Write the next schedule. Straighten and face the bills in petty cash. Count the coins.

Four piles of sorted paper clips later, a knock sounds on the office door.

"It's open."

The door opens and Mandi steps in with a glowing smile on her face. Hiring her had been a great choice. She may be young, but she is pure sunshine. Exactly what the customers should see when they walk through the front door.

"Hey, Lessa. Sorry to interrupt."

"No worries. What's up?"

Mandi stands silent in the doorway, her smile falling away as a frown takes its place and she fidgets with the strands on her apron. The look doesn't match the young lady I know. Restless and dejected are not traits I'd use to describe Mandi, and I don't want to start. Whatever brought her to the office, it can't be good.

"There's an angry customer out front. Says I purposely spilled coffee on her white top." She worries her lower lip. "Swear it was an accident. I stubbed my toe on the rubber mat with the coffee in my hand and I couldn't help it. I tried to steer it away from her and—"

I hold up my hand and halt her ramble. If I didn't, Mandi would apologize and defend herself until her lips turned blue. To the wrong person.

Mandi has worked here long enough that I have a firm grasp of her integrity and personality. She goes out of her way to help everyone. Is always the happiest person in the room. And seeing her down and panicky upsets me.

I rise from the desk and come to stand beside her, resting my hands on her shoulders. "Mandi, I will handle this. Comes with the job. Don't you let it bog you down." I dip my head to make eye contact with her. "Okay?"

She worries her lip again then nods. "Okay."

We wander out to the service counter and I spot the woman in question. Her crisp white top stained with maybe five drops of coffee, smaller than the size of a peanut shell. A stain that will come out easily with a little TLC.

But she won't make it easy. She is one of *those* people. The kind who loves to stir up drama.

Lip curled up in disgust, she stands in the center of the café, pointing to her top and speaking in an unnecessarily high volume given the situation.

Someone save me.

"Ma'am?" She glances my direction and narrows her eyes. "If you'd step up to the counter, I'd be happy to assist you."

She puckers her lips and plants a fist on her hip. "Why? So you can spill more coffee on me? Ruin my clothes and burn my skin?" Her voice escalates to fifteen on a scale of ten.

"Ma'am, please."

I refuse to be confrontational. Refuse to raise my voice or get into a debate. She will not get the best of me or tarnish my business.

The woman stomps up to the counter, steering away from Mandi and maintaining a five-foot berth from the counter. She looks me up and down, silently appraising my appearance.

"And how will you help me?" she bites out.

I wish I could just slap her. Match her stomp, march around this counter, and slap her. Hard. But that would definitely be bad for business.

"I apologize for the accident. Unfortunately, they happen. I am more than happy to pay for the cleaning bill to have the stain removed."

She huffs and glances past me to Mandi and points a mani-cured finger. "And what about her? You going to fire her?"

Is this woman serious? She wants me to fire one of my best employees over a spilled cup of coffee? A spill that barely made contact with her precious white shirt. An accident. This woman is clearly off her rocker.

"Ma'am, I will have a discussion with my employee. Quite frankly, how I handle the situation is my call. Not yours."

Well, this pisses her off in point five seconds.

Her face goes from pale to pink to red in a blink. Others may concede and give in to this woman's demands when she behaves with such mightiness. But I am not other people. I don't bend to bullies or their hostile tendencies. Instead, I picture steam spitting from her ears with a loud whistle. Picture her cheeks and face swelling like a red balloon.

I bite the inside of my cheek at the comical mental picture and do my best to not laugh in her face.

Then she steps up to the counter and points her finger in my face, an inch from my nose. "If you don't fire her, I'll never return."

And just like that, I am done. No one threatens anyone in here. No one tells me how to run my business. I sure as shit don't give in to ultimatums that hurt good people.

Plastering on my best *fuck-you* smile, I say, "Sorry to hear that. It was nice having you as a customer. Sad to hear we won't see you in the future."

She lunges forward, her hands near the counter, prepared to hoist herself over. But she never makes it. A hand wraps around her biceps, tugs back, and halts her.

"Best you don't do that," a deep baritone advises.

And although I can't see his face, I know who the voice

belongs to. Well, at least what he looks like. Never got his name.

The viper of a woman spins on her heel and hisses. "Get your filthy paws off me." He lets go of her as she glances over her shoulder to me, adjusting her purse higher. "You'll be sorry for this."

She storms past several customers who cannot help but stare. Like a whiny child, she causes a raucous to create a scene. To have all eyes on her.

"Ridiculous," I mutter.

The second she exits, I take a deep breath and let it relax my tense frame. Then I peer up and look into a pair of fiery amber eyes I never thought I would see again. A pair of eyes loaded with sincerity and a gentleness I don't see often in others. Eyes I got lost in for hours.

He opens his mouth to speak and I hold up a finger to stop him. "Give me a moment." I spin to face Mandi. "If she comes in again, let me know. You did nothing wrong. Just let it go and be yourself."

"Thanks, Lessa."

"You're welcome." I peek over my shoulder a smidge. "I'll be back in a moment. Just need to handle one more thing."

Mandi smiles as if the nasty woman was never here. "Sure thing."

And then I walk around the counter, ready to go talk to a man I haven't seen in six months. A man I never intended to see again. Ever. My one-night stand. The best sex of my life. A guy I can't get out of my head.

Awkward party of two? Check.

CHAPTER 3

BRAYDON

The likelihood of me running into her again was inevitable. She does live here, after all. I just didn't think it would be on my first day back.

Off to the side, I stare after her as she talks to the young woman behind the counter. Secured in a ponytail, her dark-blonde tresses trail down her spine and stop near the base of her shoulder blades. Memories of how my fingers curled in and tugged those strands send a wave of heat through my veins.

Taking a deep breath, I force the memory down. Shove it as deep as it will go.

She is not why I am here.

She steps around the counter and ambles in my direction. My eyes lock on hers as she enters my personal space, stopping within arm's reach. The heat from moments ago resurfaces. My fingers twitch at my sides as I fight every instinct to touch her.

"Let's find a table and talk," she suggests.

Snapping out of my lust haze, I nod. "Sure thing."

As she guides us through the dining area, I use every ounce of effort to keep my line of sight above her waist. I fail miserably. Her hips shift as she sidesteps around a chair. Without a second thought, my gaze drops to her denim-clad curves. Curves my hands and lips memorized in a single evening. For three breaths, I don't look up. Hypnotized by the sway of her hips, I gawk like a pervert. Until she comes to a stop and I all but slam into her back.

Thank goodness for quality sneaker traction. Although, the squeak of rubber against the floor probably gave away my proximity.

My cheeks sting as I smile and take a seat across from her. Scooting in the chair, my eyes lift to meet hers. My smile falls away at her expression. A chill replaces the heat on my skin as I sink deeper into the chairback.

She leans forward, arms stiffly crossed under her breasts, inadvertently pushing them up. Her mouth opens to speak but then snaps shut. In the periphery, I spot the rise and fall of her chest. And without thinking, I inch closer.

Don't look down. Whatever you do, don't look down.

A gentleman, I keep my eyes trained on hers. Brilliant and bold and blue. A spellbinding blue. The hue reminds me of a photo I took years back in Olympic National Park. Only once had the sky and water been *that* blue. I'd stayed in that spot for hours, soaking in the sights. And just like then, my eyes refuse to look away.

But the hypnotic spell she has me under vanishes the second she opens her mouth.

"What are you doing here?" she whisper-hisses.

I study her for a beat. Try to read the emotion in her expression. Decipher what she *isn't* saying aloud.

Her brows scrunch together and create a puffy *V* in the

middle. The action is more adorable than it should be. Her eyes widen more with each breath, occasionally darting to other tables as if she worries what people will say if we are seen together. With a subtle shake of her head, she tells me I cannot be here. Not Lake Lavender, but *here* with her.

It's obvious my being here makes her nervous. She wasn't this fidgety when we met. Thinking back, the memory of her exudes confidence. Boldness. Fire. What changed?

Does she have a boyfriend? Wouldn't surprise me in the slightest. Any guy would be lucky to have her on his arm. She is stunning, addictive, a force to be reckoned with.

A voice niggles in the background. Tells me a boyfriend isn't what has her in panic mode. No, it is something else. Something just out of reach. I may not *know* her, but I learned enough in the hours we spent together.

Like her addiction to food—calories, fat and sugar be damned. Where she lives and how easy it was for her to invite me into her home. The cute whimper that spills from her lips when she comes unraveled. And the feel of her fingers and nails as they bruised and clawed my flesh.

God, I don't even know her name. We remained tight lipped when it came to identities, knowing it would be one night. And damnit, missing the single detail lights a fuse in my chest.

I shake my head and refocus on her fierce eyes. "Actually, I came in for coffee and a bite. The town guide said this place is the best." I shrug, not adding anything further.

She huffs and a loose strand of her golden hair floats up before landing in the same place. I bite the inside of my cheek to hide my smile. No need to goad her further. After dealing with the crazy lady, she doesn't need anyone else ruffling her feathers.

"Thank you and sorry."

"What are you apologizing for?"

She leans back in the chair and I immediately miss her proximity. Miss the subtle scent of fresh-baked bread she wears like perfume. But I shove my feelings aside.

Serious equals heartache.

"Not really sure," she says with a laugh. "My curtness, I suppose. I'm not generally so harsh."

Had she been harsh? Not in my opinion. Hell, she'd been too sweet to the woman throwing a tantrum. If anything, she appeared more shocked than rude at the sight of me. I'd be surprised too.

Before I'd left her, we'd agreed one night would be it. Had the memory of that night been a frequent companion these past six months? Yes. Too many times to count. The memory of her was constant.

But I wouldn't go back on our deal. With her name a mystery, it isn't difficult to ignore her.

Sure, I could do the weird stalker thing and Google her address. Type the business name in a search engine and scour every link to pop up. But I am not that guy, nor do I want to be. Last thing I need is to get sucked into hours of internet stalking. The idea makes me queasy.

I mimic her actions and lean back in my chair. "Well, you just dealt with that woman." I point a thumb over my shoulder. "No doubt she spiked your blood pressure."

"Ugh." Her hand dips beneath the table then reappears with the tie string on her apron. She rolls it between her fingers over and over. "We don't get many people like that in here. But every once in a while, they crawl out of some secret hibernation cave and growl at us."

My eyes dart between hers for a beat. Then, out of

nowhere, I laugh. Loud and throaty and so hard my stomach cramps. A few people at neighboring tables glance our way. I taper my laughter and wave in apology to the onlookers, then refocus my attention across the table.

For a split second, the deal we made months ago fades into the background.

What would it be like to wake up next to her every day? A simple glimpse at a daydream and I see the answer a little too clearly. My arm around her waist as I tug her back flush to my front. Nose buried in the crook of her neck, inhaling her sweet scent. Tasting and touching every inch of her body until we're both breathless.

There would be no bad days if they started with her.

But it isn't reality. Just a fantasy. A whimsical dream.

"So, what's good here?" I break eye contact and focus on the wall-to-wall chalkboard menu. Look anywhere but at her.

"How hungry are you?"

I pat my stomach as a grumble sounds loud enough for her to hear. "Hungrier, now that I'm thinking about it."

"Coffee or tea?"

"Coffee with stevia and oat milk."

She hums as her eyes narrow and assess. "Interesting."

"What?"

"I have a knack for figuring people out by what they order. Call it a gift."

I lean forward and prop my elbows on the table. She watches my every move; eyes drifting along my forearms, up my chest, and taking a brief pause at my lips before meeting my gaze. The way she locks on to me says more than any verbal exchange.

She, too, battles with her urges. The urge to not let this—

whatever it is—become more than a fun night between the sheets. The urge to remain nameless acquaintances.

Is that what we are? Hell if I know. Feels like we are somewhere between strangers and acquaintances. Strangers who have caressed the other's skin. Tasted the other's lips. Heard the other's moan as they came undone. Strangers, but so much more.

A timid voice in the back of my head questions if friendship is possible. But I shut that voice down. Now isn't the time.

"A gift, huh?"

Her eyes dart between mine, searching. She swallows and inches closer to the table. "Yep."

Is it wrong for me to enjoy how nervous I make her? To enjoy seeing her fidget in my presence?

"And what does this gift say about me?"

She gravitates closer and rests her forearms on the table. I bite back a smile as she tilts her head left and right in observation. Her scrutiny is far from uncomfortable. Honestly, I *enjoy* her examination. The way it holds me captive. The intimacy—so different from our previous connection. With a single look, she digs deeper. Searches for the unspoken truths in my soul. Will she find them?

She snaps her fingers and I recover from my introspection. I zero in on her and her growing smile.

"You have a gentle nature, but don't broadcast it openly. And you believe in traditions but are open to updated versions. Modernizing them, if you will." She pauses and pinches her chin between her finger and thumb. "Do you sip your coffee throughout the day or drink it quickly?"

"Throughout the day," I answer, mesmerized by her first assessment. Her very accurate first assessment.

"Ah, yes. As I suspected." I open my mouth to ask what

she means, but she holds a hand up to stop me. "A thinker. Someone who likes to simmer over things."

Personality deciphered via coffee order—unlocked.

This is one of the strangest experiences I've had with a woman. Or any person, for that matter. But... her assessment of me, all by what and how I drink in the morning, is spot on. Freakishly so.

Warmth blankets me as I take in another side of her. The sentiment is odd and comforting and harrowing. For the first time in years, part of me wants more than an anonymous fling. More than one night of unbridled passion between the sheets. Just not anything serious. No promises. No attachments. Only sex with a dash of affection.

"Uh... not quite sure what to say."

"Am I right?" She inches closer, eyes fixed on mine, eager, waiting.

"Surprisingly, yes."

Leaning back in the chair, she brings her hands to prayer position near her mouth and claps in quiet, rapid succession. Her glee causes me to laugh.

Then the legs of her chair scrape the floor and pop the bubble I hadn't realized formed around us. She rises and wipes her hands down her apron. I track every move, fascinated by her nervous extroversion.

She was correct in her presumption—or prediction, whatever she calls it. I am a thinker. Always in my head. Processing everything I see and hear. Listening to my instincts.

I assumed it was part of being a good journalist and photographer—my eyes and ears and intuition were always aware of my surroundings. But maybe I'd always had those traits.

I remember hiding behind Dad as a child. Being his

shadow when unfamiliar faces filled the room. I'd picked up on every side conversation, every shift in the room. I thought it was my way of knowing when and where to hide, but maybe it was my own gift.

The bell over the door jingles and she looks up, ready to greet whoever entered. She opens her mouth, her welcome on the tip of her tongue, then she snaps her mouth shut. A sudden flush creeps up her neck and across her cheeks. Her eyes widen as her fingers go to her apron strings.

"Shit," she mutters as she turns to face the opposite direction.

"Lessa!"

I glance over my shoulder and spot a woman looking in our direction, a man at her side with an arm around her waist.

"Double shit," she groans out, and I can't help but laugh. She spins to face me, panic all over her face.

"What's the matter, *Lessa*?" I tease. In the window reflection, I spot the couple heading our way. More like Lessa's way. With each heartbeat, her anxiety becomes this massive bubble around us. "Hey."

Her dilated pupils slap me in the face. "What?"

"Just let them believe I'm a customer. If that'll make it easier."

Immediately, her shoulders loosen and she exhales her held breath. "Thank you."

I open my mouth to respond but snap it shut as the couple reaches us and stops behind my chair. If only I had my own magic ability. Being able to read her thoughts would be a cool superpower. Maybe.

"Will that be all for you, sir?" Voice in professional mode, she pleads with me to play along.

"Yes, thank you."

"Be back with your order soon."

She spins on her heel and strolls with ease back toward the counter. The couple starts to follow, but I don't miss the *"that was weird"* comment from the woman.

Now, I find myself more intrigued. Intrigued by a woman who was brave enough to invite a complete stranger back to her home but now seemingly fears what people will think if we're seen in public together.

Again, does she have a boyfriend? My gut still says no. If anything, she seems *anti-boyfriend*. So why the show?

I shift in my seat and home in on her. Study her body language and facial expression.

Eyes downcast, she taps on a screen—probably entering my order. From across the room, I note how hard she bites her bottom lip. The occasional bounce of her frame as she shifts her weight. How she twirls the loose apron strand around her finger, again and again, like she did at the table.

Nervous habit.

The couple approaches her and she immediately brightens. Dashes around the counter, yanks the woman closer, and hugs her with severe enthusiasm. They share smiles and laughter for a moment before the man steps closer and hugs Lessa.

Although the couple is clearly together, the moment he hugs Lessa, a ball of fire expands at the base of my sternum. It twists my gut and steals my breath. My eyes lock onto her and refuse to look away until he releases her. My pulse whooshes behind my ears and robs me of sound.

The second they step apart, the frenzy in my chest dissipates. The erratic rhythm of my heart settles back to a steady pace. And I suck in a breath to alleviate the burn in my lungs.

"What the hell was that?"

CHAPTER 4

ALESSANDRA

Happy as I am to see Mags and Geoff, now is the worst possible time.

Most of the time, Mags is off in her own world when Geoff is with her. Still in the first year of their relationship, Mags and Geoff live inside their own foggy love bubble. Doe eyes and frequent touches consume their daily lives.

Bliss bubble aside, Mags is still perceptive as hell. She sees and hears things most people miss. As a counselor at Statice, a youth center for minors who've lost parents, those traits are essential. She would never judge me for my choices, but the idea of her seeing me with someone when I haven't dated in years makes me twitchy.

She wouldn't belittle me for how I live my life, so why does telling her I hooked up with someone make me nervous? My fingers toy with my apron strings then drop them. Mags knows my tells. Knows when I keep secrets. And each atypical move I display is an open invitation to ask questions. Uncomfortable questions I am not prepared to answer.

Highly doubt she thinks I am celibate. I flirt with the best of them. Dance with whoever is willing when we enter the Black Silk nightclub. But she has never asked about my dating life. Ever. And maybe that is what makes my skin crawl under her scrutinous gaze.

The longer she stares, the more I see the growing list of questions.

She may not ask me for details in front of Geoff or paying customers, but she will ask. Save them for girls' night. When it is just me and her and Lena. Girls' night is when she will release the floodgates, and Lena will join in. Tag team me into divulging my secret sex life.

Great.

"Who is that?" Mags tilts her head in the direction of my nameless one-night stand.

"Didn't catch his name. Don't think he's from the area." I shrug and put on my best uninformed face. Whether or not she buys it is anyone's guess.

"Hmm." I don't like the sound of that, but before I question it, she moves on. "Geoff and I wanted to say hi and grab a bite before the concert."

Since the centennial celebration, the quaint town of Lake Lavender decided we needed more festivities. Annual activities for adults and children, young and elderly, fun and noteworthy. Festivals, concerts, free movies in the square, and tons of food gimmicks. In the off-season, the small events have more of a kinship vibe as the townsfolk gather. It's a wonderful way to stay connected as a community.

I love the endless list of activities. My business loves the occasional opportunity to cater some of the events. The town of Lake Lavender is always good to its citizens and small business owners. We pride ourselves on being a small-knit community, a family. We all look out for one another. Share the love and lend a helping hand whenever possible.

Although Mags is too invested in looking out for me at the moment.

"Glad you stopped by." I hug her again, then return to the working side of the counter. "What's tantalizing your taste buds this morning?"

Mags looks to Geoff in a silent plea to order first. He kisses her forehead then smiles as if she is the reason the earth rotates.

"I'll take the Fluffed and Stuffed with bananas, scrambled, and fruit. Also, a hot Heavy Hitter."

"Cream or sugar?" He shakes his head before we both focus on Mags. "Decided yet?"

She twists up her lips. "You'd think I'd never been here before." We laugh and Geoff kisses her temple. "I'll go with Sun's Out, Buns Out—extra hollandaise—and lavender lemonade."

I tap her selections, grab a numbered table tent and hand it to her after I input the number on the order. Geoff thrusts cash my way, but I wave him off.

"You guys don't pay, so don't pretend like you do."

"Let me pay every once in a while," Geoff protests.

"Not happening."

He drops his hand and harrumphs. But as quickly as his grumpiness appears, it vanishes. A wicked smile kicks up one side of his mouth and I narrow my eyes at him. Before I discern his motives, he takes the wad of cash and shoves it in the tip jar. Mixes the bills with the others and makes a show of it.

No way to return the money now. Don't know how much

he had or how much was in the jar beforehand. Whatever. More to distribute among the staff later.

"Stubborn ass."

He smiles in victory. "It's one of my best traits."

Mags and Geoff wander off in search of a table. Thank the heavens above they choose a table outside and away from my still-nameless guest. The one whose eyes are pointed right at me. And to be honest with myself, I don't mind one bit.

Not sure if it is the golden glow of his irises or the black-framed glasses that have me rooted in place. Perhaps both. Don't know what it is about glasses, but they always make a man sexier. Edgier. More sophisticated. And my favorite... a little nerdy.

I help Mandi at the counter until Sharon signals orders are ready.

"You good while I deliver these?"

Mandi waves me away. "I got this."

I balance two plates on my left arm and hold another on my right. Near the front, I drop off one plate and collect the table tent. I do the same with the second. Then, I head for Mystery Man's table in the far nook of the dining area.

"Your breakfast, sir." I set the plate in front of him and watch as his jaw drops.

"Jesus."

"Not quite, but I can get you there," I joke with a wink.

Why the hell did I just say that?

He narrows his eyes then shakes his head before staring at the plate again. "How am I supposed to eat all this?"

By *all this*, he means the largest breakfast plate in the house. The brawny regulars don't even finish it—no one finishes it— but it amuses me to see people try.

I pat his shoulder. "I have faith."

"Glad someone does."

I spin away from him, ready to walk off, when a warm hand takes mine and tugs. I stop breathing.

"Can we meet later? When you aren't working," he says and my brows shoot up. "Not a date," he adds quickly. "I was sent here to write an excerpt on Lake Lavender. An insider's perspective would be wonderful."

Meeting up with the guy I hooked up with once sounds like more. Like trouble. Like a *date*. Maybe I am reading too much into it. Exaggerating ideas. Overthinking. He is here for work, to publicize the town, nothing else. His story also means free publicity for Java and Teas Me.

No harm in giving him the inside scoop—and extra tidbits about the town's beloved coffee café.

"Sounds like a non-date. Let me know before you leave and we can plan for later."

He stares down at his plate. "May take time, but will do."

I pat his shoulder again and laugh before walking off to deliver more orders.

When I deposit Mags's and Geoff's food on their table, she yanks me down beside her. Gives me a side hug and kisses my hair. We chitchat about the concert until the line inside grows and I have to step away.

One order after another, the line dwindles down. When no one is looking, I peek over to two tables. One outside and one in the nook. I pray they both don't finish at the same time. That Mags doesn't find a way to *bump* into him and dig. Not that I think she would, but you never know.

Since she met Geoff, Mags has been a new woman. Not as quiet and frail as she once was. No, now she has this undeniable strength and bravery. She gets out and lives her life to the fullest. Watching her crawl out of her shell warmed my heart. I

commend her and Geoff for everything they went through—
on their own and together.

Perhaps one day, I will be so lucky to have what they do.
An indisputable bond and a love to stand the test of time. One
day. When life slows down.

Not a day in my life has passed where I worried over my
outfit, hair or makeup. If anyone fretted over such things, it
would be Lena—bestie number two.

Yet here I am, tossing shirts over my head and onto the
floor. All in the hopes I find *the one* to match my jeans. *Hello,
dumbass! All tops match jeans.* I roll my eyes at myself.

Why is this happening? The stress of looking my absolute
best is taxing.

Just another reason to add to the list of why not to date.
Not that tonight is a date. Nope. Because I, Alessandra Marie
Everett, do not date. Tonight is just dinner with an out-of-town
journalist who may give me free publicity. It is strictly business. Something I can write off on my taxes.

Maybe it'll be another night of smoking-hot sex.

As long as he—goal one of the evening, learn his name—
agrees this is not a date, sex is still on the table.

I spin in circles and stare at every shirt I own on the floor.
Maybe I should close my eyes, stick out my arm and twirl until
I get dizzy. Whichever direction I point to when I stop decides
the shirt I wear. Pretty decent idea, if you ask me. Better than
calling Lena or Mags and asking them for advice.

I love my best friends. Love them as if they were my own
flesh and blood. Heck, we grew up together. Practically lived

together most of our adolescence. But seeing as I have *never* talked about my hookups or "love life" with them, asking now would stir up more questions than I care to answer before leaving the house.

Like a small child, I close my eyes, raise both arms and spin, spin, spin. When I start to get dizzy, I slow and lower one arm to my side. As I come to a stop, I grip the floor with my toes and remind myself I am no longer moving. Once I feel stable, I peel my eyes open and look at the shirt I chose.

A teal swoop-neck tee. Perfect. The color will pop against the dark denim. Plus, it will look great under my jacket.

After I slip on the top, I gather the rest of the shirts and stuff them in the closet. "I'll deal with them later."

In the bathroom, I brush on a hint of eye shadow then highlight my cheekbones. A few swipes of mascara and baby-pink lip gloss later, I am ready to go.

I fetch my jacket from the closet and purse from the bed then head for the door. As I crank the doorknob, I look to the oval mirror by the door and take in my appearance.

Other than ladies' night on Fridays, I don't recall the last time I got dolled up. Especially for a man. Not that I never make an effort to look nice, but it has been years since I got so worked up over dinner with a guy.

This is not a date. This is just two people getting together and eating food while discussing the town I live in.

Maybe if I repeat it enough times, the idea will stick.

No romance. Just fun.

I lock up, hop in my SUV and crank up the radio. On the drive to the restaurant, I sing along with the music. Distract my wayward thoughts of sex with my mystery man. Unfortunately, no song is powerful enough to divert my attention. Each time the chorus ends, my mind drifts.

Thank goodness the restaurant is close.

Two songs later, I pull into the lot at Catalina's Cantina and search for a parking spot. With today being Saturday, the Mexican bar and grill is more crowded than usual. Fantastic.

How many familiar faces will be here tonight? How many will gawk and whisper?

Like any city or town, small towns have their ups and downs. I love living in this quaint place where the population is small and residents are friendly. I love living where I have known Rosie from the florist shop or Jacob and Terrance from the pet store for most of my life. The familiarity is comforting. The knowledge that you can rely on people and vice versa is a stress reliever for the soul.

But with that familiarity comes the gossip gang. The eldest townsfolk whose parents founded Lake Lavender. The ones who sit in small groups on Sunday mornings at the Lake Lavender Diner and share every new development—no matter how big or small. They sip mug after mug of coffee, eat the same boring breakfast, and gossip worse than school-age children. And it isn't just the women, but the men too.

The worst part about the blabbermouths is they don't care who knows about their not-so-whispered tales. The gossip-mongers blather with pride.

Will any of them be in the Cantina tonight? Will I be the center of the town's attention tomorrow?

God, I hope not.

Under the red, yellow and green paper lantern lights near the door, I spot my mystery man. He stands under the canopy and checks every person that passes. His hands jammed into his front pockets as he rocks slowly from heel to toe. He flicks his wrist and checks his watch.

There are still another five minutes before we said we'd

meet, but seeing him like this—nervous and antsy—is a breath of fresh air. Because it isn't just me who questions tonight and our non-date. He does too.

I step out of the shadows and he spots me. The right corner of his mouth kicks up and I stop breathing for one, two, three erratic heartbeats. The second my lungs remember how to work again, I do my best to disguise the subtle gasps.

"Sorry to make you wait."

I toy with the hem of my shirt for a beat but stop when his eyes follow the action. He flashes me a full-on smile and it whacks me in the chest, half an inch to the left of my breastbone.

No romance. Just fun. No romance. Just fun.

"I haven't been here long. Hungry?"

For you or Mexican food? That is what I want to ask.

Instead, I keep my lips pressed together and nod. We need to order food and drinks now. Something to occupy my mouth. Something to stop me from blurting out the wrong thing—which will, without a doubt, happen before the end of the evening.

"Starved."

He gestures for me to walk ahead. As we enter the cantina, I feel the weight of countless stares on my face. Heat crawls up my neck and blooms on my cheeks. Hesitantly, I lift my gaze and scan the restaurant. Relief washes over me when I discover no one paying us any attention.

Thank goodness.

The host leads us to a booth near the windows and hands us menus. A tall glass-jarred candle burns at the heart of the table. Music plays loud enough in the background to hear but is often drowned out by the chatter and laughter of the other diners. The scent of fresh-made tortillas, grilled peppers and onions, chili powder, and cinnamon floats through the air and makes my mouth water.

If I wasn't hungry for food minutes ago, I am now.

The host tells us the server will be with us soon then walks off. Before Mystery Man picks up his menu and gets lost in the mile-long list of deliciousness, I have a question. One I feel ridiculous asking, but need to.

I slap a hand over his menu and pin it to the table. "What's your name?" I fire out the question. His name will still be Mystery Man in my head, but I shouldn't say that aloud. At least not in public.

His eyes hold mine as he reaches up and pushes his glasses up the bridge of his nose. Then, out of nowhere, he laughs. I watch him a moment, unsure if he is laughing at *me* or the fact we still don't know each other's names. Well, he kind of knows my name. I decide it must be the latter and join his laughter.

Because it is funny as hell to ask a man who has known you intimately what his name is. A man who asked you to dinner—not as a date, but for work—and you accepted… without knowing his name.

His laughter fades and he gives me another lopsided smile. The one that steals more than one of my breaths.

Is it odd my first thought is he can have all my breaths? Yes. Yes, it is.

"Braydon." I narrow my eyes at him. "My name. It's Braydon."

Oh, right. *Jesus, Lessa, get your shit together.* "Braydon is so much nicer than Mystery Man." I mentally slap myself for sharing something I swore I'd keep secret.

"Mystery Man?"

I nod and decide to go with the punches. "Yep. What else was I supposed to call you?"

He lifts a hand and grips his chin. "Hmm. I kind of dig Mystery Man. Makes me sound like a superhero or something."

"Or something," I tease.

"At least Mystery Man sounds better than the vague name I had for you. That is before I learned your name."

"Oh, yeah? And what's that?"

His cheeks redden beneath his glasses and I love his sudden embarrassment. *Is it really that bad?*

"Uh…" He reaches up and scratches the scar in his brow. "Firecracker," he mumbles.

I hear him loud and clear, but for shiggles, I pretend I don't. "Sorry, what?"

He meets my gaze—eyes wide—and swallows hard. "Firecracker," he says a little louder. He hangs his head and shakes it once before straightening. "God, this is embarrassing."

I laugh and he just stares at me with those hypnotic amber eyes. He may be horrified by his admission, but it is funny.

First off—we never thought we would see each other again. Second—we never exchanged names. He learned mine on a whim. Well, the abbreviated version of my name. Hearing the nickname he gave me is… intriguing.

I reach across the table and grab his hand. "Please don't be embarrassed. It is what it is. And it's better to laugh than dwell. If I'm laughing over it, you should too."

On that note, his smile returns and I find my eyes fixated on his lips for far longer than appropriate. It isn't until he swipes his tongue across his lower lip that I snap out of my Braydon-induced haze. His eyes simmer as they watch me watch him.

Those eyes simmered for me once before. Above me as he rocked his hips in time with mine.

Gah! Snap out of it, Lessa. Get your shit together.

I lift the menu and block him from view. After a deep breath, I skim the menu I memorized long ago. I don't miss the soft chuckle across the table.

The server delivers a basket of fresh-made tortilla chips with salsa and guacamole. After we order, she rushes off to fetch our drinks. Zero alcohol will be drunk tonight. Not after how ridiculous I have behaved without it. Last thing I need is to be inebriated around this man. Me drunk with him in proximity may lead to us waking up in the same bed.

"So, what really has you back in Lake Lavender?" I sip my water to keep my mouth busy. Last thing I need is to blurt out how I have imagined sex with him again. On the kitchen counter, the dining table, the floor in front of the fireplace. That would not be good.

Earlier, when he asked to meet for dinner, he said he was there to write an excerpt. That he wanted to speak with a local. But maybe it is an excuse to spend time with me again. He already wrote a story about the town. At least, that is what he said when we met at the festival.

Is he really in Lake Lavender for work? Or did he return for me under the guise of work? The latter thought jars me momentarily and I mentally shake off the notion.

Braydon's unexpected appearance has me rattled. My mind overflowing with whys and what-ifs. Thinking up scenarios I *never* considered with other men. And while my head is foggy with indecision, my body is on cloud nine. Stirring back to life at the sight of him. The smell of him. At the energy pouring off of him.

I love and hate the way it makes me feel. Out of control. Wild. Alive.

All this aside, one question matters the most. How long will he be in Lake Lavender?

He leans closer, reaches across the table and presses the pad of his finger between my brows. The action startles me and I jerk back an inch. Suck in a breath and feel my brows tighten more.

He drops his hand and shrinks into his seat. "Sorry. Just wanted to ease whatever had you thinking so hard."

"I wasn't—"

He cocks his head and narrows his eyes.

"Okay, I *may* have been overthinking a bit." I sip my water then point at him after I set down the glass. "And you're avoiding my question. Again."

His shoulders sag as he exhales. He plucks a chip from the basket, scoops up guacamole and shoves it in his mouth.

Still avoiding.

I cross my arms and lean my forearms on the table. Don't know about him, but I will sit in silence until he answers. Even if it takes all night, he will answer.

When it dawns on him I refuse to surrender, his will caves.

"After my last visit, when I wrote about the centennial festival, the magazine received more interest than usual. The issue sold more than any in the history of the company." He grabs another chip and dunks it in the salsa but doesn't scoop up any tomato chunks. "So, I was sent back to write more on Lake Lavender." He eats the chip and shrugs.

So, he didn't come back to see me. He did return for work. Although this should make me happy, the twinge beneath my rib cage tells another story. The pang, plus my overall emotional state, makes me dizzy. I don't like it.

"How long will you be in town?"

Fingers crossed my question didn't come off as bitchy. But if Braydon will be wandering the streets of Lake Lavender, I need to know how long. I also need to jam-pack my schedule during his stay. Less availability equals less opportunity for round two.

Right about now, round two is tempting as hell.

Candlelight reflects on his lenses and highlights his amber irises. The corner of his mouth kicks up and I lick my lips. His eyes don't leave mine as he studies me a little too intently. I may be good at reading people, but so is Braydon. Better than he may realize. No doubt, the gift makes him a talented journalist.

"Two weeks."

I stiffen then relax and Braydon laughs. His chortle both strong and tender.

"You seem undecided."

"Undecided?" I ask with a hint of confusion.

He sips his water then nods. "Yep, undecided."

Of course, he doesn't elaborate. And before I ask what he means, the server delivers our meals. For now, I let his nonanswer go and eat my tostadas.

While we eat, I tap into my mojo to decipher the mystery that is Braydon.

He leans over his plate and tips his head sideways as he lifts a fish taco to his lips. After his bite, he sets the taco down and wipes his mouth with a napkin while chewing.

I don't know Braydon—not really—but his need to wipe his mouth clean before he finishes eating says more than most would read into. What it tells me... Braydon is a tidy person. Organized—maybe not to the same extent as me, but organized nonetheless. In tune with his appearance. Traits I enjoy, not that it matters.

No romance. Just fun.

As our plates slowly empty, my earlier eagerness for answers returns. He is here to do a story but hasn't asked a single question about the town. And let's not forget his evasive behavior.

"So, Braydon."

"So, Lessa," he parrots my tone and I roll my eyes.

"Alessandra."

"Huh?" His brows pinch in confusion.

"My name. It's actually Alessandra, but most people call me Lessa. It's easier." I shrug—unsure why I felt the need to tell him in the first place. Before I let myself dwell, I move on. "What is it you think I'm undecided over?"

He wipes his mouth again and I follow the action with my eyes. "My time here."

I tilt my head. "Not sure I follow."

Braydon slides his plate aside and leans forward. Most men would make me shrink back as they invaded my personal space. Not Braydon. Something about him keeps me rooted in place. If anything, I *want* his proximity. Want his eyes and lips closer. Want his smell to invade my space.

Braydon doesn't have an intimidating bone in his body. Don't ask how I know, I just do. If anything, his aura vibrates the opposite. Like an invitation. An unfiltered magnetism beckoning me closer. Making me eager for more. More than our one night and more than sex.

This light bulb moment alarms me most. Has red flags flying and lights flashing. But I brush it off. Take a breath and wait for him to elaborate.

"When I said I'd be in town for two weeks, your body language spoke volumes."

I push my empty plate aside, press my forearms to the table and meet his gaze. "Oh yeah? And what did it tell you?"

I clamp down on my elbows and brace myself. I dish out honesty without a second thought, but being on the receiving end is a different story.

Braydon licks his lips and I press my thighs together. Remind myself to breathe. Thank god the table is wood and hides my legs.

"The idea bothers and comforts you."

"That's as clear as mud."

He laughs and I focus on the lateral crinkle lines by his eyes, the way his Adam's apple bobs.

"Perhaps I should thin the mud a bit."

I wave a hand in his direction, encouraging him to continue.

"It bothers you because I'll be around every day. Not something you're accustomed to."

I tip my head to the side and half shrug.

"But it comforts you for the same reason." He pauses when I narrow my eyes. "Because you like me more than you're willing to admit. To me or yourself."

Well, damn. He didn't thin the mud, he washed it away. What he said isn't pure truth. It also isn't a complete lie. Either way, the brutal honesty has me unsure how to respond or act. So, I shoot for defensive.

"That's pretty presumptuous."

"Not really. We hooked up six months ago under the pretense we'd never see each other again. But don't deny the chemistry we have."

Braydon isn't pompous or egotistical. Quite the opposite.

He speaks in hushed tones but isn't afraid to express himself. Touches with gentleness and purpose, not just for the sake of contact. And the way he sees me is different from others. He sees past the exterior, past the stress and determination.

For someone who knows so little about me, Braydon sees *me*. The woman who wants more out of life, but refuses to let a relationship get in the way of business.

And the realization scares the hell out of me.

I swallow past the sandpaper in my throat and pray my voice isn't froggy when I speak. "True." The one word croaks out and I swallow harder. "I won't deny it."

He leans back in his chair and rests his hands in his lap. No cocky smile. No jerk remarks. Just a simple nod to acknowledge we are both on the same page.

And as I study the man across from me, I give in to the vitality and warmth swarming my heart. Let it take over, just a little. In the end, I pray it doesn't bite me in the ass.

CHAPTER 5

BRAYDON

The last woman I fell head over heels in love with broke my heart. When I broke off the relationship, I made a pact with myself to never feel that type of pain again. To never be so vulnerable that one person could turn my life upside down.

Yet, here I am. Schmoozing a one-nighter.

"What the hell is wrong with me?"

First of all, I don't schmooze. Ever. Hell, consider yourself lucky if I start or carry on a conversation with you more than necessary. I may be a journalist, but that doesn't mean I go out of my way to talk with people. Most of what I write about doesn't require a lot of human interaction. That is the beauty of writing about towns, landmarks, and festivities, and not people.

Second, I don't expend energy unnecessarily. Don't give all of myself to anyone—personally or in business. And since I discovered my relationship with Gabby had been masked in lies, emotional connections are a no-go.

So, what am I doing?

I met Lessa at the restaurant with every intention to talk business—hers and mine. To get an insider's perspective on the charming town of Lake Lavender. Learn more about the small town from one of its top business owners. But also, I want to know why she loves living here. What keeps her from moving to the city or somewhere outside of Washington.

We should have talked business. I should have been taking notes.

Instead, we sat across from each other for almost two hours and discussed everything except work. We flirted—more than I have with any woman—and teased. Tossed innuendos back and forth without care. And as much as we fought the pull between us, we eye-fucked each other without shame.

The whole evening had been a refreshing change of pace. A breath of fresh, intoxicating, addictive air. The high from it buzzed through my veins. Had me aching for more—of the night we shared and just... her.

Most of my weekends were spent alone, at a bar, or with family. I'd grown fond of my solitude, of not answering to someone. It meant I never let anyone down. It meant no one could tear me apart.

With Gabby, she always knew my whereabouts and I hers. I never felt smothered and thought she felt the same. Boy had I been wrong. In one night, I learned much of our relationship had been a sham. Regardless of how strong you are, when the person you love tells you the past six years meant nothing, it changes you.

It took me more than a year to kiss another woman. To touch a woman and feel desire instead of pain. I'd had to rewire my brain. Repeat the same phrase for months.

Serious equals heartache.

When it finally sank in, frequenting bars became normal.

Bar nights typically ended with an anonymous woman on my arm. I never asked for their name and never offered my own. If they asked, I gave them a fake. If they said theirs, I let it go in one ear and out the other. We always went to her place —no one set foot in my home—and had our way with each other. Less than an hour later, I hopped in my car and went on my merry way.

This isn't the life I wanted, but it's the life I now choose.

Once upon a time, I dreamed of settling down with one woman. Of having a nice home and children. Of building each other up and creating a wonderful future. I'd seen it so clearly. Love and laughter and promises of forever. Years ago, those dreams revolved around Gabby. For six years, I'd handed over every piece of myself to her and thought she did the same.

Then, she punched a hole in my chest, ripped out my heart and shredded it into confetti.

With time, the knife in my heart slowly eased out. When it finally fell away, I swore off serious relationships. I renounced romantic connections. Not because I no longer had a heart. But because I needed to protect my heart, my soul, my sanity.

No one would get the upper hand on me again.

One-night stands may be how I live my *romantic* life now, but I am no manwhore.

Four years ago, Gabby broke me. Three years ago, I hooked up with my first one-nighter. The next day, I felt dirty and ashamed. In the past, sex had always been an extension of love. Telling myself sex and love no longer coexisted in my world had been more challenging than I anticipated.

Since that first one-nighter, I'd only sought out sex when my hand no longer satiated my needs. Which isn't often, but more than I care to admit.

Thank you, busy job.

Like the others, Lessa was someone I never thought I would see again. Especially since we didn't live in the same city. We didn't exist in the same social circles. She knew none of my friends and I knew none of hers.

But fate or whatever cosmic force pulls people together has other plans. I'd be foolish to believe otherwise.

"I'm so screwed," I mumble and roll over, smothering myself in the pillow.

With a groan, I fist the pillow. Allowing myself a few minutes to wallow in this realization. To let it sink in fully.

Nothing good will come from wanting more with Lessa.

Do not get attached.

Sighing, I roll out of bed and go about getting ready for the day. No amount of procrastination will fix this.

I squirt toothpaste on my toothbrush and scrub my teeth. As the minty foam cleans my teeth, a plan for the day comes together.

Top priority… don't bump into Lessa. At all costs, avoid the coffee shop.

Slipping on jeans and a T-shirt, I swipe the town guide off the desk and leave the room.

Downstairs, I stroll into the dining room of the bed-and-breakfast. A young man steps up to the table and shares today's breakfast options.

"The two-pancake breakfast, please. Scrambled egg whites—no milk—turkey bacon, and coffee. Do you have oat milk?"

"Yes, sir."

"On the side, please."

As the server scurries off, I flip open the town guide and scan the places I marked to visit. Aside from the shops on Main Street, a few hidden gems garner my attention. The Lake

Lavender History Museum, Bradford Farms, Rescues Gone Wild, and the town's namesake lake, of course.

The server brings a mug, coffee carafe, and creamer, filling the mug before stepping away.

Before breakfast arrives, I map out my plan of attack between now and Wednesday.

Most of my time here will be spent visiting the small businesses, but I want to drive through the neighborhoods. Scour the natural landscape. See places off the main thoroughfare. The few days I'd spent here six months ago, I learned the residents are a devoted community.

Growing up and living in the city, small towns always fascinated me. They also make me twitchy as hell.

There was comfort in knowing the townspeople, in sharing annual traditions, and existing in the quiet that never happened in the city. But with that came the pack of nosy locals and older generations who weren't keen on change, even if for the good.

Regardless of where you live, there is always good and bad. The good... Lifelong friendships, endless helping hands, people who care about *you*. The bad... Everyone knows you. Really *knows* you.

From past visits to similar towns, I learned all about the gossip mills. Gossip equals drama. Neither of which I want in my life.

"Here we are." A hint of hickory and sweet cream fills my nose as the server deposits a steaming plate of food on the table. "Is there anything else I can get you? Ketchup or hot sauce?"

My stomach grumbles as I inhale a little deeper. Shaking my head, I say, "No, this is perfect. Thank you."

With a nod, he walks off. I smother my pancakes and bacon in syrup then dive in.

When my stomach is full, I tuck cash under my mug and exit the dining area. I climb the stairs and head for my room. Inside, I grab the pack with my camera, paper and pen, then venture out into the morning sun.

First stop, the town's namesake—Lake Lavender.

I arrive at the entrance to the county park within minutes, pay the attendant and drive through the paved roadways. Once I have a basic overview, I park the car and wander the grounds.

Camera at the ready, I hike a trail that leads to the lake. Tall evergreens line the path and fill in the terrain. In no hurry, I lift the camera and snap pictures of the trees and wildlife, capturing how the light filters through the greenery this time of day.

When the trees thin and the lake come into view, I press the shutter button from different distances and angles. Capture various shots of this pristine vista. Moody, snow-capped blue mountains in the backdrop. Acres of evergreens, from the mountains to the water's edge. The lake a shimmering blue green and with each step forward, rows and rows of lavender fill the foreground.

The bountiful purple meadow captures my attention first. My eyes roam the landscape, taking in what appear to be acres of lavender. A gust drifts off the lake and the fragrance hits me next. With fewer trees to filter the scent, the perfume engulfs me in its bubble. If comfort was a smell, this would be it.

I step more into the open air, close my eyes and inhale deeply. In two breaths, my muscles loosen. My mind calms as clarity sets in. I open my eyes and take in the view with a new perspective. A new sense of peace washes over me and I wonder if everyone in the town experiences this as well. The smell alone would be a reason to stay.

The lake definitely gets a check mark under the *must-see* column.

Wandering closer to the lake, I spot townspeople maybe fifty feet away, near the water. I lift the camera to my eye and snap several pictures. Too bad pictures can't capture the smell and feel of being here. Guess I will have to work some of the *magic* Dad says I have when I write the article.

I edge closer to the water and snap photo after photo. Aiming the lens toward a small group of people, I twist the focus and pause on the shutter button.

"No," I whisper-gasp.

Zooming in closer, I refocus and snap the picture. When I look at the camera screen, I close my eyes and huff in exasperation. By steering away from Main Street today, I thought I'd avoid bumping into her. Alessandra.

Ernt. Wrong.

"So much for staying away."

But she hasn't noticed me. Yet. Her attention is averted, and I don't know whether to be thankful or upset. The fire in my veins leans toward the latter.

Turning my back to her, I unzip my pack, take out a hat and put it on, tugging the bill low. More confident in my obscurity, I lift the camera to my eye and continue snapping pictures as if I hadn't spotted Alessandra within shouting distance. With a group of people. Half of which are men.

"Take your pictures and get out of here," I tell myself.

The peace I felt moments earlier is gone, replaced with a misshaped blob of uncertainty. It twirls on a wobbly axis in my thoughts. The end result... a larger mass of confusion.

I snap one final picture and pivot to leave.

On the third step, I hear, "Is that the guy from the café?" The woman's voice is unfamiliar, and I don't slow my stride.

Then I hear a man ask, "What guy?" Just as another man says, "Ooh, Mystery Man."

Shit, shit, shit.

My gait widens and I pick up steam, determined to get out of here.

As I reach the tree line, a hand grips my biceps and tugs. The hand is too small, too delicate, too soft.

I know that touch. I memorized the feel of her fingertips on my flesh.

Pinching my eyes closed, I take a deep breath. Then another before opening my eyes. Slowly, I spin around and face her. Alessandra. The woman I can't seem to shake.

"Hey." A smile stretches my cheeks and feels awkward as hell.

Her eyes dart between mine as her brows slowly pinch together. "Hey. What're you doing here?"

Avoiding you.

I hold up the camera and shrug. "Working. Thought you would be too."

And then I mentally slap myself for sounding like an asshole. *Damn, I need help.*

CHAPTER 6

ALESSANDRA

Well, that stings.

My first day off after working ten straight had started on a high note. One line from Braydon's lips and the relaxation from moments ago vanishes. It isn't *what* he said but how he said it that hurts. More than it should.

"Excuse me?"

He exhales audibly and hangs his head. When his eyes find mine again, I see his unspoken apology and… something else. His gaze shifts incrementally, looking over my shoulder and off in the distance. That unidentifiable emotion in his eyes, I see it more clearly as he takes in Logan and Owen—Geoff's business partners and best friends.

Braydon is jealous. Not *I will beat them down* jealous. More like *she isn't mine, but she can't be yours either* jealous.

I should hate it. I should remind him we have no ties. But I don't.

Warmth trickles through my bloodstream at the idea of Braydon laying claim to my body and heart. At the idea of him calling me his. It is a fool's errand, I know. Something that will never come to pass. Doesn't mean I don't enjoy the way it feels.

"Sorry," he mumbles, pushing his glasses up the bridge of his nose. "That came out all wrong."

"Try again?"

We will never be more than acquaintances that shared a scorching night together. Never more than the guy from the city and the lady from the small town. We can't be. His life exists more than an hour away. Mine will always be in Lake Lavender.

The fantasy in my head doesn't care about facts.

"Hi," he says, barely above a whisper. "It's nice to see you." His lips tip up at the corners.

"You too. Working?" I point to his camera.

He nods. "Yeah. Thought I'd capture the lake today. Walk the shoreline and let the sights spark inspiration."

Twisting, I take in the view. Try to see the mountains and trees and lake as if for the first time. Inhale the sweet perfume from the blooming lavender shrubs as if I hadn't for twenty-six years.

But it is pointless.

Though I have traveled out of Lake Lavender, it has never been long enough to forget why I love it here. People in big cities dream of moving away. Somewhere new and different from where they grew up. Maybe the opposite climate or landscape. Somewhere near the ocean or away from it altogether.

I haven't traveled much, but no other place feels like home. No other place calls to my heart the way this place does.

"Came to the right place for inspiration."

Looking back to the lake, I catch sight of my friends. Mags throws me a pleading look. A silent *who is he?* I want to say he is no one, just another tourist passing through. But she would call me on the lie.

Turning my back to Mags, I catch Braydon looking at my group just out of earshot.

"Would it be weird if I introduced you to my friends?" *What the hell am I doing?*

He scratches the small scar in his brow. Looks from me to them, then back to me. "Uh…"

Stupid, stupid, stupid.

What part of my brain thought it would be a good idea to introduce my one-night stand to my friends—two of which have known me since grade school?

"Don't worry about it." I shake my head. "I wasn't thinking."

"It's okay." He reaches out, touches my arm briefly, then drops his hand as if I burned him. He rolls his lips between his teeth and my eyes follow the action, remembering the taste of him. "I mean, what would you say?"

Huh? My obvious confusion must show because he simply smiles.

"To your friends." He jerks his chin toward the lake. "How would you introduce me?"

Fair point. Not like I often introduce my friends to random people. Just as I am about to dismiss the idea altogether, I have a light-bulb moment.

"I'll introduce you as a journalist from…" *What the hell was the name of the magazine again?*

As if reading my mind, he chuckles. "Washington's Hidden Gems magazine."

I point a finger and swish it through the air. "Thank you. I'll introduce you and tell them you're in town to write a story." Feeling somewhat victorious, I smile. "It'll also get my friend off my back."

Braydon glances past me for a beat, eyes roaming. "The brunette with twenty questions?"

"That'd be the one." I take a deep breath, count to three, then exhale. "Please don't feel obligated. When I suggested it, I was on autopilot."

His tongue darts out and traces his lips. Time stops for three rapid heartbeats as I ache to taste him again. His lips, his skin. He was the perfect blend of sweet and salty, of desire and need.

No one before Braydon made me feel the way he did.

Like the others before him, he'd told me I was beautiful. Told me he'd had an eye on me all night. Unlike the others, Braydon felt like more than sex.

His finger traces along my jaw to my chin, down the column of my throat, across my collarbone. "So damn beautiful."

Warm lips meet mine in a kiss that is somehow both hard and soft. Dropping his hips in the cradle of mine, he rocks forward and rubs his length along my entrance. A moan spills from my lips as he growls into the crook of my neck.

"Tell me you want this."

I trail my hands down his back, stopping when I reach his ass, gripping it firmly. "I want this."

"Tell me you need this." He kisses his way up my neck before sucking and nibbling my ear. "That you need me."

His words throw me momentarily, but I tell him anyway. "You know I need you."

"Thank god."

And before either of us takes another breath, he rocks his hips forward and fills me fully.

"Lessa?"

Amber fills my vision as I blink out of the memory. Rattled, I shake my head and blink more. The present filters in as embarrassment heats my skin.

Knees slightly bent, Braydon hovers a breath from my lips. If I lean forward an inch or two, our lips would meet. His hands rest on my shoulders, his thumbs drawing small, methodical circles. The touch gentle and comforting. And as his eyes dart between mine, I see true concern.

"You okay?"

I nod. "Mm-hmm. Yeah." I nod again. "Fine. I'm fine."

He straightens to his full height and inches back. I immediately miss his proximity. Miss the feel of his breath on my lips.

"Where'd you go?"

A fresh layer of heat blankets my skin as the memory from six months ago wiggles back to the surface. I bite my lower lip and shake my head.

"Nowhere. It's nothing."

Curious eyes roam my face in search of answers. As his eyes traverse my expression and skin, I feel every fiery glance on my eyes, my cheeks, my lips, my neck. Hour-long seconds pass, and then the corner of his mouth tips up.

"Do you do that often?" he asks, a cheeky smile now firmly in place.

"Don't know what you're talking about," I lie then look over my shoulder at everyone.

God, how long have I been over here?

He licks his lips and chuckles. "Playing coy doesn't suit you." The small berth he gave me, the one I missed... he takes it back. "You were thinking about the night of the festival."

At least he didn't outright ask if I was thinking about sex with him.

I purse my lips and shrug. "Whatever." I look back over my shoulder. "Do you want to meet my friends or not?"

Light laughter echoes through the trees. "Sure."

Braydon steps to the side and we walk toward the group. Everyone but Mags is carrying on a conversation. She shifts from foot to foot, waiting to see who the new guy is.

A few steps away, Braydon leans in and whispers only loud enough for me to hear. "You're not alone. I've thought of that night too. Daily."

Not a second before I introduce Braydon to the gang, my skin is an inferno.

Great. Just fucking great.

CHAPTER 7

BRAYDON

Meeting Alessandra's friends was interesting. She'd introduced me to the two women first. Magdalena and Helena—her lifelong friends. From the moment we stepped up to the group, it was easy to see their connection. The three women gravitated toward each other without effort.

The men were new to the inner circle.

Geoffrey, Logan and Owen were business partners and owned Architectural Crimson, the only architects in a fifty-mile radius. I mentally added their firm to my list of businesses to visit.

Geoffrey and Magdalena started dating around the time Alessandra and I met. Part of me itched to admit as much, but I'd kept my mouth shut. Through Geoffrey and Magdalena's relationship, Logan and Owen joined the quirky crew.

We'd chitchatted less than ten minutes before I'd excused myself—not that I wanted to leave. I'd waved as I ambled toward the lake. All but Alessandra returned the sentiment.

And I hadn't felt myself the rest of the day.

Which is why I plan to steer clear of her today. Again.

Today, the goal is to talk with some of the shop owners on Main Street. The town bakery, bookstore, diner, and ice cream shop. Strategically planned so I can also grab lunch and a couple treats. After a little research, I discovered the town has an even balance of new businesses and ones that opened not long after the town was founded. Thrill fills me at learning more about the town's rich history. History that will undoubtedly have readers eager to visit this gem.

After a quick shower, I dress and head downstairs for breakfast. The food and coffee are dull compared to what I had at Java and Teas Me, but it will suffice.

"I'm here to write a story, not gain creeper status," I mutter as I step into the bed-and-breakfast dining room.

With a full belly, I trek back to my room, toss on a hoodie, hook my camera over my head, and stow pen and paper in the front hoodie pocket.

The early morning sun greets me as I step outside. I snap darker lenses over my glasses and stroll Lavandula Lane until I reach Main Street. The farther I trek, the less I smell the lavender drifting in from the lake.

Up earlier than yesterday, surprise takes hold as I turn onto Main Street and find the road bustling with activity.

"Do these people work?"

More than half the people mulling about probably don't live in Lake Lavender. Like me, they are here as guests. Although my reason for visiting is less about fun, I plan to enjoy every minute here.

In no hurry, I wander down Main Street—in the opposite direction of Java and Teas Me. My eyes roam over each storefront and I truly take in the town as if for the first time.

Burnt-red brick accented by bright and light colors.

Wooden siding painted white or bright pastels. Wooden signs with each store's name are centered over large windows and doorways—the colors and font popping and grabbing the attention of passersby. Most of the stores along the main thoroughfare are two-story businesses on the bottom and some residential on the second story. Awnings sporadically cover parts of the sidewalk while painted images or slogans decorate windows, advertising deals or products. Tall lampposts line the sidewalk every fifteen to twenty feet, various evergreens planted between each.

I absorb each nuance. Lift the camera to my eye and capture the unique beauty of this charming town. If my story about the town's centennial festival attracted new viewers, I could only imagine what a story about the town itself would draw in.

Reaching my first destination, I open the door to One More Chapter. The tinny jingle of a bell sounds as I step inside. Closing the door, I freeze when I face forward and lay eyes on rows upon rows of tall wooden shelves. From the outside, the store looks small. I expected to see shelves along the walls and two or three in the middle, max. But what I am greeted with is so much more.

As my initial wonderment fades, I wiggle my nose at the smell. Earth and wood, a hint of musty, and something else. I aim my feet for the first aisle and the mystery smell gets stronger. Oddly, it smells like chocolate, and I inhale a little deeper. Hushed voices, the slight swish of books being removed or added to shelves, and soft classical music floating around the store.

"Good morning," a cheery older woman calls out, walking in my direction. "Welcome to One More Chapter. Anything I can help you find today?"

"Morning." I smile. "Not really. I'm actually in town to write a story."

The woman goes impossibly sunnier, clasping her weathered hands in front of her lips. "Oh, how exciting." Her hands fall to her sides. "We don't get many writers here." She narrows her eyes and gives me a once-over. "Let me guess... mystery."

Huh?

I give a slight shake of my head. "Sorry, what?"

"You write mystery novels." A dreamy look takes over her expression as she waves a hand upward. "I see it all so clearly. Small-town girl goes missing during tourist season and the town sheriff calls in the county detectives to help find her." Her eyes come back to mine. "Am I right?"

I wince and shrug. "No, ma'am." She deflates at my words. "Sorry to say, but I don't write fiction. I'm actually here to write a story about the town."

Her solemnity from seconds ago is replaced with a bright smile and delight. "Oh my!" Her eyes drift around the store briefly. "And you want to include One More Chapter in your story?"

"If you don't mind."

She lays a hand on her chest. "Not at all." Then she turns away from me and starts straightening the already tidy shelf. "Had I known you'd be here, I would've dusted and polished and better stocked the shelves."

A soft chuckle leaves my lips. "I quite like the store as is and am glad you didn't have time to change it."

Patting the spine of a book, she turns to face me. "Well, I'll let you explore." She lifts a hand and points in general directions as she speaks. "Travel, hobbies and fitness. Biographies, current affairs, and history. Cookbooks, health, and home and garden. Music, film, and the arts. Religion, astrology, and humor." She pauses to laugh and I join her. "Upstairs, you'll find all the fiction books. Romance, thrillers, fantasy, sci-fi, poetry—"

"There's a second floor of books?" I ask, cutting her off.

Straightening her spine, a proud smile turns up the corners of her cheeks. "Oh yes, and I'd have a third if the town allowed. As is, the store is jam-packed. If either store beside me closes, the goal is to snap up the property and expand. It took several years and a lot of love to earn the title *Best Small-Town Indie Bookstore, Top 50 Must-See Bookstores in the US,* and *Top 5 Bookstores in Washington.*"

I pull out the paper and pen in my hoodie and take notes. Later, I will look up these lists to reference in the story.

"That's incredible. Congratulations!"

She waves off my sentiment. "Pishposh. I didn't open the store for awards." Leaning closer, she adds in a whisper, "But I won't complain about the business it brings in." Straightening, she continues. "I'll let you have a look around. If you need anything or have questions, just holler for Ida and I'll find you."

Before she walks off, I ask, "Do you mind if I take pictures of the store?"

"Take as many as you like, dear."

I open my mouth to offer my name but don't get it out before she disappears.

The next thirty minutes are spent roaming the first floor of the store. I take a few pictures from different angles then make my way up the staircase in the back corner. When I reach the top, a new dose of wonderment hits. Ida wasn't joking when she said the store was packed.

Every available inch of wall space on the second floor is

covered in bookshelves, floor to ceiling, with a ladder available for higher shelves. The rest of the space has seven-foot wooden shelves, back to back, with barely enough room for a person to walk down the aisles. I highly doubt people could pass each other in the aisles, even sideways and hugging the shelves.

A few stepladders are parked at the end of the aisles. Books line, crowd, and nearly fall off the shelves. And though Ida said she would have dusted had she known I was coming, I can't see a lick of dust in sight. Probably because the books don't stay on the shelf long. I've been here less than an hour and have seen no less than twenty people scoping out their next read.

I snap a few pictures upstairs, peruse the romance section —my secret indulgence—and head back to the first floor. In the history section, I snag a book on the town's history then amble to the register to pay. Not thinking before I left the B&B, I forgot my reusable bag in the room. Smart businesswoman that she is, Ida has a small selection at the counter and I add a large canvas tote to my order.

Ida rings up my selections. "This one's excellent," she says as she adds the romance novel to the bag. "She's one of my favorite indies. Plus, she's local."

I hand over my credit card with a nod. "Just discovered her books this year and I'm loving them. You have an incredible selection of indies. I love it."

"They don't always get enough love in those big, fancy bookstores. I proudly add them to my shelves. Some of my favorite books were written by 'lesser known' authors." She uses air quotes for the term *lesser known*.

"Agreed."

Ida hands me my card and tosses the receipt in the bag

before passing it to me. "Hope you enjoy the remainder of your visit. Stop in and see me anytime."

I shoulder the bag and walk for the exit. "Will do, Ms. Ida. Thank you."

I exit the Lake Lavender Diner and pat my stomach. The club sandwich and fresh-cut fries had hit the spot. But I need to do a bit of walking before I make it to my next two stops. All Scooped Up and Sweet Spot Bakery—both of which I won't walk out of empty-handed.

I make the trek back to the B&B and take my book purchases to my room. Setting the bag, my camera, and the pen and paper on the bed, I sit in one of the chairs near the fireplace and take a breather. Clear notifications on my phone and read a few emails.

"Time for the best part of today," I say, rising from the chair.

Forgoing my camera, I empty the bag, fold it, and stuff it in my hoodie pocket. Like the majority of the general populous, I'll snap food pictures with my phone.

Patting my pockets, assured I have what I need, I leave the B&B and head for the ice cream shop.

Word on the street is the shop makes its own ice cream and sorbet. And from what little research I'd done, All Scooped Up caters to everyone—offering nondairy creamy confections as well.

Two shops down, singing fills my ears. When I step through the propped open door and inside the shop, the singing ends and every patron claps. It isn't long before the shop employees start their next tune.

I get in line and read over the chalkboard menu. Minutes later, I locate a table near the window, whip out my phone, and snap a couple photos of the cream-topped waffle cone with the street view in the backdrop. Satisfied with the shots, I stow my phone and enjoy my after-lunch treat.

And damn, it does not disappoint.

Jovial singing continues in the packed ice cream shop as I all but devour the lavender Earl Grey oat cream. I'd been on the fence between this and the honey lavender, and I chose well. Today's visit won't be the last before I head home, guaranteed.

Exiting the shop, I turn left and walk in the direction of Sweet Spot Bakery. I scoured their social media account last night and got a tiny glimpse at what the bakery offered. I never saw a menu, but several images showed cases of baked goods and breakfast items. Hence my need for a bag.

Not only would I order sweets to last me a few days, but I'd also grab some breakfast items I could store and eat in my room. Another great way to avoid the best breakfast joint in town... and the woman who owns it.

CHAPTER 8

ALESSANDRA

"I'll be back soon."

Willow waves me off. "Don't rush. The doors are locked and everyone's doing their thing."

I scan the dining room and spot Lyndsay. Earbuds in, she bops to the music only she can hear as she wipes down tables and chairs. Sharon clears uneaten scones from the case and wipes down the shelves while August is at the kitchen prep station, slicing and dicing ingredients for tomorrow.

"Thanks, Will."

She taps on the register screen and runs today's totals before plucking the tills and heading for the office. "Tell Lucy and Fiona I say hi."

I exit through the back, hit unlock on my fob, and hop in my SUV. Rolling down the windows, I breathe in the sweet scent of spring as I drive along the alley behind the stores.

The song on the radio ends as I park the SUV. Exiting, I don't bother locking up since I won't be long. I enter through the employee entrance at Lucy and Fiona's and wave when I spot Fiona at the butcher-block table, icing a cake.

"Hey, lady. How are you?"

Fiona straightens, sets the frosting knife down, and steps around the table. In two strides, she wraps me in a hug. "Busy as hell, but good. You?"

"Same. The season is here."

"I love and hate it." We both laugh. "Thanks for coming over to pick up your order. Mia called in sick today, so Luce has been running the front alone."

"No problem. Hope Mia feels better soon. And before I forget, Willow says hi."

Fiona rounds the table and picks up where she left off. "Me too. And hi back." She twirls the cake on its pedestal and smooths the frosting. "Wasn't sure if you'd come in the front or back, so I stashed your order beneath the cases out front."

Although Sweet Spot Bakery is coveted for its cake and flaky pastries, they make a long list of sweet and savory baked goods. Not only do I offer Sweet Spot's scones, croissants, and biscuits in Java and Teas Me, every sandwich we make is on their bread.

A few years back, Lucy and Fiona had been overrun with customers during the season. They'd had the product but couldn't get everyone in and out fast enough. Unfortunately, they missed out on countless sales because tourists got impatient with the wait. When it was mentioned at the town meeting, I offered to sell some of their product at Java and Teas Me. After further discussion, we sorted out the details and hatched a plan.

Since that first day, it has been a fruitful endeavor for both businesses. Once the townsfolk heard the news, if Sweet Spot was busy, they came my way.

Fiona prepped the dough for the biscuits and scones each day, delivering it in tubs. The croissants came to us rolled out and ready for the oven. My kitchen staff formed and baked the other items per Fiona's instructions.

"Perfect. I'll go give Lucy a squeeze, grab the goods, and get out of your hair."

I push through the door between the kitchen and store. "Hey, Lucy—" My throat goes dry as I come to a screeching halt.

Three people back in the line, Braydon peers around the other guests, scanning the cases. He has yet to see me, but I won't get out of here undetected.

Damnit.

Ducking to my left, I pray he doesn't catch sight of me. But that flies right out the window when Lucy wraps up with her customer.

"Lessa," she squeals louder than usual. She spins around and ignores the line to hug the breath from my lungs. "Thank you so much."

Arms around her middle, I pat her back. "It's no problem. Really." I peer over her shoulder and release my hold, taking a step back. "Just wish you weren't so bogged down up here. Should've told me earlier, I might've been able to lend a hand."

"Pshh." She waves the notion away and steps back to the register. "You're just as busy." She rings up an order then glances my way. "But I should hire more help. At least during the busy months."

I move toward the cold cases and look everywhere except in Braydon's direction. "You know which cooler my goodies are in?"

Lucy hands a receipt to the customer. "At the end."

Farthest from the register. *Thank goodness.* If I'm swift

enough, I can get everything on the cart and wheel it out the back before Braydon reaches the register.

I dart to the end case, squat down, and sigh at my temporary shelter. Swinging the cooler door open, I hoist out the tubs, trays, and loaves. Still on my haunches, I tug the baking cart closer and load up what I can without standing.

The familiar timbre of Braydon's voice echoes down the line as he places one hell of an order. Lucy mills about behind the line and fills a few small boxes before handing them over. His mumbled "thank you" hits my ears, then a woman's voice filters in.

One breath at a time, I count to ten then assume it is safe to stand. Facing the case, I rise to my full height and learn just how wrong I am when a pair of amber irises stare back at me. Not from across the room—that would be much easier to avoid. Nope, Braydon is within touching distance on the opposite side of the case.

"Oh, hey," I say, doing my damnedest to act as if I didn't know he was here.

He laughs and shakes his head. "Should've known it wouldn't work."

I briefly look toward Lucy, but she isn't paying us any mind. "What?"

"Since seeing you in the coffee shop, I've tried really hard to avoid you."

I jerk back slightly. "Ouch," I say. Not that I should take offense. I am equally guilty of the same.

"Don't mean it to be hurtful." His eyes soften at this. "Just think it'll be easier for both of us."

I should open my mouth and voice my agreement. Should tell him steering clear of each other is for the best. When we spent the night together, a nonverbal agreement was made. One night of sex and nothing more.

I should agree... but my damn mouth won't form the words.

Every time I think of Braydon, every time I lay eyes on him, all I want to say is yes. Yes to his lips. Yes to his touch. And definitely yes to more sex.

What did I get myself into?

Tucking my lips between my teeth, I nod. "You're right." He is, really. Doesn't mean I like it. "I don't usually come here." I circle my finger in the air. "But they were shorthanded today."

He licks his lips and my eyes drop to bear witness. I swipe my damp palms over my thighs before looking back up.

Leaning into the case, he lifts a hand and beckons me closer with the curl of his finger. I stare at his hand for a beat and remember all the things he did with those fingers. Swallowing, I mirror him and lean in.

"It's not that I *want* to avoid you." He glances toward the register and I do the same. No one pays us any mind. "But it wouldn't do either of us any good if we spent more time together." At this, I feel the tension between my brows tightening. "Relationships aren't my thing." Something passes over his expression as he says this. But it vanishes before I decipher what it means. He shrugs. "It won't end well."

I hear everything he is telling me. Hear him say we should both step away and go about our lives. And I agree.

But something inside me won't let me tell him as much.

It isn't because I want a relationship and my heart is set on this man. My life is too busy. Spending time with someone I care about would be damn near impossible. I live and breathe my job. Every day.

In my head, I know this. But for some reason, my heart refuses to accept the memo.

"'Kay," I mutter. "Message received." I take a deep breath and square my shoulders. "Best way to avoid me is to not come into JTM. Shouldn't be a problem."

He sighs as his shoulders cave in slightly. His body language screams dejection while his words express the opposite. "Yeah." He nods. "No problem at all."

He takes a step back, turns his back to me, and heads for the door. I follow his every step with my eyes as my heart pounds a vicious rhythm in my chest. And when he walks out the door, a small splinter forms in my chest.

I lift a hand and press the heel of my palm to the unfamiliar sensation in the hopes it will stop. But it doesn't.

No romance. Just fun.

"It's for the best," I whisper to myself.

CHAPTER 9

BRAYDON

If I made the right choice, why have I felt this endless, deep ache beneath my sternum for the past two days? Like a fissure slowly forming in my chest, stealing my next breath.

The heel of my hand comes to my chest and I press against the twinge. Crush the sensation. Shove it down and away.

Because this feeling, this wistful pang… needs to end. No good will come of it.

Serious equals heartache.

I repeat the mantra again and again as my eyes drift across the street. Three storefronts down, Alessandra chats with customers sitting on the coffee shop patio. A towel in her hand and a dazzling smile on her face. The woman at the table says something and Alessandra lifts a hand to her mouth, covering a laugh.

Seeing her so carefree and jovial amplifies the twinge in my chest.

"Walk away. Just walk away," I mutter to myself.

I drop my gaze to the sidewalk, take a deep breath, and

shuffle forward. Put one foot in front of the other and amble toward the bed-and-breakfast.

Spending the first half of my day in the diner, I filled up on breakfast and lunch while outlining the first third of my story for the magazine. The pancake special and BLT had hit the spot, but the coffee left something to be desired.

All it took was one sip and my mind spiraled down a rabbit hole. From mediocre coffee to decent coffee. Decent coffee to good coffee. Then it shifted to my favorite coffee shop in the city. To the way my favorite barista always draws cute pictures or writes happy messages on my cups. How he always adds the perfect amount of oat milk and stevia to my coffee.

And then, as if second nature, my mind strayed in the wrong direction. To the morning I walked into Java and Teas Me. To the boisterous woman with silky blonde hair, radiant blue eyes, and a smile I won't soon forget.

It never takes much for my mind to drift to her. We may have only spent one night together, but damn was it unforgettable.

Problem is, I need to forget her. Need to not set myself up for another trip down anguish avenue.

"A little more than a week. Peruse the town, take some pictures, and go home," I remind myself. "Eight more days. Only eight."

I dash into the B&B, drop off my notes, snag my camera, then leave. I hop in my SUV, crank the engine, and drive out of the lot. When I reach Main Street, I flick on my blinker then turn. Away from the heart of this town. Away from her.

I just need air.

Rescues Gone Wild is nothing short of brilliant. A place where previously injured or displaced animals can heal and live the remainder of their lives in a safe environment similar to what they would experience in the wild, with exceptions.

Majority of the animals here have their own habitat—each a little different depending on the animal. Visitors to the habitat have options on which tour they want to embark on. Aside from the petting farm, aquariums and reptile rooms, there is also the option to drive through the habitats of the larger animals.

On the far outskirts of Lake Lavender, I choose bravery and pay for the driving self-tour.

"Thank you for your support, sir," the young woman at the ticket booth says. A toothy smile brightens her expression. "Would you like to feed the animals throughout the tour?"

Sounds fun. "Sure."

She holds up a large loaf of thickly sliced bread. "This bread is made specifically for the animals here. Please do not feed them anything other than the bread." She pauses and I nod. "One loaf or two?"

Lifting a hand to my chin, I scratch at the stubble there and shrug. "What would you recommend?"

"Two." A chuckle leaves her lips as she shakes her head. "Some of the animals are quite greedy and you may run out with just one."

"Then two it is."

She tallies my order and I hand over my credit card. Twenty dollars later, she passes me the bread then holds up a small map and tells me about the setup. I listen to every word and rule she says. When she points to the bison area, she taps the map with more gusto.

"When you reach the elk and bison area, you'll see two sets of gates. One will not open until the other is closed. While driving through this area, no matter what, do not stop. The only exception is if you're having car trouble. If you stop, your car or person may incur damage, which we are not liable for."

My eyes widen as I nod. "I understand."

"You may choose to skip this enclosure and are given the option before gate one." She staples my receipt to the map and hands it over. "If you need assistance anytime during the tour, our phone number is on the opposite side of the map."

Though it is a cool fifty degrees out, sweat dampens my underarms. *Sheesh, I hope I don't need assistance.*

Thanking her, I lightly press the accelerator and aim my SUV toward the start of the tour. I unfasten the twisty tie from both loaves of bread and drive uphill to the first observation area on the map—sika deer and prairie dogs.

As I crest the hill, I spot a young doe near the trees. I roll down the window halfway then fish a piece of bread from the bag. Pressing the brake, I stop and hold out the slice of bread. The deer doesn't approach the car but eyes the bread. Not wanting to make her uncomfortable, I toss the bread in her direction and watch as she dashes for the piece once it lands.

Twenty feet ahead, I pause beside a sectioned-off area where the prairie dogs live. A few heads pop up when I stop and eye me in the hopes I will toss them bread. I throw a slice toward each end and in the middle of the enclosure.

Smiling, I press the accelerator and head for the next area. Llamas.

"Oh shit," I blurt out as I enter the section.

My finger goes to the window button and I quickly roll up

the window, only leaving a crack large enough to slide a piece of bread through. At the sight of my vehicle, several llamas charge forward. Until this very moment, I didn't know charging was something llamas did.

Learn something new every day.

Shoving a piece of bread through the window crack, I press the accelerator a little harder and reach seven miles per hour. Not that it seems to help much.

One by one, the llamas hover around the car. Tongues licking the windows, a few sneaking in through the cracked driver's side window. And all I can do is laugh as I shove more slices through the window.

"No wonder I need two loaves," I say on a laugh as I offer another slice. "You guys may get one whole loaf."

The path rounds a small cliff, granting me a momentary reprieve from the ravenous llamas. But as soon as the path straightens and descends, the llamas run across the thin grass to beg for more.

Three more slices and I exit the llama enclosure. The next few areas are a bit quieter. The animals are interested in the bread but act a little less exuberant upon my approach. Zebras and Tibetan yaks. Brown bears and black bears.

The next section does not allow feeding. These animals either have special diets or are new rescues. Wolves and hyenas. Large cats and coyotes. Raccoons and peacocks and emu.

At the stop sign, I have the choice to exit or drive through the final enclosure. The elk and bison. I take a deep breath and aim my car to the right. As I approach the first gate, a large red sign with white letters greets me.

"No stopping in the elk or bison compound. Damage may occur."

I swallow and accelerate forward. Gate one opens and I

drive through. Elk meander nearby but aren't interested in me at the moment. Continuing forward, gate two opens; the same red sign is on either side.

"What the hell did I get myself into?"

The first minute in the paddock is lackluster. Cars farther in have elk and bison corralling them. I grab slice after slice of the bread and toss them out the window into the field. It isn't until I round the first corner in the loop that one of the bison takes an interest in my vehicle. And I may just have a heart attack.

Closing in on the car ahead of me, a bison shifts his gaze and steadily walks in my direction. Two breaths pass and that steady walk turns into a sprint.

"Oh shit!"

Heart pounding in my chest, I crack the window more and launch piece after piece out the window and away from my car. Mere feet from my car, the bison redirects and heads toward the offered snack. This happens two more times as I drive around the rest of the loop.

I exit the enclosure, drive out the main gate and park my car in the lot. Throwing the car in park, I drop my head to the steering wheel and press a hand to my chest.

"Nothing like looking death in the face... for entertainment," I mutter.

Minutes pass as I work to level out my breathing. And once it does, once my heart finds its natural rhythm, I hate the first thought that filters in.

Alessandra.

The idea of bringing her to this place and laughing as we fend off the energetic llamas and colossal bison. Of the fight-or-flight rush we would both endure driving through certain areas. Followed by the need to drive off and find somewhere secluded to quell the surge of adrenaline.

I groan. "Why, brain? Why?"

Regardless of how much distance I put between myself and Alessandra, I can't escape her.

After my first trip to Lake Lavender, it took several weeks to not think of our night together twenty-four seven. Slowly, the fantasy of her dimmed. Faded into the background as I worked all hours of the day and traveled to new towns.

The only time she snuck back in was when life got quiet and loneliness or horniness took hold.

Nights when I fisted my cock and tugged roughly, it was Alessandra who entered my mind. The image of her beneath me—head tipped back, lips parted, breasts smashed into my chest, nails digging into my back as my hips rocked in time with hers. On those nights, I swear I heard her whimpers in the room. Swear I felt the heat of her breath and slickness of her skin on mine. And when I came, it was with the name I'd given her on my tongue.

Firecracker.

Eyes closed, I bang my head against the steering wheel. Roll it side to side as I shove away thoughts of her.

Dad wants me in Lake Lavender for at least another eight days. Wants me to capture all the magic in this small town. But I may need to cut my trip short.

Six days. I have been here six days and I feel my control slipping. Control I need.

"One more day," I whisper to myself. "I'll give this trip one more day." Then, I will drive home and spend the rest of my "time away" scouring the internet and reading the book I purchased at One More Chapter. Should be enough to write a *magical* story. It has to be. Because there is no way I can spend another week in this town.

My heart won't survive.

CHAPTER 10

ALESSANDRA

"Have a great weekend," I say to Sharon as we exit the back of the coffee shop.

"You too, Lessa." She waves and jogs to her car.

Inserting the key in the dead bolt, I lock up then dash up the stairs to my apartment. Unlocking the door, I slip inside, drop my purse on the table and shuffle to my bedroom. I strip out of my work clothes, twist my hair up in a bun, and jump in the shower to wash the day away.

Towel secured around my torso, I head for the closet in search of clothes for girls' night. I tug a red top from its hanger and snag the black denim pants from the shelf, tossing both on the bed. Sifting through the top drawer of my dresser, a wicked smile stretches my cheeks when I pick up my favorite black thong and matching bra.

This is what I need.

Maybe wearing the racy undergarments will boost my chances tonight in the club. Maybe I will walk out of Black Silk with a new distraction. Someone to steal my incessant thoughts of Braydon, even if just for an hour. The sixteen-hour shifts I've pulled the last three days haven't done the trick. Every free second I have to breathe, there he is... taking over my brain like some alien invasion.

Yesterday, I spotted him across the street and a little ways down the block. He hovered near the florist shop, barely visible behind the evergreen near the street. I chatted with customers, pretending I didn't see him.

But I saw him the entire time. Counted quietly to myself as he watched me from a distance. Peeked up from under my lashes but kept my head downcast and watched as he wandered back in the direction of the B&B.

Avoiding Braydon hasn't been too difficult since our bumping into each other at the Sweet Spot Bakery. I simply stayed within the confines of Java and Teas Me and my humble apartment above the shop. Not that I'd had anywhere else to be.

Tonight, though... I am going out. And when the girls and I make our way upstairs after dinner, I plan to find a better distraction on the dance floor. Hopefully one that will distract me *off* the dance floor as well.

Dressed, I shuffle back into the bathroom. I hang the towel on the bar then step up to the vanity. Leaning in, I survey the dark half-moons beneath my eyes.

"Definitely need to cover that up," I mumble as I swipe up the foundation and get to work.

Several layers of makeup later, I sift through the few lip products I own and select the one that will surely garner me some attention. Spitfire Red. Twisting up the tube, I roll the pigment over my lips and feel the energy boost I need surge through my veins. I undo my bun, brush the tangles from my hair, and opt to leave it down for the evening.

With one last glance in the mirror, a jittery energy lifts my spirits. As I shoulder my purse and head for my car, my mantra repeats in my head.

No romance. Just fun.

After we settle the bill, Mags, Lena and I make the trek upstairs to Black Silk's nightclub. As the walls transition from charcoal to that deep red, a shot of thrill hits my bloodstream.

Feels like weeks have passed since I've relaxed. Since I've let go of stress and worry and had quality me time.

Tonight, I plan to do exactly that… let go.

The bouncer steps aside and grants us entry. "Enjoy your evening, ladies."

We weave through the crowd and tables, Mags surveying the room for Geoff. The moment she spots him, she reaches for my hand and tugs me forward. After a jolt, I manage to take Lena's hand in my other and tow her along.

"You'd think she hadn't seen him for months," Lena shouts over the music.

Coming to an abrupt halt, Mags drops my hand and goes right to Geoff, plops on the leather couch beside him, and kisses him with more PDA than I have ever seen from her. Neither Lena nor I move as we watch the most reticent person we know act without restraint.

"Yeah… can't say I know this Mags."

I tug Lena toward a vacant couch and sit. Geoff and Mags are to our right, while Logan and Owen sit on the couch across from us. A woman is on Logan's left and Owen casually sips his whiskey. I lift a hand and wave.

"Hey, guys." I tip my head in Logan's direction. "Having fun already, I see."

Logan lifts his beer bottle in cheers. "Absolutely."

I twist in my seat to face Lena. "Want to dance?"

She shakes her head. "Not yet. A little more wine first."

Pushing out my bottom lip, I give her my best pout. "Fine," I huff out. "Order me one?" She nods. "Thank you." I kiss her temple and rise from the couch. "I'll warm up the dance floor."

As I weave through the crowd, Lena says something I don't hear. I lift my arms over my head as I reach the middle of the room, my hips swaying to the beat. The bass rattles my bones. The treble wakes up my soul. And the hypnotic voice of the man singing lights a fire in my chest.

This. This is what I needed.

I close my eyes and dance. Let the music pull me in, stir me to life. Bodies move in time with the beat, occasionally brushing my side or back. From time to time, heat blankets me from behind. A firm body pressed against me. I don't pull away. No, I lean into them. Press my body flush with theirs as we move to the beat. And when they step away, I dance more. Wait for the right person to step up.

And then he does.

Warmth surrounds me as strong hands grip my hips. He drags me closer, his hold on me tightening as he grinds himself against my ass. One of my hands drapes his on my hip while the other reaches behind me to his nape. Neither of us says a word as we all but fuck on the dance floor.

Lost in his heat, his touch, the feel of his body against mine, I let go. For the first time in too long, I surrender to what I feel and disregard all the rampant thoughts I've had this week.

His free hand drifts from my hip and trails the hemline of my shirt, stopping low on my belly. He flattens his palm, spreads out his long fingers, and pins me in place as he grows hard beneath his zipper. Soft lips kiss the skin where my neck and shoulder meet and I moan. Give him more of my weight. Grind against his thick erection.

My skin hums as he kisses his way up the side of my neck. With each press of his lips, the room and people and music fade more into the background. When he reaches my ear, his tongue slowly glides up the shell. I shiver and he tightens his hold.

"This week has been the worst and best week in years," he says just above the music and I freeze. *Braydon.* "God… all I've thought about is you."

His other arm bands around my middle as he rocks his hips, wordlessly asking me to keep dancing. My body caves to his will. My head screams to resist, but my body… she is a traitorous bitch.

"No matter what I do, no matter how hard I try to avoid you, at every turn you are there. In person or in my head." His lips dance over the skin beneath my ear. "Why can't I stop thinking about you?"

Thank goodness we are in public. Thank goodness my friends are here to pull my attention away. Otherwise, I'd probably take Braydon's hand and haul him back to my loft. Have my way with him. Break one of my cardinal rules— nothing more than casual hookups.

"Wish I knew," I answer. Slowly, I spin to face him. His hands drop to my ass, one of his legs pushing between mine as he pins my front to his. My hands trace the tops of his shoulders and my fingers drift up into his thick locks. "Much as I hate to admit it, I can't stop thinking about you either."

He groans, dropping his forehead to mine. "This is bad."

"So bad."

"Have dinner with me. Tomorrow."

It isn't a question, more like a demand. Braydon may be somewhat reserved with most people, but when he feels comfortable with someone, another side of him comes out. A side I met once... six months ago. A side I like a little too much.

"Why?"

He inches back, his eyes darting between mine. The corner of his mouth kicks up as he shakes his head. "Never really had that work dinner." His lips push out slightly, his shoulders lifting in a shrug. "We should try again."

His proposal for dinner sounds more like a date than two professionals meeting for a meal to discuss business. I want to pass up his offer. I want to tell him no.

But when I open my mouth to say as much, it doesn't happen. Instead, I say, "Where?"

A slow smile plumps his cheeks and I want to squeeze my thighs together. Leaning in, his breath hot on my ear, he says, "Give me your number and I'll message you in the morning."

I close my eyes and pray to whatever deity will heed my call. *Please, please, please... don't let this become something it can't be.*

Inching back, I open my eyes and breathe deeply. Mentally shove down the building ball of anxiety beneath my diaphragm. Then I do the unthinkable. I hold out my hand in a silent request for his phone.

Please don't let this be a mistake.

And then I give Braydon—the only one-night stand I've thought about past one night—my phone number.

God, I am an idiot.

CHAPTER 11
BRAYDON

I have no idea what came over me last night. Seeing Alessandra dancing in the middle of the club, hips swaying to the music, other men too damn close... I was a man possessed. Wanted no one dancing near her, with her.

No one touched her but me. At least, that was my mindset as I slid off the barstool and walked onto the dance floor— something I'd never done.

I may have the occasional burst of extroversion, but at the end of the day, I curl in on myself. Keep my overflowing well of thoughts and feelings inside.

Rolling onto my stomach, I groan into the pillow. "God-damn fool," I mumble.

I push up on my forearms and reach for my phone on the nightstand. Going through my typical morning routine, I open my email, delete almost all without reading, and respond to one from Dad. Instead of sending texts, Dad sends emails more often than not. It isn't a generational thing. He just spends more time on his laptop than his phone and typing out

Good morning, son,

> *Hope the first week conjured up more of your magic. Let me know when you'll be back and we'll have dinner at the house.*
>
> *Love you,*
> *Dad*

I type out a brief reply and hit send.

Morning Dad,

> *I'll call when I head home. Love you too.*

The next hour goes by in a blur of social media posts. Procrastination at its finest and the perfect form of avoidance. But I can't put off the fact I asked Alessandra to have dinner with me tonight. Details need to be sorted out. Messages need to be exchanged.

Dragging myself out of bed, I shuffle across the room and grab the town brochures off the desk. Parking myself in the chair near the fireplace, I sift through the pages and scour over the local food establishments. Familiar with some, I skip the places I've already dined in.

Three places stand out when I reach the end of the list. J's Sushi Bar, Trixie's Thai House, and Black Silk. Although I was in Black Silk's upstairs club last night, I hadn't dined downstairs. Maybe I should just throw all three options in a message to Alessandra and see which one sticks.

Opening the messaging app, I type out a text and stare at it for three breaths, thumb hovering over the send arrow before tapping the screen.

> Morning. Looking at places to meet up.
> Japanese, Thai or Black Silk?

I stare at the screen, my eyes losing focus as I wait for her to read and respond. The screen dims and I close my eyes. Mentally shake my head at the attachment already forming.

Don't get attached. Attachment leads to serious. And serious equals heartache.

I toss the phone on the table and push out of the chair. Amble toward the bathroom and crank the hot water in the shower. Strip out of my boxers and step under the spray. Press a palm to the tile while the other wraps around my thickening cock and tugs.

My morning routine hasn't changed much since my relationship with Gabby. If male virginity could be restored, mine would have in the year after we split. Not only had I not been with another woman, I'd also not touched myself. The idea of feeling pleasure after the person I loved rejected me seemed beyond wrong.

We were in love. She *loved* me. And then she broke me in a way no one else could.

Finishing in the shower, I cut the water, step out and dry off. I fetch a graphic tee and pair of jeans from the dresser. Slipping my glasses on, I brush my teeth and hair before putting on socks and shoes.

Today is a lazy day. No work and no agenda other than seeing Alessandra. Part of me wants to hole up in the room and watch meaningless television or read the book I purchased. But I doubt I'll be able to stay put all day.

I pick my phone up and tap the screen. No notifications.

A pang twists beneath my diaphragm and I immediately despise the sensation.

"She's working. Just stop."

Unable to bear another bad cup of coffee, I slip my phone, wallet, and keys in my pockets, grab a hoodie, and exit my room. I dash down the stairs and out the front door of the B&B. One foot in front of the other, I pull my hoodie on and head for Main Street. To the one place I've avoided all week. Toward the one person I've tried my damnedest to stay away from but keep running into.

As I bite down on my breakfast sandwich, Alessandra sidles up to the table, hands on her hips.

"The Hook Up, huh?"

I chew the bite in my mouth, trying not to laugh, then swallow and chase it with coffee. I lift a napkin to my mouth and wipe.

"Pretty damn good." I shrug and cock a brow. "I'm not the one who named the menu items. Don't want people hooking up in your restaurant, don't make it so easy."

Her neck and cheeks pinken as her eyes widen. She yanks out the chair across from me and takes a seat. Forearms on the table, she leans in.

"Really?" Her eyes dart around the room then lock with mine. "Yes, I named everything with an ounce of dirty humor." Her palms lift off the table then slap the surface. "It's meant to be funny. Not taken seriously."

I grab a fresh napkin and wipe my hands clean. Then,

without thinking, I reach across the table and lay my hands over hers. The contact sends a ripple of energy over the surface of my skin. Heat spreads from the tips of my fingers, travels up my arms, and weaves its way to the center of my chest.

My eyes roll shut as I absorb the sensation. As I allow myself to feel the burn that only her touch generates. And then I draw my hands back and lay them in my lap.

"Sorry," I mutter.

I may have wrapped my arms around her in public last night, but I'd had a couple beers and seen one too many men get close to her. I wanted to be the man she clung to, not some random guy.

But isn't that what I am? Some random guy.

We don't know each other. At all. So who am I to be jealous? Who am I to think that she belongs to me?

I am no one.

She taps the table and I blink out of my momentary realization. "Hey," she says, trying to garner my attention.

But I keep my eyes on the table, on her hands. Again, she taps the table, then leans forward and lower so her line of sight aligns with mine.

"Hey," she repeats. "Don't worry about it." Her eyes survey the room, pausing at the counter. She inhales deeply, leans back in the chair, and crosses her arms over her chest. "Just saw your text. Weekends are busier."

I mirror her position and nod. "Figured as much." Although I knew she'd be busy, I still wanted to see her name pop up on my screen. Still wanted the small connection. And I hated myself for desiring such an indulgence. "Seeing as we're having dinner tonight, didn't see the harm in stopping by for breakfast."

A groove forms between her brows and I clench my hands under the table. I take a deep breath to stop myself from leaning forward and touching the spot with my thumb. The gesture is too comfortable, too intimate. Something we don't share.

"You could've stopped in throughout the week." The corner of her mouth kicks up in a smirk. "I don't bite." At this, I cock my brow and her face pinks again. She clears her throat. "In public," she says, a breath above a whisper.

Silence stretches between us for one, two, three breaths before we both laugh. And just like that, the tension surrounding us thins. It never fades completely, but at least now I breathe easier.

Straightening in my seat, I scoop up my breakfast sandwich. "Thoughts on dinner?" I shove the messy sandwich between my lips and take a bite.

For a beat, I stare at her as her eyes stay fixed on my lips. I swallow and she blinks, eyes lifting to mine.

She shrugs. "I've been to all three. Would prefer Japanese or Thai since I ate at Black Silk last night."

"One or two?" I blurt out.

She lifts a hand and rubs her jaw near her ear. "W-what?"

I lean in. "One or two?"

Her hand slides back and squeezes the nape of her neck. "Um… one, I guess."

Leaning closer, I lower my voice. "Wasn't thinking something gross or dirty." I laugh. "Just a way to randomly choose dinner."

At this, her entire frame relaxes. I bite my cheek to refrain from laughing harder. *Where was your mind at?*

"Thai food it is. How's six thirty?"

Chair legs scrape wood as she scoots her chair back and

rises. Her eyes grow hazy as they drift around the room. She nods.

"Six thirty is good. I'll let you know if it changes."

"Cool. Meet you there?"

She nods again and takes a step away from the table. "Yeah. Meet you there."

CHAPTER 12

ALESSANDRA

I park a few spots down from Trixie's. My gaze roams the sidewalk until I land on Braydon.

Clad in dark denim, a rich-green Henley, and Chucks, he rocks back on his heels. Hands shoved in his pockets, he eyes each person as they pass, giving an abrupt smile to each.

Inhaling deeply, I cut the engine, shoulder my purse, and exit the car. When I hit the lock on the fob, he looks down the sidewalk and smiles wider. He takes a step in my direction, pulls his hands from his pockets, and pushes his glasses up the bridge of his nose.

I reach him in ten strides, lips trapped between my teeth. Like a nervous twit, I raise a hand. "Hey."

"Hey."

"Ready?"

He nods and I step toward the door. As I reach for the handle and pull, warmth lands on my lower back. I suck in a breath, my stride faltering for a beat. Three hour-long seconds pass before normal breathing resumes and I lead us inside.

This is not a date. Business. This is just business.

His hand remains in place until we reach the table. His hand falls away and I immediately miss the contact, the weight, the buzzy connection. The host hands us menus and tells us a server will arrive momentarily.

I lift the menu and pretend to scan the selection. Considering I eat from Trixie's almost weekly, I knew what I was ordering the second Braydon said Thai. Spring rolls, Tom Kha soup, and green curry chicken. I have a rotation of sorts with each restaurant in town. It's usually more than a month before I circle back to the top of the list.

Angelica sidles up to the table, her brightest smile in place. "Hey, Lessa. Nice seeing ya."

I return her smile. "You too. How's your dad?"

She rolls her eyes. "Stubborn as ever. The day that man actually accepts the help he knows he needs, I swear the earth will stop spinning."

A few months back, Teddy—Angelica's father—was constructing a new house on the outskirts of town and slipped off his ladder. Broke his right radius, the bones in his right wrist, and got a hairline fracture in his femur. Needless to say, he is not happy.

"Well, I hope he heals soon."

"Thanks, Lessa. I'll pass along the love." She looks between me and Braydon. "Can I start you with drinks and an appetizer?"

Braydon lays down his menu. "I'm ready to order if you are."

I wave a hand in his direction. "By all means."

Angelica scribbles down our orders then wanders off.

Leaning back in the booth, I futz with the hem of my shirt. "So…" I purse my lips. "How's the story coming along?"

Before he answers, Angelica returns. She sets our drinks on the table and tells us the appetizers will be out soon. Soft music drifts back in the moment she leaves. We both reach for our drinks, me downing half my wine while he sips his beer.

"Not bad." His gaze drops as he picks at the label on the beer bottle. "Think I've hit up most of the touristy spots." Then his gaze snaps up, an unfamiliar glint in his eyes and animation in his expression. Leaning forward, his fingers fall away from the bottle. "Have you been to Rescues Gone Wild?"

Was definitely not expecting that question. Laughter bursts from my lips and I slap a hand over my mouth. Kind of a silly question, considering I live here.

Last time I visited the animal rescue was during high school. The teachers swore the trip was for educational purposes. A way to teach us about wildlife in person. To respect nature. My friends and I thought it was a great escape from the mundane school day. What we didn't know was how terrifying it'd be to have bison charge the car. And since no one can drive faster than ten miles per hour in the place, we all thought we were going to die. The teachers wouldn't admit the glee they felt at seeing us frightened, but I caught them laughing under their breaths. Saw the smiles they tried to hide.

As a teen, I hated how much they enjoyed our fear. As an adult, I understand the kicks they got from the trip.

I nod. "It's been a while, but yeah."

"First off"—he holds up a finger—"those llamas are fucking crazy."

I drop my chin to my chest, cover my mouth and laugh.

"Second, I almost pissed my pants in the bison enclosure."

This makes me laugh harder, only because I know where he is coming from.

"I mean, shouldn't they tell guests to use the bathroom

before entering? And no one should go in that place alone." His hands fly to either side of his face. "One person should be focused on the road while the other tosses out bread." Eyes wide, he shakes his head. "Damn llamas tried to corral me off a cliff."

At this, I snort-laugh and clutch my stomach. I don't remember the llamas as much as the bison, but I easily picture the man across from me, terrified in his car as llamas swarm and veer him toward the edge of the road.

"It's not funny."

I laugh harder. My vision blurs as tears spill down my cheeks. My hand clamps down over my mouth as I try to think of something, anything, to make me stop laughing. But every time I look across the table, it kicks into the next gear.

He huffs. "Okay, fine." His eyes shoot toward the ceiling. "It's a little funny." He joins my laughter for a moment, then points a finger in my direction. "Go there alone. You'll see."

Angelica steps up to the table and deposits our appetizers. The scent of fried spring rolls and chicken satay hits my nose and my stomach grumbles. She tells us to enjoy then walks off.

The table goes quiet as we dig in. An unsuitable-for-public moan leaves my lips as the flavors hit my tongue. Across the table, Braydon freezes. His satay skewer midway between the mini grill and his open mouth.

I cover my mouth with my hand and mumble, "Sawee," then swallow the bite. Dropping my hand, I take a sip of my wine. "Thai food's my favorite." I shrug and take another bite, not knowing what else to say.

Braydon bites a piece of chicken from the skewer and hums.

Why can't I be that restrained? Instead, I am over here moaning like spring rolls are better than sex. Well, sadly, they are better than some of the sex I've had. But not better than sex with Braydon.

Mentally, I shake my head. *Shut. Up.*

The rest of dinner goes by with good conversation, more drinks, and less moaning. I never realized how vocal I am over food until tonight. Mags and Lena should have shut that shit down a long time ago.

Braydon tells me about all the places he has visited in his first week here. I chime in with what I know about each store, restaurant or adventure and the people who own them. He asks about Java and Teas Me. How long it has been open. When I came up with the idea. What inspired me to want to run a restaurant.

The more we talked, the more comfortable I felt with him. Though we know next to nothing about each other, Braydon feels familiar. Safe. Easy. Without effort, I picture us beyond this. Beyond a one-night stand. Beyond two acquaintances getting together to chat over a meal.

This may be a *work* dinner, we may be discussing the places he has visited for work while he's here, but this is so much more than job-related.

When Angelica sets the bill holder on the table, Braydon snaps it up before I can. A half smile tugs up one corner of his mouth.

"I got this." He slips his card in and hands it back to Angelica. "After all, I did invite you."

Much as I want to argue—because this is *not* a date—I keep my lips sealed.

With the bill settled, we exit the restaurant and he follows me to my car. A beep echoes around us as I press the button on my fob. I step off the curb and move toward the driver's side door, opening it and tossing my purse inside.

Sweat dampens my skin as I shut the door and take a step closer to him. Nervous energy forms a ball in my throat and I swallow. My fingers pick at the hem of my shirt as I take another step, leaving inches between us.

This is not a date.

I meet his gaze and, in my periphery, he swallows.

"Tonight was nice. Thank you," I say softly.

I lick my lips, unsure what to do or say next, and his eyes drop to follow the action. He swallows again, shuffles a little closer, and nods imperceptibly.

"Was nice." His amber irises come back to mine, fire simmering just beneath the surface. "Should do it again."

Immediately, my mind drifts to something other than food. When he suggests we *do it again*, flashes of him hovering above me, hands pinning mine above my head, our moans filling the room come crashing in.

My feet move of their own volition, inching me closer. And with this singular move, we are but a breath apart. We have yet to touch each other, but I *feel* him. Feel his heat, his need, his desire. They mirror my own.

And damn, I want to kiss him. I want to feel the softness of his lips and subtle scrape of his stubble. The rise and fall of his chest as our lips start to move together. As we taste each other for the first time in six months. As we give in to the obvious attraction between us.

I shut down every thought except one. Him. For once in my adult life, I just feel.

Pushing up on my toes, I lean in and press my lips to his. And damn, it is so much better than I remember.

CHAPTER 13
BRAYDON

For months, I fantasized about the possibility of this moment. Of my lips on hers again. My hands on her skin, her curves.

In less than a minute, the fantasy became a reality.

When I returned to Lake Lavender, I had no expectation of seeing her again. Though the town is small, the likelihood of bumping into her seemed slim. Thousands of people lived here, and with the start of warmer days, tourists trickled in from bigger cities and out of state. Traffic isn't bumper to bumper, but plenty of cars line the streets and fill the lot at the bed-and-breakfast. Each day, I greet new faces as I walk through town, many of them with the same curious eyes as they take in the stores and scenery.

I'd returned to Lake Lavender with an agenda. Two weeks to visit the town, see the sights, meet the townsfolk, and write a story to entice readers.

Seems my agenda may change.

Whoosh, whoosh, whoosh.

My pulse thrums in my ears as my lips taste hers. Once

twice. My hands come to her cheeks, tip her head back and to the side. Softly, slowly, I kiss her. Relish in the suppleness of her lips. Revel in the weight of her frame as she presses her body against mine. Lose all sense of control as her lips part and the tip of her tongue traces my bottom lip.

My hold on her tightens. Fingers curling at the ends, digging into her hair and soft skin as I gasp.

Then her tongue strokes mine. Stokes the embers of the fire she lit inside me months ago. A fire I never let fully extinguish. A fire that, with each new taste, morphs into an inferno.

"We should…" *Kiss.* "Go somewhere." *Taste.* "Or…"

She sucks my tongue and I melt—literally—and back her up against the car. A groan vibrates my chest as I bruise her with my fingertips. I deepen the kiss and savor every piece of her she lets me have.

Her boundless intensity and fierce desire. Her stubborn strength and endless ambition. Her willingness to take what she wants, even if it will shred us in the end.

Because there is no way this will end well.

She breaks the kiss and inches back. "Braydon, I—"

My lips drop to hers and kiss her chastely. "Whatever you want." My thumb strokes her cheek and she leans into the subtle touch. "Your call."

Much as I hate handing her all the power, I have to. Because this time next week, I will pack my bags and drive away from here. Away from her. And though going our separate ways will undoubtedly hurt us both, I won't be the one living with the visual reminders when I look at landmarks or beds or parking lots. She will, and it is cruel of me to not take that into account.

Her fingers fumble with the cotton of my shirt. Tighten and loosen, only to repeat the motion again and again. She bites the corner of her bottom lip as her eyes dart between mine in search of answers or clues or anything to help her decide.

"I want to," she says softly and I don't miss the hint of reluctance in her tone.

"You want to, but…" I inch back and take a slow, deep breath.

Her eyes drift down the sidewalk as a *V* forms between her brows. Light laughter and conversation echo around us as people exit stores and restaurants. I don't concern myself with any of them. Don't shift my gaze from Alessandra's face as my thumbs continue to stroke her cheeks. But I witness every ounce of unease to mar her expression. Every facet of uncertainty.

Which is why I refuse to decide what happens next. Were it left up to me, my decision would be instantaneous, irrational, and lust induced.

Plain and simple, I want her. More than I have wanted anyone. And that terrifies me the most.

Alessandra and I will never be more than this. Undiluted chemistry, insatiable hunger, and unwilling to commit. And it would serve me well to remember as much.

Midnight-rimmed cobalt-blue irises search my eyes. Silently asking where we go from here. What step we take next. If this is a good idea. If this—us caving—is smart.

The answer is no, this isn't smart. But damn, I have never been this willing to be an idiot.

She shakes her head and straightens her spine. "But nothing." Her fingers loosen their hold on my shirt. "Follow me?"

My eyes narrow infinitesimally. She doesn't move, doesn't speak. Her shoulders square in my periphery, but I also note the uptick in her breathing. Confidence and surety light her expression. She does her damnedest to let it show in her body language too. But I see past her mask.

Subtly, I nod. "Yeah. Sure." I drop my lips to hers for three breaths then pull back. Meet her eyes one last time. Give her one last opportunity to change her mind.

As suspected, she doesn't. She purses her lips, holds up her key ring and jingles it, and spins to face her car.

The fifteen seconds it takes to walk to my car, the same five words cycle in my head.

I should have walked away.

Obviously, I prefer pain.

Complete. Dumbass.

I park next to Alessandra and stare up at the building through my windshield. Stare at the brick structure I was too lust drunk to pay any attention to last time. Curse under my breath at the fact I've sipped coffee and eaten breakfast a floor below the place where we had sex and been none the wiser.

Hell, not only are the walls of her home painted with the memories of our night together, the fire between us lingers in the air of the entire place.

Did I taint her home and business in one fell swoop?

We never said as much, but I assume she wants commitment as much as I do. Which is not at all.

So why bring me here? The first time and now. Why not go to the B&B and leave memories in a place neither of us calls ours? Or find some secluded spot away from the main thoroughfare and hook up in the back of the car?

I exit and lock my car. Amble in her direction with my

hands shoved in my pockets. Trek up the stairs and do my damnedest not to gawk at her curves as her hips sway inches from my face. Suck in a deep breath as she unlocks the door, steps inside, and I follow. She flicks a light switch near the door and soft amber light fills the space.

Out of nowhere, answers smack me square in the chest.

We are here so no one sees us together. Not because she is embarrassed to be seen with me but because small towns talk.

If we walked into the bed-and-breakfast together, someone might recognize her. Might watch us as we take the stairs to my room, silently casting their judgment on her. Criticism no one has the right to dole out, but will nonetheless. In a small town, some folks make it their business to share other people's secrets. All it would take is one misstep or keen observation from a gossiper and Alessandra's reputation in her hometown would be tainted.

We may never be anything more than acquaintances or bed buddies, but I respect her enough to not drag her through the mud.

"Drink?"

"Please."

Stashing her keys in her purse, she hangs it on a hook above a mudroom bench, toes off her shoes and tucks them in a cubby beneath, then walks off.

Three breaths pass before I take a step. Before I allow myself to look around and glimpse her personal space. Something I didn't do on my last visit.

Six months ago, we fumbled through the door with our lips stuck together. My eyes closed and hands roaming her body, she led the way to her room. The next several hours were nothing but lips and tongues and teeth and skin on skin. Not a single light got flipped on and I left before the sun rose.

Nothing about her home is familiar because I didn't want to remember. I didn't want to get attached. Because attachment inevitably leads to heartache, and I've had my share.

I toe off my Converse and place them in a cubby. Follow the path Alessandra took and step into the kitchen. The space is small but bigger than my kitchen in the city and big enough for a single person.

She drains wine from a glass then adds more before placing the bottle in the fridge. Spinning around, a hand flies to her chest.

"You startled me," she whispers.

Shuffling farther into the room, I pick up what I assume to be my glass. "Sorry. Didn't mean to." I lift the glass to my lips, sip the burgundy liquid, and watch her over the rim of the glass.

Why is this so damn awkward?

Because the lights are on. Because we are sipping wine and standing casually in her kitchen. And because this moment feels less like a hookup.

Tonight feels like more. Tonight feels dangerous.

She chugs the rest of her wine and sets her glass on the counter. Eyes on hers, I down the rest of my glass and set it next to hers. In the next breath, her hand wraps around mine. Her grip is as tender and firm as her personality. Goose bumps trail up my arm as a shiver rolls down my spine.

Before I get the chance to read into my reaction to her touch, she is on the move. Hauling me out of the kitchen and through the main living area. Down a short hall and into a bedroom. Her bedroom.

Stepping past the threshold, she drops my hand, walks to the side of the bed, and turns on a Himalayan salt lamp. Soft-pink light filters through the room, stealing some of the security the darkness provides. Alessandra remains rooted beside the nightstand, her back to me, while I linger near the door.

God, how I want to demolish the distance between us.

Three strides. In three strides, I'd wrap my arms around her middle. Press my lips to the soft skin where her neck and shoulder meet. Kiss a trail up the side of her neck. Nip at her ear as my hands roam down her belly and slowly peel her top off.

Step.

Removing the elastic from her hair, blonde strands sweep down her spine. She tosses the hair band on the nightstand.

Step.

Her hands drop to the bottom hem of her top and fist the fabric.

"Don't," I whisper and she grants me a glimpse of her profile.

Step.

My hands rest over hers as I press my front to her back. Audible breaths float through the room as her chest rises and falls faster. A shiver rolls through her as my fingertips lightly trail up her arms. Sweeping her hair aside, I dip down, run the tip of my nose across her shoulder, and inhale deeply. My eyes roll back as I reach the curve of her neck, my lips parting and tongue darting out to taste her.

One touch, one taste, one hit and she melts.

My hand trails over her collarbone to the front of her throat. Fingers splayed, I tighten my hold and tilt her head to the side. A moan reverberates in the room as I palm a breast and sink my teeth into her shoulder. She covers my hands with hers. Adds more pressure. Squeezes. Claws.

Ripping my hands away, she spins around, removes my glasses and sets them on the nightstand. Then her hands are in my hair, fingers fisting the strands, yanking me down and crashing her lips to mine. My arms snake around her middle and haul her impossibly closer. I walk her backward until she bumps into the bed.

My hands slide down either side of her waist to the bottom of her shirt. Mouth devouring hers, I fist the cotton of her shirt and slowly drag it up her body. The kiss breaks long enough to yank the shirt over her head and toss it aside. Followed by her bra. With deft fingers, I pop the button on her jeans and pull the zipper down the teeth.

Her hand dips beneath my shirt, fingertips ghosting over the skin at the waistband of my jeans. I suck in a breath, rest my hands on her hips, and curl my fingers. Hard.

"Fuck, firecracker," I breathe out. She has barely touched me and already I need to detonate.

Nails drag up my chest, pushing my shirt up and over my head. It hits the floor in a whoosh. We crash back together— lips and tongues tangling, fingers and hands fumbling. My jeans hit the floor with a thud, followed by hers.

Six months ago, I spent hours memorizing the softness of her skin. The flare of her hips. The curve of her breasts. And the way she fit perfectly against the length of my body. Everything about that night was perfection. Our chemistry was fire and vital and undeniable.

We will never be anything except passion. At least, that is what I keep telling myself.

A hand on her hip, I press a knee on the mattress and guide her down onto the bed. She scoots back and lies down, her hands framing my face. Her legs band around my waist, heels digging into my glutes and forcing me forward. My fingers bruise her hip as I rock my weight and length against her center.

She tips her head back and gasps. "Oh god."

I lace my fingers with hers and drag her hands up the bed. I kiss along her jaw, down her neck. Lick the length of her collarbone before drifting down and kissing the swell of her breast. Her grip on my fingers tightens. Her chest heaves as her heavy breaths float in the air.

Savoring every inch of her skin, I take my time. But when my mouth wraps around her nipple and I suckle the pert bud, her back bows off the bed. When I add a little teeth and lightly tug, her hold on me turns painful. Soft whimpers mingle with her heavy breaths as I rock my hips and grind my hard length against her middle.

I pay equal attention to her other breast then kiss my way down between her breasts and over her belly. I release her hands as I drag my lips and tongue over her navel. When I reach the band of her panties, I nip and kiss my way to one hip, then move to the other.

Her fingers dive into my locks and tug up until our eyes connect.

"Please, Braydon," she whisper-begs.

I press a kiss to the skin just above her panties. "Please what, firecracker?"

"Stop teasing already."

The corners of my mouth tip up as my fingers trail down either side of her. Fingertips dip beneath the band of her panties and tease the flesh hidden beneath the cotton.

"Not teasing," I say with a shake of my head. I drop a kiss on the center of her panties, over her mound. Hovering over the cotton, lips parted, I take slow, methodical breaths. Let her feel the heat of my breath, how close I am. "No, not teasing." I tug her panties down an inch. "Foreplay, firecracker."

She groans as I inch her panties down a little more. "More like torture."

I chuckle. "But damn is it delicious."

She opens her mouth to say something but snaps it shut when I lick the partially exposed area of her bare mound—something that surprised me on our first night.

Until Alessandra, I hadn't been with a woman with no hair between her thighs. After the initial shock had faded, I'd licked from the bottom of her seam to the top of her mound. Soft and smooth and euphoric.

Her fingers in my hair loosen and tighten before she yanks me up again. "Braydon," she pleas.

"God, I love my name on your tongue."

I shouldn't have said that.

"Know what else is great on tongues? Me on yours."

Her blue irises darken, the midnight blue of the rim blanketing the cobalt. Need dilates her pupils as her chest rises and falls.

Eyes on hers, I curl my fingers under the band of her panties and slowly inch them down. Her lips part when I expose her fully. Rocking back on my haunches, I tug the cotton down her legs and toss them to the floor.

In the dim light of the room, my eyes roam every inch of her exposed flesh. Take in the sight of her as she waits for me to make the next move. The slight rise and fall of her breasts as her breaths grow heavier. How her fingers clench and flex in the comforter. And the soft whimper in her voice as I rise from the bed.

I bend down and pick up my jeans. She shoots up onto her elbows, eyes wide. When I remove my wallet from the back pocket and drop the denim, she falls back on the mattress. I take out the condom and drop the wallet. Shoving my briefs down, I step out of them and tear open the foil packet.

Her eyes heat as I roll the condom down my length. "I have condoms in the nightstand."

I mentally freeze for a breath. The idea of Alessandra having a stock of condoms in her nightstand momentarily throws me off track. Though we dove into that drawer a few times six months ago, we were not the same people then. What we were doing was obvious. One night of sex and nothing more.

But tonight is different. Tonight makes *us* different. Not in the sense that we will be more than this. More than sex. The fact that we hooked up and neither of us was bothered by the lack of information exchange is answer enough. Neither of us expects more. Still, the drawer of condoms bothers the irrational side of me. The side that thinks of her beyond sex.

Maybe the box is new. Maybe she bought them on a whim. Maybe she was hopeful when I walked into the shop.

Whatever the reason, I need to forget it. Live in the here and now. In the moment, with her.

"Good," I say as my knee hits the mattress. I crawl my way up her body, kissing up her breastbone, the column of her throat. "We'll need more."

My lips crash down on hers as I bracket her head with my forearms. Nails scratch down my back and dig into the muscles of my ass as I glide my cock over the seam of her wet pussy. I snake an arm around her waist and, on the next rock of my hips, press my tip inside. She rocks her hips in a silent plea for me to give her more.

But damn, how I love it when she begs.

I rear back and out of her. She whimpers, her nails sinking

deeper into my flesh. As her lips part to beg me for more, I rock forward and fill her fully.

So. Fucking. Tight.

One hand in her hair and the other at her hip, I bruise her body with my touch. Crush her lips with mine. And then I move. Each stroke of my cock is deliberate and meticulous. Weighted and thick. I break the kiss and hover above her. Watch her eyes roll back and jaw fall slack as I drive forward a little faster. Memorize this moment—this tiny blip of time where she belongs to only me—and store it in a safe place.

Nails claw up my back and I hiss. "Trying to mark me, firecracker?"

She wraps her legs around my waist and locks her ankles. Grabs hold of my hair and fists the strands. Tips my head to the side, sinking her teeth into my shoulder. It's borderline painful and only serves to push me harder. Faster.

Releasing my shoulder, she runs her tongue over the indentations. Licks her way up my neck, clamping down on my earlobe. "If I want to mark you, I will."

I growl and tighten my hold on her.

"Now…" She licks the shell of my ear. "Fuck me like you mean it."

CHAPTER 14
ALESSANDRA

For days, I have made it my mission to avoid Braydon. I kept myself busy with endless tasks at work. Spent time with friends. Left work and home sparingly.

Mission: Avoid Braydon at all costs. Mission status: Failed.

Three nights ago, I met Braydon for dinner. This time, we actually discussed work and his story. We opened up a little to each other. Shared great conversation and laughs. Got comfortable in our own bubble. Had sex again.

Repeats… something I never do with one-nighters.

I am not promiscuous. Okay, maybe I am to a certain extent. I don't double-dip. At least, I haven't in years. Not because I don't want to. Not because none of the guys haven't satisfied me. Most nights my body needs release, I take care of business on my own. When it isn't enough, I seek relief with someone new. With my hectic schedule, it's easier if my time with men is one and done.

Then Braydon came along.

It's difficult to pinpoint what exactly has me wanting more with him. What has me caving on a rule I enacted years ago. *No romance. Just fun.* My life is too busy for anything else.

Yet, somehow, I have made time the past three nights for Braydon. And damn, I want him more each day.

We woke late Sunday morning in a mess of tangled limbs. He pressed his lips to mine and I deepened the kiss. He rolled me onto my back and gave me two more orgasms before releasing his own. And when we were both breathless, a foreign statement left my lips.

"Come back tonight."

And he has been in my bed every night since. An unspoken *acquaintances-with-benefits* agreement between us.

"What has you so cheery this morning?" Lena asks as I tap in her breakfast order.

I peer up at one of my best friends and temper my cheek-stinging smile. I shrug. "Slept well." More like I have been boneless when Braydon leaves each night. But she doesn't need to know the minor details.

Her green eyes narrow. Inspect. Question what I am leaving out.

I keep my expression the same and stiffen my spine. One flinch and the floodgates will open.

"Well, it looks good on you."

My shoulders and spine loosen. "Thanks. Be back in a sec." I take her reusable cup and walk off.

Down the line, I pour oat milk in a shaker, add matcha powder, vanilla, sweetener, and ice. I clamp the lid on and shake. After several vigorous rattles, I transfer the drink to her cup and rinse the shaker.

As I approach the register, my mouth opens to tell Lena her food should be ready in a few minutes. Instead, my feet stick to the floor. I snap my mouth shut. White noise floods my ears.

My rib cage tightens around my lungs. My heart pound, pound, pounds against my breastbone.

What is he doing?

I take a deep breath and unstick my feet from the floor. Take one step, then another, and step fully into view. Pushing his glasses up the bridge of his nose, Braydon's eyes dart to mine for a fraction of a second before focusing back on Lena. He smiles then offers his hand.

"Thank you, Helena. I'll swing by your shop in a bit. Saving the best for last."

He winks at her and a knot twists beneath my diaphragm. I ball my fingers and resist the urge to say something I will regret. Something that will hurt my friend and garner the attention of everyone here.

Braydon is not mine. Braydon will never be mine.

I take another calming breath and set Lena's latte on the counter. "Large, iced vanilla matcha latte with oat milk."

"Ooh, another oat milk drinker," Braydon says with a hint of excitement.

Lena puts her metal straw in the cup and lifts it to her lips. One sip and she sighs. "So good." Her eyes meet mine. "Thanks, girl. I'll be on the patio." She starts for the patio, then pauses. "Later, Braydon."

The casual way they speak has me on edge. Irritated. Borderline jealous. Okay, maybe slightly over the border. Which pisses me right the hell off.

One—Lena is my best friend. She would never do anything to hurt me. Mags, Lena, and I... we'd take bullets for each other. We'd crush anyone who tried to hurt any of us.

But she has no clue about me and Braydon. The fact we slept together last fall. The fact we've been having sex—lots of sex—since Saturday night.

Two—Braydon isn't doing anything wrong. Neither is Lena. They were talking. Casual conversation among familiar faces. Him planning a stop at her shop for his story, his job.

Get a grip.

Braydon is not mine. I am not his. And in half a week, he will go back to Seattle. Back to his life. One that does not include me. None of this is news.

I swallow back the restless thoughts and smile up at him. "Morning."

The corner of his mouth kicks up in a half smile. "Good morning." His eyes drift up to the menu board, his teeth nibbling at the corner of his bottom lip. "Hmm." A hand presses his stomach. "Pretty hungry today." A devilish smirk lights his face. "Been… exercising more than normal."

I snort as my teeth clamp down on my lips. "Best fuel up then."

"Right you are." Another quick glance at the menu. "Breakfast of Champions. Meatless sausage and scrambled whites. My usual coffee, but large today. Need a caffeine boost."

Eyes on the screen, I shake my head as I tap in his order. "I'll get your coffee."

I fill a cup with coffee, stevia, and oat milk. Add a protective sleeve and lid. Take a deep breath and walk back to the register. I hand him the coffee and he hands me cash. With his change, I give him a numbered table tent. He tosses the bills and coins into the tip jar.

He takes a step back, then stops. Amber irises lock me in place and the twisty feeling from minutes ago comes back, but this time different. A bundle of nervous energy. I like and hate how edgy it makes me feel.

"Go to a movie with me tonight. The cinema updated the

marquee." He licks his lips. "Popcorn, candy, moody Robert Pattinson."

I snort-laugh and slap a hand to my mouth. "The *Twilight* movies must be back."

"Yep. There's a double feature option, too."

Now I am intrigued. "You have a secret crush on Pattinson?"

He shrugs. "I like indie movies and he's done a bunch. I'm not ashamed."

"No?"

His lips purse as he shakes his head.

"Favorite *Twilight Saga* film?"

He lifts the coffee to his lips and takes a sip. "Way to put a guy on the spot." He taps his lips with a finger, his eyes darting around as if in deep thought. "It's a toss-up between *New Moon* and *Breaking Dawn, Part 2.*"

"Well then."

"*New Moon* is moodier. Darker. I resonate with the vibe more."

This has me mentally jerking back. His response is not what I expected. Then again, neither is Braydon.

"*Breaking Dawn, Part 2* is when everything finally comes together. Plus, the battle scene was pretty great."

"So, not team Jacob?" I tease.

He chuckles. "Werewolves and shape-shifters are cool, but nah. More team Alice and Jasper."

A ding echoes from the kitchen bell and snaps me back to the fact I am openly flirting at work with Braydon. Mandi grabs the order and wanders to the dining room.

Much as I'd love to sit in a dark theater, eat hundreds of empty calories, and curl up to Braydon in the seats, it isn't a good idea.

This—us—is temporary. Just two people with undeniable chemistry, connecting on a base level.

No romance. Just fun.

"A movie would be fun," I say. His eyes widen with surprise. "But it's not a good idea." His shoulders cave forward. "Sorry."

He takes a step and I *feel* his retreat more than see it. And damn, it is a knife to the heart.

"No." He shakes his head. "I shouldn't have." Another step back. "Talk to you later."

Before I get another word out, he all but runs across the dining room, sits at the farthest table, and aims his back toward me. I stare after him. Watch as he futzes around on his phone. Mentally berate myself for allowing things to get this far.

I should have left it where it was—one night. I should have sucked it up and stuck to my guns while he was in town. Instead, I kissed him outside of Trixie's. I initiated this whole fiasco. And it will be me who cuts it off. It will be me who hurts him.

CHAPTER 15

BRAYDON

I cut the engine and glance up the stairwell that leads to Alessandra's front door.

"What *am* I doing?" I mutter.

Yesterday, Alessandra put me back in my place. Reminded me of who we are. What we are. Where we stand. Yes, we've had mind-blowing sex the last five nights. But we will never be more than two people using each other. A fact I need to carve into my brain and remember.

Tonight and tomorrow night. Then you won't see her again.

I scoop up the bag from the passenger seat and second-guess if buying us dinner was a good idea. Whether or not she eats it, that is up to her.

Exiting the car, I lock it and make my trek up the stairs. The memory of last night, of me taking these stairs, flashes in my mind's eye. How it took me an additional few minutes to make the small journey. How I questioned whether or not seeing her again at all was a good idea. Hell, tonight I still question if I am making the right choice.

Probably not, but I don't want to turn back.

At the top of the stairs, I lift a hand and rap my knuckles on the grain. Quiet surrounds me for two breaths before I hear the security chain scrape and dead bolt disengage. The door swings open and a smiley Alessandra stands an arm's length away.

"Hey." She glances down to the bag. "Food?"

"Yeah. Didn't have time to eat before heading over."

Partial truth. We never agreed for me to come over at a certain time. But if I wanted any time with her, I had to arrive before the sun sank beneath the horizon.

She steps aside. "Come in. Smells like you brought tostadas."

I wave the bag as I step inside and toe off my shoes. "Indeed. Hope you're hungry."

We move to the small table between the kitchen and living room. I remove the food from the bag while she goes to the kitchen and fills two glasses with ice water. She sets the glasses on the table and takes a seat. Silence stretches between us as we open the boxes and take the first bites of our dinner.

The moment feels so normal. Easy. Domesticated. Comfortable. I love how effortless it is to sit in her company. How painless it is to exist alongside her.

"How much do I owe you for dinner?"

And just like that, my thoughts from seconds ago fade away. Because no matter how easy things are between us, Alessandra will never be more than a borderline friend with benefits.

I lift the bottle to my lips and down half the contents. "Don't worry about it."

Dinner passes in awkward silence and shoptalk as we eat. It feels static, clinical, cold. We clear the table and toss the recyclables in the bin. As we exit the kitchen, I open my mouth to say I should go back to my room at the bed-and-breakfast.

But as the words form on my tongue, her fingers dance down my spine. I stop moving, stop breathing, stop thinking. All I do is feel. Not just the warmth from her touch but also the buzz under my skin.

I should go. I should walk out the door now and not come back. But, of course, I choose to stay.

Like every other night I've walked up those stairs and stepped in her home, I let her lead me to the bedroom. Let her give me another dose of her addictive high. Let her take control—of not just my body but also my heart.

Glutton for pain and punishment, that is what I am.

"Shit."

Yanking the pillow out from under my head, I groan and toss it over my face.

"Shit," Alessandra repeats. "Braydon." She nudges me in the ribs and I groan again. "You need to get up. You need to leave."

I push the pillow down and squint as light from the bathroom steals my vision. "What?" I ask, sleep thick in my voice.

Alessandra tugs her jeans up her legs, then yanks a shirt from its hanger before slipping it over her head. "We fell asleep. It's morning. Some of my staff are already here."

At this, I bolt up and hike the sheet to my navel. "What? Where?"

Peering over her shoulder, she rolls her eyes. "Not in my apartment, crazy. Downstairs." She shuffles into the bathroom and brushes her hair. "Everyone parks out back." She secures her hair in a ponytail then pins me with wide, fearful eyes. "Your car is out back."

I whip the sheet off, swing my legs over the edge, and rise from the bed. One article at a time, I gather my clothes and slip them on. Amble into the bathroom, wrap my arms around her waist, and kiss the side of her neck. Watch her in the mirror as she applies a light layer of makeup. I don't need my glasses to know that Alessandra doesn't need any; she is beautiful either way.

"Everything will be fine."

After a swipe of lip gloss, she steps out of the bathroom. I close the door and go about my morning business. Once I wash up and borrow her brush to tame my sex hair, I exit and go in search of her.

Alessandra bounces by the door, the tip of her thumb between her teeth. I slip my shoes on, step up to her, and hold her at arm's length.

"You go out first. Make sure the coast is clear. I'll peek out and you wave me down."

Her head bobs while she stares off into the distance. "Yeah. Okay." My favorite shade of blue pins me in place. "That should work."

Before either of us takes another step, I lean in and press my lips to hers. Sticky gloss paints my lips, but I don't care. I need one last taste of her before the facade slips into place. But as quickly as I go in for the kiss, she breaks it.

She twists the knob and pulls the door open. "Lock the handle please." Then she disappears.

The cold from last night filters back in. Yes, we are not a couple. Yes, doing the overnight thing is not really part of the deal. So, I get why she is in freak-out mode. But damn, her dismissiveness is like a punch to the solar plexus. One hit and I am done.

I suck in a slow, steadying breath. This serves as a reminder of why I no longer do serious relationships. It was wrong for me to come here every night. To slip into her bed and connect more with Alessandra. Each time our lips met, each time we connected physically, she cracked the walls around my heart. The walls that kept the hurt out.

I'd let a piece of her slip through the cracks. Now, I will pay the price. Because she appears completely unfazed by my leaving.

I peek out the door to see a wide-eyed Alessandra. She waves me down. I lock the door, pull it shut, and trudge down the stairs. When I reach the bottom, I breeze past her for my car. Hit the button on the fob and unlock the door. Grab the handle and yank the door open.

"See you later?" she asks.

My eyes look everywhere but at her. I give a noncommittal shrug. "Maybe."

Then I slip behind the wheel, crank the engine, and back out without a second glance in her direction. If she wants to be cold, I will give it right back. Because this time tomorrow, I leave Lake Lavender. I leave her. And there is no turning back.

CHAPTER 16

ALESSANDRA

A chill rolls down my spine and I shiver. I hug myself and rub my hands up and down my arms through the thin sweater. The chill has nothing to do with the dip in temperature and everything to do with not seeing Braydon the rest of the day.

No matter how I spin it, something about the way we parted this morning doesn't sit right. Was I short with him as I bustled to get ready? Yes, but it hadn't been intentional.

Waking up and seeing the time, knowing I should have already been in the office crunching numbers or in the dining room prepping for the day, I panicked. The last time I woke up late for work, I didn't own Java and Teas Me. I'd worked at Lakeside Grocer, the town's family-owned grocery store, and I'd been ten minutes late. Ten minutes is nothing compared to two hours and the whole staff depending on you.

I spot Lena's car as she pulls into the parking lot of Black Silk. As I exit my car, Geoff drives into the lot and drops Mags off near the door. Lena and I converge and stroll up to meet our friend for girls' night. After hugs, we head inside.

Conversation and dinner go by in a blur. I hear everything my friends are telling me but don't absorb a word. Can't. Not with the nauseating twist beneath my diaphragm.

"Want to skip upstairs tonight?" Mags asks.

I blink away my dazed state and glance up at my friend. Lines mar her forehead, a deep *V* between her brows. She has no idea what is going on, but knows something is off. Mags has never been keen on the club or being in the thick of the crowd. Nor has Lena, she just goes along with it because she doesn't want me alone.

I shake my head. "No, I'm fine." I am far from fine, but maybe dancing or the vibe upstairs will distract my thoughts. Get me out of my head. Stop me from driving to the B&B and doing something irrational.

We settle the bill and Mags texts Geoff. He and Logan are in the club; Owen opted to stay at the office and work another few hours.

The trek up the familiar staircase settles some of the anxiety I've felt all day. The dark walls and tantalizing images in frames add another layer of balm. And when we enter the nightclub, a sense of freedom blankets me head to toe. Maybe it's the slight anonymity the darkness of the club provides. Maybe it's because I am comfortable letting go and being myself in these four walls. Or maybe it's because this place speaks to my soul.

There is no judgment here. No worries. No tasks to juggle.

Here, I get lost in the music, in the sway of my hips, in someone else's body pressed to mine.

We catch up with the guys for a few minutes. I sip water and scan the club. Though I can't see everyone, no one in my line of sight resembles Braydon.

"Going to dance." I set my water down and rise from the couch.

"Want me to join?" Lena asks.

"Only if you want to."

Her eyes dart to the dance floor and I spy the answer written on her face. "Think I'll stay here for a bit."

"Cool." I kiss her forehead, then Mags's crown. "Be back in a bit."

Digging in my pockets, I check that my fob and wallet are snug. I weave through the crowd, hips already swaying and arms up before I reach the dance floor. Embedding myself in the throng of bodies, I close my eyes and get lost in the music. Let the bass vibrate my bones and treble steal the endless what-if thoughts.

Sweat pricks my skin as one song transitions to another. I dance by myself. I dance with strangers. But with each new song, I feel more myself. At ease and comfortable in my own skin.

Then a familiar scent hits my nose. An oddly specific smell. Like hot ink—the smell when your printer finishes printing hundreds of pages. A weird mix of soot and lavender.

And only one person wears the smell like a cologne. *Braydon.*

I spin around to see him inches away. Standing stock-still, his eyes trail down my body and then back up. Fire lights his amber eyes as he steps closer and fists my hips.

As he leans in, another smell hits. Beer. And if I smell it over the sweaty bodies and the scent he naturally wears, he's had quite a bit.

"What're you doing here?" I ask over the music.

He dips lower, his lips at my ear. "Hoping to see you." He leans back and meets my gaze. "DTF?"

Whoa, whoa, whoa.

Do I pick up men in the club? On occasion, but it isn't the sole reason I come here. Sometimes, it is nice to just be desired. To feel wanted. Do I hook up with strangers over familiar faces? One hundred percent. In a small town, the last thing I need is all the men thinking I am easy. Because I'm not. A woman not in a committed relationship but enjoying herself does not make her any less. If men can hook up without being shamed, so can women. Period.

But I don't throw myself around like a whore. I don't fuck every stranger I meet. And I certainly don't flaunt my debauchery.

I steer Braydon away from the crowd. Lead him to a quieter corner where fewer eyes will be on us. Park him on a stool and step between his legs with my hands on my hips. Lock onto his slightly glazed-over eyes.

"What the hell, Braydon?"

He tilts his head to the side. His eyes narrow and study me momentarily before widening. "Oh." He slaps a hand on his forehead. "You don't know what it means. Sorry." He lifts a hand to cover his mouth and snickers. "Down to fuck?"

I inch back, my eyes darting between his, then shake my head. *Who is this guy?*

"Yeah, I know what it means. Just didn't think that was your MO."

He throws his hands up then slaps his thighs. "Well, you don't really seem to care for the softer side." He looks to the side, stares at the growing crowd for a beat, then brings his eyes back to mine and shrugs. "Either way, I lose."

Someone, I beg you, please save me.

Stepping back into him, I rest my hands over his. Lightly stroke the soft skin of his hands. Weave our fingers together.

Inch impossibly closer and close my eyes. The heat of his beer-tainted breath coats my lips and sends a delicious shiver down my spine.

Braydon makes me feel more than anyone. Though he shouldn't be, Braydon has always been more than sex. All it took was one night and a piece of him permanently etched itself in my bones.

Unfortunately, this is all we will ever be—two people with a connection that lead separate lives.

"We both lose, Care Bear."

He jerks back. "Care Bear?"

"Soft, cuddly, comforting." I shrug.

He leans forward and presses his forehead to mine. "I'll be your Care Bear, firecracker." Then his lips drop to mine in a chaste kiss.

I unthread our fingers. Fist his shirt with one hand and cup his cheek with the other. Stroke the rough stubble along his jaw. Stare at his lips just a breath from mine, the bottom fuller than the top. Tightness builds in my chest the longer we stay like this. My heart beating a painful rhythm beneath my rib cage.

This shouldn't happen. This can't happen. Nothing will come of it. Nothing but hurt.

Going against every logical cell in my body, I drop my lips back to his. Kiss him as if we aren't standing in the middle of a public venue. As if hundreds of onlookers won't see us. As if Braydon is mine. Only mine.

My hand on his cheek falls away. Both my hands fisting the cotton of his shirt as his hands go to my hips. Fingertips bruise as he hauls me closer and deepens the kiss. His tongue strokes my tongue, a feral growl vibrating his chest.

He scoots to the edge of the stool. Slides a hand up my

spine and grips the back of my neck. Drops the other hand to my tailbone and forces me forward. The thick bulge behind his zipper presses against my lower belly. Begs for attention, for release.

Lust heats my blood as bravery steps into the light. Fingers loosen from his shirt and drift down his abdomen. I flatten my palm as I reach the waistband of his jeans. Curl my fingers as my palm settles over his erection. Add pressure as I squeeze and rub the length of him through the denim.

He gasps and breaks the kiss but doesn't back away. "Firecracker…" His nickname for me is breathy and feral on his tongue. "Fuck," he groans out.

"Come home with me, Care Bear." I lean in, kissing his lips once, twice. Stroke him through his jeans. "One last time."

His fingers at the back of my neck drift into my hair and curl. Pin me in place. Send a shiver down my spine and heat my skin.

Lips ghosting mine, he answers, "Yes." He presses his lips to mine and doesn't move for a beat. "One last time."

CHAPTER 17

BRAYDON

From the foot of the bed, I stare down at her.

On her belly, dark sheet bunched at her waist, the creamy skin of her back bare. Blonde strands strewn across the pillow. Eyes closed and lips slightly parted. Profile facing the now vacant side of the bed. Fingers fisting the edge of the empty pillow.

I don't want to leave. Don't want to go back to my empty room and pack my bags. Don't want to drive home to my empty apartment and live with nothing but memories of something I can never have.

But this is how it has to be. How it will always be.

I may not have been completely sober when I came home with her, but I will remember everything. Even her rejection. Less than an hour has passed, but the gut-wrenching moment plays on repeat.

"Use my number after I leave." I tuck hair behind her ear. Brush my knuckles over her cheek. *"Stay in touch."*

Uncertainty taints her cobalt blues as they hold my ambers. She ~~su~~ ~~zes~~ *"Not sure that's a good idea."*

Fire licks my veins, but not from desire.

An idiot, I am not. This—us—would never be anything more than casual. The woman from the small town. The guy from the city. Two polar opposite people living in two dissimilar worlds.

But is it such a horrible thing to keep in contact? To be friends? Alessandra seems to think so.

"Whatever." I roll away from her and sit up. Prop my elbows on my thighs and drop my head in my hands.

The sheets rustle and the bed dips behind me. Soft fingers trail around my waist as she scoots closer. I flinch and hate myself immediately for my negative reaction to her touch. A touch I crave more than is healthy.

"Sorry," she whispers against my shoulder. Her lips kiss the top of my shoulder blade and I clamp my eyes shut.

I shake my head. "Don't apologize." My fingers drift to my hair and tug. "I wasn't thinking." Shrinking out of her hold, I rise from the bed. "Be back in a sec," I say as I head for the bathroom. Eyes forward, I feel hers on me as I leave the room.

The door closes with a soft snick. I flip the light on and use the toilet. Crank the cold water and cup my hands under the sink faucet. Splash my face and snap myself back to reality, to the fact that nothing good will come from wanting the woman in the other room. I turn off the water, dry my face, and stare at my reflection in the vanity mirror for far too long.

Flipping off the light, I take a deep breath and exit the bathroom. Pad across the bedroom and stop when soft snores hit my ears. Minutes pass as I stare after her. Watch her chest rise and fall in time with those sweet snores.

An ache sparks beneath my sternum and I jab the heel of my palm to it to the dull pain.

"Time to go." Before I lose the will to do so.

I step around the bed, lean down, and press a kiss to her spine. "Maybe in another life," I whisper.

Then I pad across the room, taking one last glance before walking out the door. At the front door, I slip my shoes on. Unlatch the security chain, twist the dead bolt and handle lock, then turn the knob right. A whoosh of cool air sends goose bumps across my skin as I step out the door. I engage the lock on the handle and slowly close the door.

The latch clicks softly, but it is the loudest sound I've heard. The din of the end.

CHAPTER 18

BRAYDON

The cursor taunts me as it blinks on the blank page. Notes and brochures and photos lie scattered across my desk. My project outline a blur of nonsensical places and moments and ideas. Words bounce around in my head. Images from weeks ago play on repeat. The scent of pine and lavender still fresh in my memory.

Yet, every time I rest my fingers over the keyboard, not a damn letter gets tapped. Not one. The words are there, just on the tip of my mental tongue, yet I can't get them out. Can't speak them. Can't write them. Can't set them free.

And it is all because of her.

Alessandra.

The woman overrides every damn thought I own. And she shut me down when I pushed for something beyond acquaintanceship with benefits.

I wholeheartedly believe she doesn't have a cruel bone in her body. Hurting me wasn't her goal when she'd said it wasn't a good idea for us to keep in contact. The truth of her words stung—still sting—and faulting her for being honest makes me cruel.

The pang in my chest… that is on me. It is my burden to carry. My wound to heal. My hurt to mend.

What I need is to write this damn story. Get it over with and move on. Wrap up this small chapter in my life and squash the artificial feelings I associate with it.

Everyone and everything I hold close is here. In Seattle. My family, my job, the small group of people I call friends. All of it is here, not in some small town an hour south. Not in a brick building on Main Street in Lake Lavender.

A knock on my office door snaps me from my mental tirade. I blink at the screen then lift my gaze to see my father in the doorway.

"Mind if I come in?"

I gesture to the chair on the opposite side of the desk. "By all means."

Dad takes a seat, props an ankle on his knee, and stares across the desk. I close the lid of my laptop and give him my full attention. Lace my fingers in my lap and lean back in my chair. Wait for him to say something. Anything. Dad isn't a boisterous man, but he isn't the type to shelter his thoughts.

His sitting in silence serves a purpose. What the purpose is, I have no clue.

"What's wrong?" he asks, a soft timbre in his voice.

Of all the people to recognize I am far from myself, I should have known it would be Dad. When it comes to his son, nothing gets past Edward Harris.

When my relationship with Gabby fell apart, he was the first person to sense something was off. That I needed more than an ear to listen, but also a shoulder to cry on. A shoulder he offered without hesitation. A shoulder he let me cry on and didn't make me feel less than because I displayed emotion. If anything, Dad encouraged tears. Coaxed me to share what society says to bottle up. Because real people *feel* it all, and there is no shame in being human.

Dad and I have always had this indestructible bond. An invisible tie, unlike most parent-child relationships. For five and a half years, Dad was the only parent I had. A depressed soul mourning the loss of the woman he loved. The woman I never had the chance to meet. My mother.

Those five and a half years weren't dark, but they definitely weren't filled with light. On more than one occasion, I listened to my father cry as he lay in bed at night. Heard him talk to my mother as if she were in the room. Overheard him ask her for advice on the rougher days. More than anything, I remember those years being packed with love. Many kids shoved their parents away when they got hugs. Not me. No, I held on tighter.

No one has a heart like my father. Though he loves my stepmother fiercely, he still reserves a piece of his heart for Brenda Olson, the woman I've only met in photographs and videos. Thankfully, my stepmother doesn't begrudge him his past or love for another woman, a ghost.

Tipping my head back, I stare at the speckles in the ceiling tiles. Look for patterns in the randomly placed spots. Mull over what to say to my father. How much to share.

He is aware I haven't been in a relationship since Gabby. He'd be the one person I'd tell. That said, he is unaware of the bed habits I've had since my relationship with her ended. Dad is no fool. I highly doubt he thinks his son is celibate. Just because his son's ex-girlfriend said no to a marriage proposal doesn't mean the world ended. Sure, I went through a period of darkness. Same as Dad did with Mom. Sure, I have trouble trusting people now. Who wouldn't have trust issues after their best friend and love of their life broke their heart?

But life keeps moving forward. And eventually, we heal.

Eyes still on the ceiling, I say, "I met someone in Lake Lavender."

A creak fills the air as Dad shifts in his seat in my periphery. "And this is a bad thing?"

Inhaling deeply, I straighten in my seat. "Yes and no." His eyes narrow. "Met her on the first trip." I close my eyes, take another deep breath, then level my gaze with his. "We had a one-night stand."

Dad leans forward and rests his forearms on the desk. "No judgment here, son."

I nod.

"So, I assume you saw her again during this last trip."

"Yes."

"And?"

"And at first, it was awkward. I didn't know her name. She didn't know mine. Seeing her again was pure coincidence." My fingers dive into my hair and I laugh. "God, we tried like hell to avoid each other the first week."

"I take it that didn't go according to plan."

Lips pursed, I shake my head. "Nope." I lean forward, slide my laptop aside, and mirror Dad's position on the desk. "One week in, we both caved. Decided acquaintances with benefits was a smart move." Just saying the words out loud, I hear how foolish they sound. "News flash... it wasn't."

Elbows on the desk, Dad lifts his forearms and clasps all but his forefingers, pressing them to his lips. His eyes roam the desk, looking but not really seeing the scattered papers and photos. He processes what I've said and mulls over how to respond.

"Is she why you've been so down these past weeks?"

I nod.

"Sorry to hear that, son." He drops his hands back to the desk. "Wish I had the perfect piece of advice." A sad smile tugs at the corners of his mouth. "Give yourself time. If you choose to let her go, it won't happen overnight."

Choose to let her go? Not as if I have much of a choice in the matter.

As if he hears my thoughts, he says, "There is always a choice. Both of you may have chosen what feels like the easier route." My brows pinch together. "Sex without love or commitment," he clarifies. "But, son, life always throws us curveballs. Tosses out challenges when we least expect them. In the end, the choice is ours. We either rise up or falter."

We either rise up or falter.

God, he makes it sound so easy. Choose to let her go or go after what I want. The notion is so simple. Will enacting it come with the same level of ease? Only time will tell.

Above all else, I need to figure out what it is I want. While my head says to forget Alessandra, my heart whispers she will always exist in my life. The memories I have of her will never fade. Our time together will continue to haunt me.

Is it wise to preserve and protect those memories? Hold out hope that one day we will see each other again and create more. Or should I shove them in a bottle and toss them out to sea?

Either way, it isn't only about what I want. She, too, has a choice in the matter. And based on our last words, I foresee our future only going one way. Further apart.

CHAPTER 19
ALESSANDRA

Batshit crazy. The two words sum up my life the past month.

Since the morning I woke up and discovered Braydon was gone, everything feels *wrong*. Sleep is a joke. The shop is busy from when the doors unlock until the sign is flipped to closed. Mandi got the flu and passed it to Sharon, who gave it to Lexi. My car broke down two weeks ago on the way to girls' night and had to be towed to Abel's Garage—something about a head gasket, and let's not forget the oil needing to be changed and a tire rotation. That put a major dent in my savings.

The cherry on top of the sundae... the expansion construction for Java and Teas Me starts in five days.

Why the hell did I decide to start construction during the season?

Because my head hasn't been straight since Braydon was last here.

Originally, I'd asked Geoff if Architectural Crimson would help with the expansion project. He turned me down and gave me the business card of a fellow architect associate. Someone he trusted. I'd stashed the card in my office, swearing I'd call when the time felt right. I never reached out.

At the time, I didn't know Geoff had been seeking out Mags. He'd been interested in her but wasn't sure where things would go. When he suggested the other firm in Tacoma, it was his way of not mixing business and personal.

The Friday before my car crapped out, everyone met in the club after we ladies had our usual dinner. Geoff asked if I'd reached out to the architect and I said no. Out of left field, he and the guys offered to take on the project.

"Why the change of heart?"

Geoff drapes his arm over Mags's shoulder and tugs her into his side, kissing her temple. "I thought it would be a conflict of interest." He shrugs. "Things are different now."

I need this slice of good news. "Count me in."

The next day, Logan came into the shop and we talked logistics. By the time he left the shop, a heavy weight had lifted from my shoulders.

Little did I know, the weight would return and bring a few of its closest friends—ton and boulder.

A knock echoes through my office. Sighing, I lift my head from my hands and plaster on my best smile. "Come in."

The door swings open and Lyndsey steps in, shifting from foot to foot behind the guest chairs. "Sorry to interrupt, but…"

I wait for her to continue. She doesn't. "But…"

"A few of the customers are complaining about the noise." A sheepish wince dons her face.

I close my eyes and count.

One, two, three. This will all work out.

Four, five, six. Today is a one-time issue. They start working overnight tomorrow.

Seven, eight. Everything will be fine.

Nine, ten. Everything is *fine.*

I open my eyes and push my chair back. Rise from the seat and walk over to Lyndsey. Resting my hands on her shoulders, I give her a sympathetic smile. "I'll handle the grumblers. You worry about the orders. This won't be an issue after today."

"Okay."

As we exit the office, I slip on my invisible armor. The whirring and screeching of drills and power tools hits my ears before we step into the main part of the shop. Lyndsey returns to her spot at the register and I ask her to point out which customers are upset.

She juts her chin to a couple in the center of the dining room, then to a man in the far corner. When my eyes drift to the man, I blink a few times. His back to the counter, his brown hair and semi-slouched posture are familiar. I squint and look for any other similar qualities. Screeching fills the air and the man peeks over his shoulder, irritation flooding his expression with the flare of his nostrils and curl of his lip.

It's not him.

The simmering pang I have felt the past month boils to the surface. I press the heel of my palm to my breastbone, trying to stave off the ache that never disappears. Not fully.

"Thanks, Lyndsey," I say as I head for the dining room.

Like the noise from the construction, the throb in my chest won't last forever. At least, this is what I keep telling myself.

I take a deep breath and focus on what's in front of me— disgruntled customers. People I need to make happy. Fingers crossed, I attempt to win them over with long-winded apologies, promises of a better experience in the future, and offers of free food and drinks on their next visit.

"I don't like seeing you like this," Mags says.

Death would be preferable to how I feel right now.

Sleep had been shit before construction started. Now, an hour of sleep is a luxury. While the town sleeps in their cozy beds, I lie awake, staring at the ceiling, and regretting every choice I have ever made. The construction is just the tip of the iceberg. Because while the saw buzzes and drills squeal and the bang, bang, banging of hammers happens from ten in the evening to three in the morning, I get maybe an hour or two of sleep.

Since the overnight construction began, I have fallen asleep in the office each day following. It's a good day if my eyes stay open and the makeup masking my dark circles doesn't fade.

"Just exhausted," I say on a yawn. "The construction will be done in a few weeks. I'll sleep like the dead on day one."

Mags hits pause on the remote and leans into my left side. Lena sets down her fork and adds her weight to my right. When Mags came in for breakfast this morning, she took one look at me and said we should cancel girls' night. When I said no, she countered. If I refused to cancel, then we'd do girls' night at her house.

Takeout from J's Sushi Bar, a cheesy rom-com, and pajamas. It sounded like heaven and I said yes without hesitation.

She surveys the lines of my face then shakes her head. "No, there's something else you're not telling us."

Every stressor I've experienced in the past four weeks, Mags and Lena know of them. All but one. Braydon. And I don't know if I have the energy to bring him up.

Lena knocks my shoulder with hers. "We love you, no matter what."

With a heavy sigh, I nod. "Same."

"Then tell us what has our brightest friend so glum," Mags says as she lays her head on my shoulder.

As we fill our bellies with sushi, udon noodle soup, and katsu chicken, I rehash every sorted detail about Braydon. From our first night during the centennial celebration to his most recent visit to his abrupt departure.

I spill my heart and they listen to every word without interruption. And when I finish, they cocoon me in the tightest hug. Squeeze all the hurt out and replace it with the love only they provide.

My eyes grow heavy and Mags tells me to stay tonight. Sleep in the spare room and get a good night's sleep. I cave the moment the words leave her lips.

I needed tonight. Needed to share the hurt Braydon unknowingly left in his wake. A hurt I didn't think was possible. I'd put up walls for years and no one made a dent. Not even a scratch.

Then Braydon waltzed into town with his charming smile and nerdy boy next door swagger. Without effort, he cracked my foundation. I tried to fight what I felt. I said things I didn't mean.

In the end, I hurt myself as much as I hurt him. The worst part... there is no way to say I am sorry. No way to reach out. No way to beckon him back. Because I said no contact. I deleted our texts and his info from my phone, and it was the stupidest decision.

CHAPTER 20
BRAYDON

My phone buzzes in my pocket and I pull it out to see a new social media notification.

[beh0103]: Java and Teas Me added a new post to their feed

Another notification pops up.

[beh0103]: Java and Teas Me added to their stories

Yep, I am officially *that* guy. The stalker guy. Well, not *really* a stalker. An avid follower with alerts in place. I mean, if the option is available, then it isn't wrong. I never comment on any of the posts. Most of them are pictures of food or drinks or the café. Occasionally, one of the employees will pop up in a picture with food or a drink.

Alessandra has yet to appear in any images. Every time an alert comes through, I hold my breath as I open the app. And each time, disappointment seeps in.

"No phones at the table."

My eyes snap up from the screen as I lock my phone and stuff it back in my pocket. "Sorry, Mom."

Gretchen gives me a soft smile. "We have plenty of time outside of these sporadic dinners to scroll sites and answer emails. Time for us is important too." She spears a piece of chicken and some green beans. "Shawn, have you gotten updates on your fall classes?"

My half brother rambles on about his upcoming term at University of Washington. Like the rest of us at the table, Shawn will have a position at Washington's Hidden Gems after graduation. Aside from journalism, business marketing is on his roster. Only eight years separate us, but the marketing tools I learned in college are vastly different from what he will learn. His knowledge will open up WHG to a younger demographic. Something we sorely need.

"Braydon?"

I blink up from my plate and look across the table. "Sorry, Dad. What?"

He flashes me a pained wince, and I hate the pity behind that look. "Asked how the story was coming along."

Oh. Right. The story.

An eye-twitching grating noise fills the air as my fork scrapes across my plate. I scoop mashed potatoes onto my fork then spear the green beans. "It's coming," I say before shoving the bite in my mouth.

In reality, the story is moving along slower than a snail's pace. Considering it will be the featured story in next quarter's issue, the story should be around five-thousand words. This includes details on specific shops, restaurants, and destinations within the town.

A story of this size... I should have wrapped it up a week or two ago. As it stands, I crested the halfway point yesterday.

All because I can't get out of my damn head.

Every time my fingers graze the keyboard and I reminisce over the quaint town packed with welcoming residents and charming storefronts, my mind drifts to her. And each time it drifts, all the wonderful things I want to say about Lake Lavender disappear.

"Writer's block is a nasty little bugger," Gretchen admits. "We've all been there." She lifts her wineglass and tips it in my direction before bringing it to her lips. "Maybe you need a scenery change while you write." Her eyes lose focus as she nods. "Always worked for me. Some days, the office was so claustrophobic and I had to get out. I'd take a pad of paper and pen to the park. Stare at the trees or water or animals and just let my mind go. Forget about the pressure of the story. Forget about word counts and eager readers. More often than not, it worked."

Not sure the park is really where I want to go. The closest parks are inundated with screaming children and adventurous adults. I need quiet when I write. Or brain-stimulating music without lyrics. In order to find the quiet, I'd have to leave the city. Drive to one of the state or regional parks. Bring a cooler of food and drinks and sit among the trees all day.

I miss the outdoors. Can't remember the last time I hiked in the mountains or got away from all the chaos that is life. I need a few days of silence, of stillness. Just me, food and gear, and the clothes on my back. I need a reset.

"I have an idea," Shawn chimes in.

"What's that, lil' bro?" I pick up my glass and take a sip of water.

"If the words aren't flowing, maybe you need to go back to the source. Back to Lake Lavender."

Water slides down the wrong pipe and I choke at the table.

I set down my glass, cover my mouth with one hand, and smack my chest with the other.

"Oh, shit." Wood bangs wood as Shawn bolts up from his chair. *Whack.* "Cough it up, B." *Whack, whack.*

I flail my arm in Shawn's direction as my face heats and lungs burn. "I'm..." *Cough.* "Fine." *Throaty hack.* I pick my water up and hold up a finger as I take a sip. Another sip and the raw burn in my throat calms. I set the glass down and take a deep breath. "Not sure that's such a good idea," I croak out.

Shawn takes his seat. A solemn look paints his face. "Oh." He picks his fork up and pushes food around the plate. "I just thought..."

That came out all wrong. The idea *is* good. But because I haven't disclosed much of my trip to anyone but Dad, neither Gretchen nor Shawn understand my need to stay away.

"Let me rephrase." I lay a hand on his forearm. "It is a good idea." The shadow darkening his expression slips away. "Personal reasons stop me from wanting to go back." I shrug and catch Dad's sympathetic look out of the corner of my eye. "Thank you for the suggestion, though."

The dinner table quiets. All eyes downcast on our respective plates as we nibble away at our food. It is not until I set my fork down that Dad speaks up.

"I like Shawn's suggestion."

"Dad..."

He holds up a hand. "Hear me out."

I huff and sag into my chair. "Fine."

"Go back to Lake Lavender, hole yourself up in a room, and just write." He says the words as if it is just that simple. "Plenty of writers do it. Book hotels to escape the day-to-day and give themselves a different view." He leans forward and lays his hands on the table. "Go. Lock yourself in the room. Order room service. *Let go* of what's weighing you down."

I don't miss the hidden meaning in his last words. *Let go of her.* Or maybe he means to quit fighting what I feel. Either way, it is time to let go and live my life, with or without her.

CHAPTER 21
ALESSANDRA

My jaw drops as I stare at the screen.

Seven unread messages from user beh0103.

Social media isn't really my jam, but I have accounts on a couple platforms for the shop. In the beginning, I posted live each day. Now, Willow or Mandi schedules posts through a website. They snap perfectly laid-out pictures and edit them so the vibe is cohesive in the feed. Using the site, they also respond to comments. No one logs into the actual account on the app except me, and I typically do that once or twice a month.

Of course, there are other notifications. Customers sharing pictures of Java and Teas Me, their coffee, tea or breakfast, the fun names on the menu board.

There is one other message.

ReDh0t8: I remember.

"Creepy." I swipe left and press the delete button.

My finger is hovering over the unread messages from beh0103 when Lena knocks my shoulder with hers. "Put it away." She lifts a brown bottle to her lips. "Whoever it is, they can wait."

"You're right." I lock my phone and stash it in my back pocket. I pick up my own beer and point the neck of the bottle at the makeshift stage. "Who is this?"

Lena leans in as the guy behind the mic strums his guitar. "Some garage rock band from Stone Bay. Don't remember the name."

Bone-rattling booms fill the room as the bassist and drummer join in. "They're good."

Since girls' night at Mags's house, the ladies have been adamant about taking me out every other night. The first two nights, I complained. Swore it would mess with my sleep schedule—which was already a hot mess—or throw me off at work.

They weren't having it.

After getting the best night's sleep in weeks that night, Mags all but packed my bags and had me temporarily staying at her house until the construction finished. I didn't fight her. Since the construction was estimated to last a month, maybe a little longer, I said yes in a heartbeat. Dust and dysfunction, I could handle. Not getting enough sleep and dealing with those things, plus the day-to-day tasks, I'd scare everyone away with my growly temperament.

On my second night at Mags's, she and Lena declared the three of us—and maybe the guys every once in a while—would be going out every other night. Not like we do on Fridays, but just for a drink or dinner. I put my foot down and said no. Going to work hungover is worse than going in without enough sleep.

Obviously, I did not win the battle. And I am happy I didn't. Because the past two weeks have been a little lighter. A little easier. And I have my two favorite people in the world to thank for that.

"Onion rings and chicken wings, ladies." The server deposits two large baskets on the table.

"Thanks, Denny."

He tosses me a wink. "Any time, beautiful." He deposits a stack of napkins and wet wipes between the baskets. "Let me know if you need anything else." And then he heads back to the bar.

We dive into our fried bar food while the band transitions from one song to the next. Muffled by the music, patrons continue to chatter and whistle for the band. The bar is dimly lit except near the stage where bright lights shine down on the two guys and one woman on stage. Sweat and hops mingle in the air with fryer oil. And this invisible energy vibrates around the crowd—something only the excitement of live music creates.

My cheeks sting as warmth hugs my heart. In this moment, I am happy. Thanks to the two most remarkable women in my life, I feel free.

"Evening, ladies," an unfamiliar man says as he steps up to our table. He sets down a pint glass and leans over the tall top, resting his arms on the table. "Enjoying the music?"

None of us say a word. We simply eye the man invading our personal space.

He is older—not quite my dad's age, but definitely older. His salt-and-pepper hair is shaggy and pointing in every other direction. Eyes dark and glassy. Facial hair thick and unkempt. A light-colored flannel covers his weathered skin. If he cleaned up a little and found a better approach, he'd be ten times more attractive. As is, he has a slight wobble when he's not leaning on the table.

Great, a drunk.

Mags shrinks into my side. I bet she wishes the guys were with us tonight. Not that she is afraid, she just doesn't like to deal with hasslers. Lena does her damnedest to ignore him— eating wings and watching the band.

Guess that leaves me to reject the guy. *Joy.*

"We were." I purse my lips and give him what I hope is a *please leave* look.

He straightens and I do a mental victory fist pump. Taking a step back, a lopsided smile tugs at the corner of his mouth. Then he steps around the table and my eyes go wide.

"Don't be like that, sugar," he says, stepping up behind us.

Anxiety ripples off Mags and I get the sense Lena is trying to flag down someone from the bar.

Why can't we enjoy a night out without the guys and not get badgered, for crying out loud?

I rise from my stool and take two steps away from the table, away from my friends. I deal with more disgruntled people than they do. Somehow, I will get this guy to leave.

"One," I say and hold up a finger, "don't call me sugar."

He shuffles closer. "You know you like it… sugar."

I roll my eyes. "Two, if a woman doesn't invite you to her table, don't come over. We're here for the food and music and nothing more."

He reaches out and takes hold of my arm. I try to pull out of his hold, but he tightens his grip. "Only 'cause you've never had a real man. I've seen you flirting in your little apron.

Come on, sugar." His lip curls and the air around me goes cold.

My eyes scan the room, searching for Denny or any of the other bar staff. But before I find any of them, I land on a pair of seething amber eyes near the door. Before I can mouth *help me,* he barges through the tables and small crowd in front of the stage. In three erratic breaths, Braydon steps up behind the man, grabs his bicep and tears him away.

"Get your fucking hands off her," he bites out as he steps between us.

Drunk Man stumbles back and holds up his hands in surrender. "Whoa, man. I didn't do shit. She came on to me. Was flaunting her cleavage—"

Thwack. The man staggers back a few steps and bumps into a table. Braydon curls and straightens his fingers as he shakes out his hand.

"What the hell is going on here?" Denny asks as he runs over to us.

Drunk Man opens his mouth, but I beat him to the punch. "Guy was harassing us. Braydon stepped in when he wouldn't back down."

Denny pats Braydon on the shoulder. "No fighting in the bar, man." He gives Braydon a sympathetic smile. "But I appreciate you looking out for the ladies." He tips his head to Braydon's hand. "I'll get you some ice." Denny twists to face Drunk Man, his smile gone as he points toward the door. "As for you, get the hell out of here."

A few patrons help Denny shuffle the man to the door. Every set of eyes in the bar watching, the crowd parting and the band playing a little quieter. Drunk Guy shouts, "I'll destroy you." Then he is out the door, and it is as if the volume dial gets cranked back up and life in the bar resumes.

I twist and take in the man in front of me, knuckles red and swollen, chest heaving. He looks the same, maybe a bit more haggard—dark circles under his eyes and a bone-tired wilt to his frame, like me—but very much the man I remember. Brown locks long enough to grab a decent fistful. Black-framed glasses accentuating his fiery amber irises. A layer of stubble on his angular jaw, a bit thicker than when I last saw him. And the scar in his eyebrow that says he has lived a little.

A storm brews beneath my diaphragm at the sight of him. A whirling uproar. A chaotic commotion slowly expanding and spreading and swallowing me whole. Beckoning me forward. Edging me near the cliff. Begging me to jump, to fall.

And god, I love how alive he makes me feel. But damn, am I terrified of what happens if I take the leap.

At every turn, I fight my feelings for Braydon, but I have missed him on an unhealthy level.

"What're you doing here?"

His eyes stay on his hand as he continues to bend and flex his fingers. Closing his eyes, he sucks in a lungful of air, holds it for one, two, three seconds, then releases it and lifts his gaze to mine. Hundreds of unspoken words fester in his amber irises. Pin me in place and steal my breath. They are words we both refuse to give a voice. Emotions we refuse to declare, to own, to give life. Because the moment we do, there is no going back.

Pink colors his cheeks as he looks over my shoulder. No doubt, Mags and Lena are watching our exchange. Ready to step in and steer me out the door if need be.

"I, uh…" He hangs his head and rubs the back of his neck. "I messaged you online," he says, voice barely audible over the noise of the bar.

He shifts from foot to foot while I remain tight lipped. I toy with the hem of my shirt as I wait for him to look up. For our eyes to reconnect and spill all the confessions our lips refuse to speak.

As if he hears my thoughts, his hand falls away and he straightens. Uncertainty clouds his amber irises as they hold me prisoner. Braydon may not be a man of many words, but his eyes, his expression, the way he carries himself speaks volumes.

I shuffle forward and wince. "Sorry. I'm really bad at checking messages."

One confession each and the air around us shifts. Lightens. Charges. Vibrates.

"Promise I wasn't creepy." He lifts a hand and scratches the scar in his brow. A ragged chuckle spills from his lips. "I mean, I did look at the account every day, but I'm not some weird sycophant." His brows tug down as his lips stretch into a thin line. "Maybe I should shut up."

Fear widens his eyes when I don't respond right away. He nibbles the corner of his bottom lip as his eyes dart between mine. And as he opens his mouth to say something else, I laugh. Hard and loud.

A hand goes to my stomach while the other covers my mouth. Tears prick my eyes as my belly cramps. Without effort, the laughter continues to bubble to the surface. The more I laugh, the harder it is to stop. After the past month, I need this release. This catharsis. This means to expel all the pent-up emotion festering beneath the surface.

"Sorry," I get out between fits. "Not laughing at you." I press both hands to my belly and try to take a deep breath. "Things have just been..."

"Shit," he answers.

My laughter dies down. "Yeah." I nod. "Things have been shitty."

"Sorry I left the way I did." He looks off to the side. "My head was a mess."

Inching closer, I reach for his hand, take it in mine and give it a little squeeze. "And now?"

His jaw works side to side. He swallows and swivels his head until our eyes lock. "Still a damn mess," he confesses just above the music. Warmth paints my skin as he cups my cheek. My eyes fall shut as his thumb strokes the line of my cheekbone. "Which is why I'm here." His breath coats my lips. "To let go."

I almost miss the last three words, but they ring loud and clear. *He needs to let me go.*

The thought should make me happy. Should set me free. Should bring me some form of comfort.

Instead, pain stabs my breastbone. Twists. Digs deeper. Adds a shadow to my heart.

I let my hand fall away, drop my gaze to the floor, take a step back, and nod. "Yeah," I mutter. "Okay."

Before I take another step back, he steps into me, pinches my chin between his thumb and finger, tips my head back, and shakes his head. "You misunderstand."

My bottom lip trembles. "W-what?"

"I don't need to let go of *you*." He shakes his head. "Not sure that's possible."

I furrow my brows. "I-I don't understand."

His hand slides around to the nape of my neck and he drops his forehead to mine. Soft, strong fingers massage the back of my neck. "I need to let go of the past. Of the hurt someone else inflicted. The painful reminders that keep me from what I want."

I suck in a ragged breath. "And what is it you want, Braydon?"

The answer lingers between us, thick in the air, but I won't assume.

He presses his lips to mine for the briefest of seconds. "You."

CHAPTER 22
BRAYDON

Vulnerability, party of one.

Can't believe I said that. Can't believe I opened myself up and laid my heart in her hands. May not have been a proclamation of love, but it wasn't far off.

And love isn't something I can do, not after last time.

The man returns from the bar with ice wrapped in a towel. "Here you go." He lays a hand on my shoulder and squeezes. "Thanks again. Don't usually have trouble like that. Probably an out-of-towner."

I bite my tongue and refrain from saying I too am from out of town, but not a pushy jerk. I definitely don't pursue a woman after she makes it known I make her uncomfortable or she's not interested. That's a dick move.

"No worries." I hold up my hand and the ice towel. "Thanks for this. Not my usual style."

He waves me off. "What can I get you to drink?"

"Uh…" Not my place to assume Alessandra is okay with me joining her.

Before I turn down his offer, Alessandra sidles up to my left and hooks my arm with hers. "He's a pale ale kind of guy," she tells him with a wide smile.

"House pale ale, coming up." And then he disappears into the crowd.

Arm still hooked in mine, Alessandra spins us around and leads me to the table with her friends. Their eyes rake over us without judgment, but I don't miss the way they fix on our connection. On the way Alessandra holds on to me tighter than acquaintances or friends hold on to one another. On the way Alessandra walks with a slight bounce in her step and the smile I see in my periphery.

When we reach the table, Mags moves to a stool closer to Lena, leaving the two vacant stools side by side.

"Hey, Braydon. Didn't know you were in town," Mags says.

I park on the stool, flatten my hand on the table, and set the ice on top. "Was a spur-of-the-moment decision."

"Oh. Any updates on the story?" She plucks an onion ring from the basket. "Can't wait to get my copy," Mags says, then dunks the onion ring in sauce and bites it.

I cup the back of my neck with my uninjured hand and massage the muscles. "The story is part of the reason I'm here." All three of them watch me, waiting for me to expand. I shrug. "Struggling with a bout of writer's block. My family suggested coming back and holing up in a room at the B&B. That maybe being back will inspire all the words."

At this news, Alessandra sags. Visibly deflates at the table. And a hint of sadness shadows her friends' faces.

I lean into her side, bringing my lips to her ear. "Said it was part of the reason," I whisper and she licks her lips. "But the biggest reason is you."

She visibly shudders as I straighten in my seat. Denny

deposits a foam-topped mug of pale ale in front of me. In an awkward attempt to reach for my wallet, he stops me and says it is on the house then walks off.

The table quiets as the ladies munch on finger foods. I lift the mug to my lips and sip the pale ale. Hum at the light but hoppy flavor. Take a larger pull from the glass and tune in to the band. Take a deep breath and do my damnedest to settle the turbulent beat of my heart and cacophony in my head.

Because this... it feels easy. Natural. Something I could do every day and not tire of it.

Sit at a table with Alessandra and her friends. Chat, eat food, and listen to rock music. I see it all so easily. Smiles and laughter and whispered words—both sweet and vulgar. My hand on her thigh under the table. My lips on her temple, the angle of her jaw, her chin, the tip of her nose. The public display would be effortless. Like heartbeats and breaths. The undeniable need to be close, to touch, to taste.

Alessandra's hand grazes my thigh and I jolt. A soft chuckle leaves her lips as she leans into my side. "Stop thinking so loud."

I turn my head to take her in. *She's so close.* Breath painting my lips. Tip of her nose brushing against the side of mine. If I lick my lips, my tongue would taste her. And if I taste her, a public display would make an appearance sooner rather than later.

"And what is it I'm thinking of?"

"Oh, I think you know."

At this, I laugh. "Of course I do." Unable to resist, I lick my bottom lip. The tip of my tongue skims her lip, sending a shiver down her body. "But do you?"

"Braydon, I—"

My lips press to hers before I overthink the idea. She

freezes. Stops breathing. Gives no indication of whether or not she wants this. Wants me. I start to count in my head but don't retreat. *One.* Her lips are so soft and perfect. *Two.* Heat and deep affection radiate off her. *Three.* She sparks the dying embers in my soul. When I reach four, she inhales, hooks her finger in my pocket, and deepens the kiss.

This, I did not expect. But when it comes to this woman, I should never set expectations.

In the middle of On Tap, we kiss like desperate partners. Like lovers reunited after years apart. Like our souls have finally found each other and refuse to let go.

And it only makes me want her more.

I shoulder my laptop bag, grab my phone, wallet, and keys, then exit my room at the bed-and-breakfast. When I reach the bottom of the stairs, a woman at reception waves and wishes me a good day. I return the sentiment.

Bypassing my car, I walk toward Main Street and the café. My hair ruffles in the warm, late-spring breeze. The lavender a hint stronger than the pine in the air. Children's laughter and dogs barking is the musical backdrop as I turn on to Main Street. Pedestrians fill the sidewalk while cyclists pedal on dirt and gravel paths. The street isn't inundated with cars, but plenty roll by in search of an empty parking space.

At the crosswalk, I press the button then make my way to Java and Teas Me. There is a line to the door, but it moves steadily as I step inside. Every time I shuffle forward, my eyes find Alessandra. And when our eyes catch, my pulse thumps faster, harder.

A young woman takes my order while Alessandra does her best not to smile in my direction. Her resistance briefly tugs at the corner of my mouth. I pay for my breakfast, take the numbered table tent, and weave through the tables, deciding to sit on the outdoor patio.

I opt for a table nearest the street. All the tables are covered by an awning and enclosed by a three-foot metal fence. With the wide sidewalks, the patio seating still allows pedestrians to pass without disruption.

"Perfect," I whisper as chair legs scrape the concrete.

Leaning back in the chair, I set my laptop bag and the numbered tent on the table but don't unzip the bag. Instead, I let my eyes wander. Take in the town after being away for weeks. Shut out all the pressure and worry and anxiety of not meeting my deadline.

For as long as I can remember, I have loved the city. Loved the tall buildings and go, go, go buzz in the air. Loved being near the bay and having endless activities to occupy my time. No matter which direction you head, there is a sight to see or a place to visit. There are no dull days in the city.

During my time at Washington's Hidden Gems, I have traveled to countless cities and towns within the state. Many were small, like Lake Lavender, but not all of them held the same charm.

On my first trip here, I sensed how different this town was from others I'd visited. People were friendly in all the towns I'd explored, but Lake Lavender just felt like coming home. No one treated me like an outsider. The smiles here are genuine, as are the welcomes.

I never pictured myself as a small-town person, but the more time I spend here, the more at ease I feel.

"So, you like saucy meat on your buns, huh?"

I jump in my chair, knock the table with my knees, and twist to see Alessandra next to the table with a huge plate of food and a steaming mug of coffee. Lips bunched, she tries not to laugh at my reaction.

"What can I say? I am a man of simple pleasure."

She places the plate in front of me, followed by the mug. "Hmm, I'm not so sure."

To my surprise, she takes a seat across the table. I crane my neck and look inside. The long line from minutes earlier is no more. So this may be one of the few times she has a break, and she chose to have it with me. I won't ask why she took a seat. Won't ask if she has better things to do. Asking questions may lead to her walking away, not that I don't deserve it.

Instead, I sip my coffee and eat my breakfast. My eyes never leave her face, and hers only leave mine to smile at or greet patrons.

"So…" she says.

"So…" I parrot.

"You returned to write?" She tilts her head toward my laptop bag.

"I did. The words are there." I tap my temple. "But for whatever reason, I can't seem to get them out." My gaze drifts down the sidewalk and I lose focus. "It's the oddest thing, not being able to give them life."

"Does that happen often?"

I shake my head. "No. The last time it did, my ex and I had recently split. My head was a mess and I didn't know which way was up."

She reaches in my direction and flattens her palm on the table. "So sorry."

"It was years ago. What's done is done."

"Is it too forward of me to ask what happened?"

I spear home fries on my fork then dunk them in the gravy. Shove them in my mouth and keep my eyes on the plate. Shortly after my relationship with Gabby ended, I'd been embarrassed by her rejection. Her denial of my marriage proposal ate away at me, provoking dark thoughts. Had me believing I wasn't good enough to be in a lifelong commitment with another person.

It took many stern conversations with Dad and some time with a therapist to see the truth. That I shouldn't be embarrassed or made to feel less than. Instead, I should be relieved. Had Gabby said yes when her heart wasn't on the same page as mine, the acceptance could have led to years of unhappiness.

"Not at all," I say after I swallow my bite. I lift my gaze and find solace in Alessandra's rich cobalt blues. "Four years ago, I asked my girlfriend of six years to marry me." I pause and take a breath. "She said no."

Alessandra winces. "Ouch."

"Pretty much."

The table falls quiet. I take small bites of my breakfast, not wanting to hinder the possibility of more conversation.

"I've never been in a long-term relationship," she confesses.

My entire expression scrunches to my nose as I look at her. "Seriously?"

She nods. "I don't count the guys from high school who lasted less than a year." She shrugs. "No one held my attention for long or exuded that forever kind of feeling. Then college happened and I was super focused on doing well. The idea for the shop came up shortly after graduating. I had so many ideas from other places I'd seen. I wanted to incorporate them all. Mags and Lena gave me the push I needed and backed me financially." Her fingers drum the table. "Since then, life has been too busy to have a relationship."

"Is it still too busy?" The question slips out before I stop myself.

"Yes and no."

"Well..." I pick up my mug and tip it in her direction. "Glad we cleared that up."

Whimsical laughter floats through the early morning air. A few people look our way then turn their attention back to their table.

"So long as I own this place, my life will always be busy. Comes with the territory." Her hands lift from the table then drop. "But each year, business is better. Income exceeds expenses more and more. I'm able to hire more staff and lighten my workload."

In this moment, I want to be selfish. I want to ask what this might mean for us. If there is a chance at an *us*. Gabby may have made me swear off commitment because of *her* doubts, but with Alessandra... I am willing to put my heart on the line again.

This time around, it feels different. Less scary.

Maybe it is the fact I walked the path that led to heartbreak. Maybe it's that we are both mature and have solid ground beneath our feet—well, in everything except relationships. Whatever the reason, this ache in my chest... I don't feel it when she is near. When she is near, life feels right. Serene. Stable. Complete.

I don't want to let her go. So I dip my toes in the shallow end of the selfish pool.

"Would you be willing to try?" I ask and her brows tug at the middle. "A relationship."

She rolls her lips between her teeth. "I, uh..."

I hold up a hand. "You don't have to answer right now." I spin the mug on the table, my eyes homed in on the action. "Just think about it. It'd obviously be semi–long distance. Your life is here and I live in Seattle." *For now*, I want to add but don't. We barely know each other, best not to jump the gun.

"Yeah, I'll think about it." Wood scrapes concrete as she rises from the chair. "Probably should get back. Will you be here a while?"

My eyes roam the street. Men and women trail the sidewalks, pausing at storefronts to peek through windows. Some with bags on their arms, others with frozen confections or pastries. Children skip ahead while parents walk hand in hand. It is the perfect backdrop to stir my creative juices. Sitting in the middle of town while I write, the words should flow without trouble. And if I get stuck, I simply need to take in the sights.

"If that's okay."

"Of course it is." Her fingers fumble with her apron strings. "Talk to you later?"

"Later."

And with that, she tucks the chair in and walks off.

Coming back to Lake Lavender was the right move. I should send Dad a quick thank you. Without his and Shawn's push, I wouldn't be here. I wouldn't have seen Alessandra again. And I wouldn't have another opportunity at whatever this is building between us.

Try as we might, there is no denying our connection. If I am lucky, she will say yes. Give the long-distance thing a shot. See if our chemistry is equally strong outside the bedroom. She may be reluctant to say yes, but her eyes tell another story—as does her body—and she wants more too. Fingers crossed, she will take the leap.

CHAPTER 23

ALESSANDRA

"What the hell?"

I throw the car into park, shoulder my purse, and exit the vehicle. Eyes glued to the building, I press the lock button on my fob as I walk toward the end of the building. I shield my eyes from the security light on the top corner of the building as I near the corner. Squinting to get a better look, my jaw falls open at the bright-yellow spray paint on the brick.

The construction crew left a little more than an hour ago, but nothing they are doing in the café involves yellow paint. This isn't them.

When I reach the spot, I lean in closer. The paint appears to still be wet. *Maybe one of the workers saw something before they left.*

I pull my phone from my purse and scroll through my contacts. Landing on the general contractor's name for the project, I hit call and hold the phone to my ear. As the phone rings, I pace toward the patch of grass and garden between Java and Teas Me and the next building.

Years ago, this was a side service alley. To beautify Main Street, the town changed how delivery vehicles accessed the backs of the stores. Many of these offshoot service alleys were turned into gardens or outdoor seating. Between Java and Teas Me and Harvey's Homemade Candies, the town planted two evergreens and an array of flowers. The old crosswalk was now a wide sidewalk. And with the closing of the service alley, I was able to add a little more space to my outdoor seating— the small extension housed an additional four tables. During the construction, this section of the patio is expanding and more than half the seating will be enclosed. Large windows will give the feel of being outside, but customers will be protected from the elements.

On the third ring, the call connects. "Hey, Lessa. What's up?" Sheila answers, voice thick with sleep.

"Hey, sorry to call so early." I pivot and turn back toward the building. As I do, my eyes go wide. "Oh my god," I mutter as I lift my hand to my mouth.

Rustling sounds on the other end of the phone. "Lessa, what's wrong?"

I rotate my head. Look left then right. Look for any sign someone may still linger nearby. But there isn't a soul in sight. Most people aren't awake at dark-thirty in the morning. My gaze drifts back to the building, eyes examining the mass of yellow spray paint on the brick.

Ruined.

The single word steals my breath. By the looks of it, this wasn't done by someone that uses spray paint often. The job is sloppy. Excess paint still drips beneath the letters. Some letters have a wider spray radius than others.

My free arm wraps around my middle. Although the job looks juvenile, a chill rattles me to the bone.

"Lessa?"

"Sorry, Sheila." I wander toward the sidewalk lining Main Street. "Did you or any of the crew happen to see anyone outside the café before you left?"

When I reach the sidewalk, I look left then right. Shift my gaze to the opposite side of the street and do the same. Everything appears normal. Nothing broken or out of place. No spray-painted words on any of the other businesses, from what I can tell.

"I didn't, and no one mentioned seeing anyone. Did something happen?"

"Someone vandalized the side of the building." I turn and head for the back. "Spray-painted what I assume is a message. Not that I know what it means." I reach the back door, slide my key in the lock, and twist. "Not the way I wanted to start my day, with police surrounding the café."

"Let me know if I can be of any help. Even if it's to clean the paint off when the police are done."

"Thanks, Sheila."

"Welcome. Sorry I couldn't be of any more help."

Disconnecting the call, I look up to see August at the prep table in the middle of the kitchen. His hands still as he looks up from the fruit he's cutting. Confusion knits his brow as he studies my face.

"Everything okay?"

God, the same question popped up far too often over the past month.

Is something in retrograde? Because every damn thing in my life is off-kilter right now. If it's not one thing, it is another. Sick employees, car repairs, construction on the café, unhappy customers, not being able to sleep in my own bed, and now vandalism. All of it is taking its toll.

And then there is Braydon. Seeing him again has my mind cloudy, my heart beating harder. Am I happy to see him? Absolutely. The man makes me feel alive in a way nothing else does. But seeing him also stresses me out. I already feel stretched thin. Like no matter how hard I try, I can't catch my breath. I want to see where things will go with us, but fear I won't be able to give him one hundred percent. And that isn't fair to either of us.

"Was anyone hanging around when you got here?"

Metal clangs metal as August drops the knife and rounds the table. Red stains his white apron as he wipes his hands.

"No, why?"

I hang my head and audibly exhale. One breath, then another. I lift my gaze to his and shake my head. "Someone vandalized the building. It's barely noticeable on the back. Must've caught the light just right as I parked."

"Seriously?" August grabs the towel draped over his shoulder and wrings the cloth with tight fists. "We don't live in a place where hooligans vandalize buildings." The muscles in his jaw tighten. "If I learn who did this..."

I pat his arm then give it a squeeze. "Step in line, buddy." Holding my phone up, I wave it. "Time to start my day with a call to the police department."

I aim my feet toward the open office while August returns to his spot at the prep station. My purse lands with a thump on my desk as I roll the desk chair back then take a seat. I prop my elbows on the desk, drop my head in my hands, and count to ten.

Please, let there be some sort of evidence. Don't care how big or small. Just something to give the police a lead.

Waking my phone screen with a tap, I scroll through my

contacts once more. When I land on the police department's nonemergency line, I hit call and bring the phone to my ear.

On the second ring, the call connects. "Lake Lavender Police Department. How may I direct your call?"

Ugh. This is going to be a long day.

No amount of caffeine is too much today. Considering I own the main source of caffeine in Lake Lavender, that says a lot.

For the past three hours, Java and Teas Me has been the center of attention. Officers arrived as the sun started to pink the sky. Sheriff Blackstone arrived with her two best officers and taped off the area. They scoured the lawn, searched the ground beneath the plants, took pictures from several angles, and rummaged through the dumpster. They dusted the non-brick areas nearest the paint but didn't lift much. The brick is too textured and porous to attempt lifting prints.

Though I love the additional business because gossipers want to see what happened, this is *not* how I wanted to garner a crowd. Java and Teas Me will be the talk of the town for months to come unless the culprit is apprehended or another shop is vandalized. And gossip talk is not the type of word I want to spread about my business. From one ear to the next, the story will change. Before long, it won't resemble what really happened. Unless they figure out who pressed the nozzle on the can.

"We've pulled down the tape and packed up," Sheriff Blackstone says. "If you have someone who can clean the wall, go ahead and call them in." She hands me a slip of paper. "The case number is here." She points at the page with her pen. "If anything else comes up, anything out of the ordinary, call the station. Even if it seems unrelated, chances are it isn't."

My vision blurs as I stare down at the paper. One memory at a time, I sift through my thoughts. Look for anything out of place. Other than the recent construction, there have been no odd noises. But…

"I got a strange message on the café's social media account. Hold on." I fish my phone out of my back pocket and pull up the app. Tapping on the messages, I flip my phone around for Sheriff Blackstone to read.

She plucks a business card from her pocket and hands it over. "Don't delete it. Screenshot it and send it to my email. We'll do some digging and see if we can figure out who the user is." She makes a couple notes on her tablet. "In the meantime, might I suggest looking into cameras for the store? A few outside and inside." Closing the cover on the tablet, she tucks it under her arm. "We don't see a lot of crime around here, but during the season, something always crops up. Better to err on the side of caution. Protect you, your employees, and the town."

The idea of putting cameras up anywhere in or around the shop gets under my skin. The town isn't a hundred-percent crime-free, but it was a rarity to hear news of break-ins or theft or vandalism. It wouldn't shock me if the police station received more calls about cats in trees or neighbors planting flowers too close to the caller's yard. Sure, there was always a small uptick during the season, but it was usually shoplifting or bar fights.

"Promise, I'll look into it," I concede on a huff.

As Sheriff Blackstone steps away from the counter, the bell over the door jingles. Ready to greet whoever walked in, I turn to see Braydon striding in with his laptop bag and a fading smile. In seven quick strides, he is across the room and at my side.

His hands frame my face and he steps impossibly closer. "Are you okay? What happened?"

I sigh and lean into him, wrapping my arms around his waist. "Let me get you a coffee first."

God, will this day end already.

CHAPTER 24
BRAYDON

After she recants the horrific events of her morning, Alessandra excuses herself and says she will return with food. I don't argue. With the morning she's had, she probably needs a long soak in the tub, candles, and whatever her favorite food is.

Note to self… find out her favorites.

My laptop is open as I read and respond to emails when she returns. To my surprise, she has two plates and another drink in her hands. Closing the lid, I shove my laptop aside. She sets a plate in front of me, loaded with eggs Benedict, home fries, and fruit. Taking the seat next to me, she sets down another plate piled high with French toast, scrambled eggs, and fruit. Before either of us takes a bite, she lifts the cup and drinks half the green, creamy liquid in her cup.

"Better?" I ask.

She scoffs. "Not in the slightest. But stewing over it won't solve anything." She spears a strawberry and aims her fork in my direction. "But if you see anyone around town with yellow

I cut into my eggs Benedict. "Yes, ma'am."

Though her day started off on a sour note, I hope to make it better. After some time on the patio and writing, I need to make a few stops.

Parked behind Java and Teas Me, I second-guess every *good* idea I had hours ago.

The café closed an hour ago, but Alessandra is still here. Well, her car is parked in its usual spot in the alley. Being the owner, I don't foresee her out the door before any of her employees. Not to mention, she said the main reason she doesn't shoot for relationships is because she works more often than not.

I wrangle my phone from my pocket, open my email app, and scroll through the messages. *Delete. Delete. Save for later. Reply.*

> *Hey Dad,*
>
> *Things here are good. I'm not a hermit in the bed-and-breakfast, but I am making headway with the story. When I get back, I owe you and Shawn dinner. Send Mom my love. Talk soon.*
>
> *Love,*
> *Braydon*

Chatter snaps my head up as a woman and man exit Java and Teas Me. A few spots down from the door, they don't see me as they head in the opposite direction down the alley. They chat another moment, get in their respective cars, and drive away.

Not sure if it is safe for me to assume Alessandra is alone in the café, but as I exit the car and lock up, I surmise it to be the case. For now, I leave the bag in the car. Seeing me will shock her enough. Don't need her in freak-out mode after the day's events.

I rap my knuckles on the door, then take a step back and shove my hands in my front pockets. Two forward and back rocks of my heels and the door swings open. A frazzled-looking Alessandra greets me, brows pinched tight in the middle. She glances over my shoulder, then shifts her gaze back to mine as her shoulders sag.

"Hey." The three-letter word is laced with exhaustion and defeat.

"Hey," I whisper and jerk my chin toward the café. "Can I come in?"

Stepping aside, she holds the door wide and gestures inside. "Sure."

With a loud click, the latch hits the striker plate and the door locks behind us. Alessandra shuffles away and walks through a door off to the side. I follow in her wake but stop at the entrance of what looks like her office. For a beat, I lean against the doorjamb and watch her.

Hair has escaped her ponytail and hangs haphazardly down her back and near her cheek. Her brows scrunch then relax again and again as she stares at the papers on her desk. The faint half-moons under her eyes earlier today are now darker, more prominent. And the smile that always tugs up the corners of her mouth is nowhere to be seen. In fact, this is the first time I have seen her sullen. Truly down.

My molars grind until pain stabs my temple. My fingers curl in, nails piercing the skin of my palm. One degree at a time, my blood begins to boil.

I have never been the type of person to hate another. Yes, people irritate the hell out of me every now and again. But hate is a powerful emotion. One that smothers and steals joy without effort. Even when Gabby threw my heart in the sink and turned on the disposal, I didn't hate her.

Whoever this is, whoever has Alessandra dispirited and defeated... I hate them.

Shuffling into the office, I take a seat in one of the guest chairs. Her eyes don't meet mine as she continues to stare down without purpose. She hasn't moved an inch since her butt hit the chair. Like she is broken or waiting for something to jump out and wake her from this nightmare.

"Let's leave," I whisper into the stale air. "All this can wait."

She inhales deeply, holds the breath for one, two, three seconds, then her entire body sags, wilting on the exhale. Chin dropping to her chest, her frame begins to shake. The muted sound of her sobs takes over the silence.

Up and out of my chair, I dart around the desk, spin her to face me, haul her upright and wrap my arms around her. At this, she cries harder. Fisting my shirt and tugging me impossibly closer. Shaking in my arms as tears trail down her cheeks, dampening my shirt.

"Shh, shh, shh." I tighten my hold. "I've got you."

Hour-long minutes pass without a single word said. One hand trails up and down her spine in slow, measured strokes while the other massages the back of her neck. My lips kiss her hair often.

When her sobs quiet, I inch away from her, frame her face and tip her head back. Bring her eyes to mine and drop my lips to hers. Taste the salty tears on her lips. Kiss her soft and gentle. It's nowhere near enough but is what she needs in this moment.

"Come on." One of my hands falls away and takes her hand. "Let's go."

"I have so much to do," she whines then sniffles.

"It'll still be here." I give her hand a slight tug as I take a step back. "But we need to take care of you first."

Reluctance mars her expression, but after a beat, she takes a step in my direction. With a nod, she takes another step and reaches for her purse on the hook. "Yeah. Okay."

We shuffle out of the office and I head for the back door while Alessandra flips the lights off. She slips her hand into mine as I open the door and we walk through. A loud clap echoes around us when the door shuts.

Giving her hand a squeeze, I kiss her crown. "Head upstairs. I'll be up in a sec. Need to grab something from the car."

Her head bobs as her hand slips from mine and she drags her feet to the stairs. I watch after her until she reaches the top, unlocks the door, and steps inside. When she disappears from sight, I exhale the breath I'd been holding. The ache beneath my sternum from the past month slowly creeps to the surface. Fisting the small beating organ. Digging its claws in. Not out of longing. More out of need.

The need to fix this. Find the person wreaking havoc on her life. Punish them for stealing her light. Penalize them for vandalizing and making a mockery of her business. Hold them accountable for casting a shadow on her heart.

Taking a few calming breaths, I grab the bag from my passenger seat and head up the stairs. I twist the handle without knocking and smile at the fact that she left the door unlocked. I toe my shoes off and stow them next to hers.

Wandering toward the kitchen, I spot her as I round the corner. Palms on the counter, her head hangs forward, shoulders rising and falling with each labored breath she takes.

I pad across the room and set the bag down beside her on the counter. Sweep her hair off her neck and press my lips to her warm skin. Rest my hands on her hips and curl my fingers slightly. Watch as she visibly shivers. The almost imperceptible action tugs at the corners of my mouth.

"Got you some things." I kiss her neck again then straighten and shuffle back a step.

She spins in my arms. Lifts her puffy red eyes to mine. Swipes at her cheeks. "You did?"

"Mm-hmm." I nod and pull the first item from the bag. A bottle of her favorite cabernet sauvignon—thanks to a long list of tips from Lena. "First, wine."

Her eyes light up then water. "Y-you bought me wine?"

Opening one cabinet after another, I locate her glasses. Set one on the counter then hunt for the bottle opener. She rolls out a drawer, riffles through it, then hands me the fanciest bottle opener I've seen. In seconds and with little effort, a pop fills the air as the cork breaks free. I fill the glass and hand it to her.

"I did, and a few other things."

The nights I'd spent in Alessandra's apartment, I took mental notes about her space. She didn't have a lot of *stuff*. It wasn't that she was completely minimalist. Rather, she didn't buy things just to fill a room. Each item in her home served a purpose. From the sparse yet eclectic art on the walls to the books on her shelves to the decorative pillows and throw blankets on the couch and bed.

I pour myself a small amount of wine before corking the bottle. Sip the sweet, earthy drink and hum in appreciation.

Then dig in the bag for the next item. A jasmine-and-lavender-scented candle with a handwritten label and twine around the jar neck. I unscrew the mason jar lid, bring it to my nose, then offer for her to smell it. She leans in and inhales the subtle fragrance and hums.

"Like it?"

She nods then pretends to peek into the bag. "What else is in this bag of goodness?"

A smile tips one corner of my mouth at the lifting of her spirit. My hand dives back into the bag and comes out with a paper-wrapped bath bomb and a small book. She unwraps the paper and a hint of a smile appears. "This is almost too pretty to use. Almost." She winks then tips her head toward the book. "What's that?"

"A small collection of poetry. Something to lift you up when you have a bad day." I hand her the book.

She flips through the pages and stops on one. Reads the small poem on the page. Tears rim her eyes but don't fall down her cheeks. She looks up from the pages and locks her blues with my ambers. "I love this," she whispers. "So much. Thank you."

I cup her cheek and lean in to kiss her forehead. "Glad you like it." I straighten and go back to the bag. "One more thing."

"Really?" she asks, voice laced with excitement.

Slipping my hand under the box, above an ice pack, I turn the bag and wrangle the box free. Her eyes widen at the logo on the top of the box—Harvey's Homemade Candies. She inches closer to me, her fingers fumbling to take the box. I set it on the counter and slowly open the lid.

Her gasp bounces off the walls. "No. You. Didn't," she says in disbelief.

I press my lips to her forehead again. "Yes. I did."

In the box is an assortment of decorated, chocolate-covered bananas, cherries, and strawberries. Pink and white, light and dark brown. Nuts and sprinkles. Hearts and little animal faces on the bananas. They look too good to eat. Almost.

In a flash, Alessandra slams into me and hugs the air from my lungs. "Can't believe you did all this." Her arms constrict more. "I-I don't know what to say."

Wrapping my arms around her middle, I tap her. "Can't breathe."

She releases me in an instant. "Sorry."

I pull her back into me, frame her face with my hands, and drop my lips to hers. "Never apologize. Not for this." I chuckle. "Just make sure I have air."

Light laughter fills the room and it magnifies the warmth in my chest. I want all her laughter and smiles. Want to be the one to lift her up on the days she feels low. Want to be more than just some guy from Seattle that warms her sheets. More than anything, I want to warm her heart too.

Swiping the bath bomb and candle from the counter, I wander toward her bedroom.

"What're you doing?" Light footsteps pad behind me.

"Starting the bath." I peer over my shoulder as I turn into her bedroom. "Grab the box and your wine. Bring it in here."

Without another word, she scurries off and I enter the bathroom. I crank the water for the oversized tub, plug the drain, and let it fill. In a drawer on the bathroom vanity, I find the lighter I saw when looking for toothpaste during one of my overnighters. I light the candle and set it on the ledge near the tub.

Exiting the bathroom, Alessandra enters and gives me a big smile. "Be right back." I head to the kitchen for my glass and the poetry book.

When I return, she is in the bathroom, stripping off her clothes. The bath bomb has been tossed in the water and fizzes away. The box of chocolate confections is sitting on a stool next to the tub. Her wineglass on the same ledge as the candle. For five deep breaths, I simply watch her move. Nothing sexual, I just observe.

As the last of her clothes hits the floor, I step into the room. Set my glass and the book down. Peel my shirt over my head and toss it in the same pile as her clothes. Unzip my pants and shove them down, along with my underwear, then kick them aside. Wine and book in hand, I pad across the room to the tub. She straightens in the water, making room for me to sit behind her. I set my glass and the book by hers then relax in the warm water. She turns the faucet off then leans back and settles her back to my front.

For a beat, neither of us says a word. My eyes fall shut as my arms band her waist. Her fingers trace my skin and we just breathe each other in.

"Braydon?" she whisper-asks.

"Yeah?"

She shifts and tips her head back. "Thank you." The two words barely audible.

A small smile tips up the corners of my mouth. "Always." Then I press my lips to hers.

CHAPTER 25

ALESSANDRA

The noisy parts of the renovation ended two nights ago. Now they are moving on to more cosmetic things, such as spackling and painting. Halle-freak-ing-lujah. Much as I love my friends, sleeping in a strange bed, constantly invading their space, and waking up with unfa-miliar body aches are equally stressful.

Soon as I got the news from Sheila, I messaged Braydon. He'd gifted me the most unforgettable night with him after the vandalism incident. Put so much thought into each gift. Tended to me in a way no one ever had. And every moment since, I've wanted him in my bed. In my space. With me.

Is it about the sex? Eh, maybe a little. But there is some-thing to be said about being wrapped in his arms. Something about the innocent yet powerful touch, his hold, that calms every brewing storm in my head. He brought me up to my apartment, showered me with comfort gifts, pampered me with affection, and then took his time with me in my bed. I'd needed the noise to stop and he found a way. I'd needed my

And now, I need more of him.

Braydon accepted without protest.

Though I told him I didn't have time for a relationship, in the past thirty-six hours, I found a way to make time for him. It hasn't been a hardship, but it is also new. Staying positive, I want to say it will last. But a little voice in the back of my head says to stay level-headed. To not lose sight of what is in front of me. To not give in to the fantasy, in case it cannot become reality.

I hate the little voice.

Like clockwork, Braydon walks into Java and Teas Me at ten thirty, laptop bag slung over his shoulder. He throws me flirty eyes while ordering coffee and a breakfast sandwich. Neither of us hints at anything other than him ordering food. I hand him the numbered tent and he winks before heading for the outdoor seating.

Once the line clears, I turn to Mandi. "I'll take order fifteen out."

She cocks a brow. "What's up with you and the writer hottie?"

"What?" Not like Braydon and I have spent all our free time traipsing around town. We also haven't been masking our time outside my apartment. "Nothing is up," I add with a less-than-confident tone.

Lips pursed, she rolls her eyes. "Oh, okay." Soft laughter leaves her lips. "Should work on your delivery if you want people to believe it." Her gaze drifts to the door leading to the patio. She nods for a beat then meets my gaze. Takes a step closer and leans in. "But FYI, you don't fool me. The way that man looks at you, the way you look at him..." Lifting a hand, she fans her face. "There is definitely something going on."

Mouth agape, I stare at her. My mind suddenly a blank

slate. Fingers toying with my apron strings as I try to conjure up an intelligible response. Do I tell Mandi she must have her wires crossed and there is nothing going on with me and Braydon? Or do I confirm her suspicions and fess up?

Giving our whatever-ship a voice wouldn't be the worst thing. Right? *Braydon and I aren't boyfriend-girlfriend, but we are something.* If the notion sounds weird in my head, I only imagine how foolish it will sound out loud. Like I have no clue what is going on in my life. Like I have no confidence with men. And I guess when it comes to romantic relationships, I am somewhat clueless. Maybe. Maybe not.

My "love life" has consisted of flings and one-night stands for as long as I recall. I had boyfriends over the years. High school was filled with those short-lived, hormone-induced romances every teenager experiences. The ones you say are love but are the furthest thing from actual love. Not that I am an expert on love.

Sad as it may sound from a twenty-six-year-old woman, I don't think I've ever been in love. But then again, I haven't really asked anyone what being in love feels like. I could ask my parents—they met when Mom was a college freshman and Dad a college senior. Joan and Samuel Everett love each other, but since my brother, Anderson, and I moved out, they seem to spend less time together. When I talk to Mom and ask how Dad is, she waves off the question with a *"You know your father. He's fine."*

I'd ask Mags how she knew Geoff was *the one*, but the inquiry would prompt lots of questions I am nowhere near ready to answer. By the time I buck up enough courage, I will undoubtedly already know the answer.

The longer I remain silent, the wider Mandi's grin becomes. Whatever. At this stage of the game, I have nothing to lose.

Ding, ding. "Fifteen," August calls through the pass window.

Perfect timing. I snatch Braydon's breakfast from the ledge and place the order slip on the receipt spike. Mandi narrows her eyes at me as I walk off. Just before I exit the staff alley, I pause and look over my shoulder at her.

"Maybe there is." I smirk in her direction. "But I don't kiss and tell."

As I hit the first row of tables in the dining room, I hear her say, "Ha. I knew it."

I laugh but don't look back as I head outside. Sunshine heats my skin as I reach Braydon's table closest to the sidewalk. Brow crinkled and back hunched as he types furiously on the laptop keys, the moment I sidle up to the table, he stops and looks up.

Smile brightening his expression, he pushes his glasses up the bridge of his nose. "Hi."

"Your breakfast, sir."

He chuckles as I set the plate down. "Join me?"

I peek over my shoulder. No line and Mandi found something to do besides stare my way. "For a bit." I pull out the chair and sit, my knee brushing his as I do. I swallow and bite the inside of my cheek, fighting my smile. Jerking my chin toward his laptop, I ask, "How's the story coming along?"

He finishes chewing, swallows, and wipes his mouth. "Good, actually. Finished draft one yesterday. Now on to the *fun* part. Revisions." He takes a sip of coffee. "Considering my head was a mess during the first twenty-five percent, I have no shame in admitting it's partial garbage." I jump as he lays a hand on my thigh under the table. "But I won't publish a word unless I love the end result."

Slow, measured strokes. One, then another. And another.

His fingers dance lightly across my denim-clad thigh. Perspiration slicks my skin that has nothing to do with the late spring weather. Tingles ripple from the point of contact and spread like wildfire. Leaning over his plate to take another bite, his fingers shift up and to the inside of my thigh.

Breath caught in my lungs, I lick my lips. He gives me a devilish smile, squeezes my thigh, then leans back. The heat of him vanishes while the hum he elicits remains.

"You know," I start on a laugh. "Only minutes ago, Mandi was giving me a hard time. Said she knew something was going on between us."

Braydon shifts his gaze, stares inside the café for a beat, smiles, then meets my blues. "She isn't wrong."

Nervousness thickens in my throat and I swallow past it. "No, she's not."

God, why is that so scary to admit?

While Braydon eats his breakfast, I stare at the people walking along Main Street. Lose focus and mentally zone out for a moment. I don't want to think *why* confessing the truth flipped my stomach upside down. Why it made me a little dizzy. Instead, I look out toward the mountain and trees in the distance. Tell myself I only feel this way because Braydon and I have spent so much time together recently. That it is chemistry and nothing more.

What else could it be?

I mentally shake off the path my thoughts start to take. It doesn't matter what I feel. He lives in the city and I live here. Feelings won't change facts.

"I'm back in my apartment," I blurt out.

Braydon pushes his plate away, leans back in his chair, and kicks his feet out. His eyes roam my face. "That's good news."

It is good news. No more unfamiliar beds or disrupting my

friends. No more lack of privacy or accidentally waking Mags at dark-thirty in the morning as I leave. And no more wishing for Braydon to stay over... because now he can without anyone being uncomfortable.

"Come over when I finish up?"

He sits up and leans in my direction, his hand returning to my thigh. Sliding his phone across the table, he unlocks it and passes it to me. "Yes, but only if you give me your number again." He winces. "I may have deleted it in a moment of anger."

Sucking in a deep breath, I hold it as my hand reaches for his phone and nod in understanding. He'd had every right to be upset with me when he left. I'd cut him off. Essentially threw him away.

But he came back. Mainly for work, but he admitted I was more the reason for his return.

For five vicious heartbeats, I stare at the screen. Then my fingers dance across the screen. Create a new contact and enter my details. Type out a message and feel my back pocket buzz after I press send, so I have his number again as well.

"I'll message you when I'm close to being done." I slide the phone in his direction.

He stares down at the screen with the brightest smile on his lips. "I look forward to it, firecracker."

CHAPTER 26
BRAYDON

I don't want to leave but know in the next day or two, I have to.

Yesterday, I wrapped up the self-edits on my story. Soon as I send it to the editor at the magazine, Dad will reach out. Ask when I plan to return. Tell me the next town he wants me to visit and write another *magical* story about.

But I'm not ready. To leave Lake Lavender. To return to my cold and lonely apartment in the city. To be anywhere Alessandra is not.

Nausea rolls in my stomach at the idea of getting in my car and driving out of town. It is not a question of *if* I will see Alessandra again, but *when*.

Without effort, she had me forgetting my own rules about love. We've spent less than a month in each other's company and in that time, I got attached. Love is too strong a word to affix to what I feel for Alessandra. I'd say I am very much in *like* with her, though.

"Ahh," Alessandra groans as she rolls onto her side, fingers trailing up my chest. "Too early." She snuggles the length of my torso. "Quit thinking so much."

My frame shakes as light laughter leaves my lips. "Sorry my thinking woke you." I press my lips to her crown. "I'll try not to think so loudly in the morning."

Hooking her leg over my hip, she paints small circles over my skin with her fingers. Kisses a path from my pec to my collarbone. Licks her way up the side of my neck and sucks the lobe of my ear between her lips. With a shift of her weight, she straddles my hips. Grinds her drenched center over my thickening erection.

I fist her hips before rocking my own. Desperate moans and labored breaths fill the air. Nails dig into the flesh of my pecs as she pushes up and rocks her hips, giving me more of her weight. My fingers bruise her flesh and she glides back and forth, back and forth. Each time we're together like this, we tease with bare skin until I inevitably roll on a condom.

But the time for teasing is over.

One hand firmly on her hip, the other drifts up the curves of her torso and cups her breast. Pinching her nipple. Her back bows and I tighten my grip. Sitting up, I take her nipple in my mouth and suck. Bite the tender flesh enough to elicit a throaty moan from her. Both hands on her hips, I lick and suck and nip my way up until my lips crush hers. Cheeks spread in my grip, I grind her faster, harder against my cock.

"Need to feel you. All of you. With nothing between us."

Her hands glide over my shoulders and up the back of my neck. Fingers fist the length of my hair and yank back. Hard. Tongue darting out, she licks my bottom lip.

"I'm on the pill and clean."

I groan as she rocks forward. "I-I'm clean too."

On the next roll of her hips, I shift just enough to bump her entrance with my tip. As if neither of us is prepared for what happens next, we pause. Her fingers in my hair go slack as her hands drift to cup my cheeks. I band my arms around her waist and hold her in place. She drops her lips to mine and kisses me with unprecedented tenderness. Warmth radiates from my rib cage and I moan for an entirely new reason. A reason that has me wanting to stay. A reason I can't seem to shake. Her.

As she deepens the kiss, I pin her in place and rock up into her. Gasps fill the air as the pads of her fingers bruise my cheeks and I tighten my hold on her.

"So fucking perfect," I whisper against her lips. As her hips move, my eyes roll shut. "Damn, firecracker." I open my eyes and suck her bottom lip between my lips. Bring one hand to the back of her neck and drop the other to her tailbone. "Like you were meant for me."

Resting her forearms on my shoulders, she rolls her hips. Slow for two strokes. Then she moves faster. Glides up and down my cock, jaw slack, and eyes the darkest shade of blue as they hold me captive. The middle finger of my lower hand slithers down her ass crack until I graze her puckered hole and press lightly.

"Braydon, I—"

"Won't do anything you don't want me to." I add a little more pressure and on the rock of her hips, she pushes into the touch. "More than perfect."

She crushes my lips with hers, the kiss as ravenous as our fused bodies. The faster our rhythm, the more she accepts my finger. Breaking the kiss, she throws her head back and gasps. She grips my shoulders, my neck, my hair as her tight pussy strokes my cock, again and again. As her ass begs for more than a knuckle and a half.

And then I feel it. The slow constriction of her walls around my cock. I pump my finger faster, deeper as skin slapping skin echoes off the walls. Pain shoots through my scalp as she all but rips my hair out. It only makes my hips piston faster.

"Oh, god," she moans out.

I shift my finger inside her. "Let go, firecracker." Above me, she shudders as her body grips mine like a vise. "That's my good girl." Eyes on her flush cheeks and neck, on the next rock of my hips, I come undone. And damn, is it unlike anything I have ever experienced.

What just happened was more than mind-blowing sex. Alessandra gave me something I never truly had in previous relationships. Her trust.

And fuck, it is heady and addictive and magnificent.

"What if I don't want you to go?"

God, those words are music to my ears. "Believe me, firecracker, I don't want to leave." I lean over the table and press a chaste kiss to her lips. Take her hand in mine and lace our fingers. "But I need to at least check in with my dad. Do a few small things at the office."

"I get it." Her bottom lip pushes out. "Don't like it, but I get it."

She sips on her lavender tea latte while I cut the pancakes on my plate to share with her. Not that we generally eat off the same plate, but I will miss these moments. Me coming into the café every morning, sitting outside on the patio, having time with her—whether for five minutes or thirty.

What choice do I have?

Not like I can uproot my life. Even if I did, is it responsible to do something so drastic after knowing someone for such a short time? The connection I share with Alessandra is undeniable. But what if I change my entire life to be with her and our relationship—*are we in a relationship?*—fizzles out? I would have nothing to fall back on. Sure, I could crawl back to Dad and he would help. But I don't want it to be over losing someone. Not again.

An idea sparks and claws at my insides. Before I lose courage, I blurt out, "Want to try a long-distance thing?"

Alessandra looks up from our joined hands with wide eyes. "W-what?"

The slow-forming knot in my stomach twists. "Well, kind of long distance. An hour apart should be more like an annoying distance." I scratch the scar in my brow. "I don't want to leave. You don't want me to leave. What if we ease into a relationship?"

Her brows knit together as she nibbles her bottom lip. "How would it work?"

Good question. My schedule is more flexible than hers, but there are stretches of time when I'm away to capture the next story. I love traveling, seeing the state, and writing stories that drive others to visit places they never knew existed. Every two to three years, the magazine writes about places outside of Washington but no more than a two-hour drive from the border.

I love my job, but right now, a chisel is chipping away at that love.

I want time, *need* time, to see where this can go with Alessandra. When I return to Seattle, I will talk to Dad. Explain the situation and tell him where my head is in all of it. Ask for his advice. If left up to me, I may not make the wisest decision.

"Wish I had answers." My thumb slowly strokes hers. "All I know is, I don't want this to be it."

"Me either," she whispers, barely audible.

I spear a piece of pancake and sliced banana, swiping it through the puddle of syrup on the plate. Holding the loaded tines in her direction, I feed her.

"Then it won't be. Promise."

Whatever it takes, I plan to stick to my promise. Even if it means me driving back and forth between Seattle and Lake Lavender throughout the week. Though I want more, I will take whatever I can get until we figure out a better solution. Until we get every day together. No matter how long it takes, Alessandra is worth the wait.

CHAPTER 27

ALESSANDRA

"Java and Teas Me, Lessa speaking. How may I help you?" Subtle white noise fills the phone line. Pain lances my knuckles as I squeeze the phone handset. "How may I help you?" I repeat with more gusto.

This is the fifth call this week where the person on the other end says nothing. When I asked the employees if they'd answered any similar calls, they shook their heads. Mandi had a few hang-up calls this week, but we got those every now and again. I always assume those are solicitors or wrong numbers. But maybe they aren't either. Maybe it is the same person that makes my mouth go dry. That makes me pick at my cuticles until they bleed.

"Must be a bad connection," I lie. "Try calling back from a different phone." I drop the handset in the holder, lean back in the chair, close my eyes, and exhale the breath I'd been holding.

I inhale and exhale a few steadying breaths then open my eyes. Straightening in my desk chair, I shake the mouse next to the keyboard. The sunset dipping below the horizon of the lake flashes to life on the screen. I take another cleansing breath and try to locate my zen.

A fraction calmer, I double-click the Mission: Watchdog Security app on the desktop. A dashboard pops up on the screen with alerts, communications from the security company, and a few of the many live feeds from the installed cameras.

After the spray paint vandalism, I caved and had a security system installed. Enough cameras outside to catch anyone approaching from any angle. A handful of discreet cameras inside, nestled in the crooks of machinery and sandwiched between art. Sensors on the windows and doors are only disengaged during business hours. And my least favorite... three panic buttons—one in the office, another under the service counter, and the last hidden under the kitchen prep table near the ranges.

I want my employees to feel safe. I want everyone who thinks about coming into Java and Teas Me to feel safe. But this all feels too much. Cameras and sirens and panic buttons. One unanswered call or bad password given to the security company and police will flock to this place like the FBI's most wanted is inside.

Whoever the hell this is—the weird social media messages, the spray paint, the bizarre phone calls—I am over it. At my wits' end. Done.

Perusing the overnight camera feed, I see nothing out of the ordinary. I close out the app, pay a few of the vendor bills, and exit the office.

"Where's that smile I love?" August says as I step into the kitchen.

His presence has always been a burst of sunshine. Aside from his skills in the kitchen, his radiant energy is the top reason I hired him. August might be having the worst day on the planet and he still finds a reason to smile. Who doesn't want that kind of joy in their life?

I lift my hands to my face, rub my eyes, drag my fingertips to my temples and sigh heavily. As the last of the exhale leaves my lungs, I use every muscle in my face to tip up the corners of my mouth.

"It's only been a couple weeks and I am tired of all this extra security nonsense." I step around the prep table and wash my hands in the sink near one of the ranges. "Logically, I know having the cameras and alarms protects all of us and the business." I shut the water off and tear off paper towels from the holder. "But it makes me feel like *I* did something wrong. Like *I'm* being punished instead of the person causing the damage." I toss the towels in the bin. "Ugh. It irritates the hell out of me, but there's no alternative."

August wraps an arm around my shoulder and hauls me to his side. Beside him, I feel small. It's not that August is feet taller. More like his spirit makes him larger than life.

"Baby girl, there will always be someone trying to knock you down. And each time they do, you stand right back up and flip 'em the bird." He hugs me a little tighter. "Life is way too short to give your energy to someone who doesn't deserve it." He releases me and smirks. "Save your energy for that handsome fellow. The one that makes your whole body smile." I cock a brow at him. "Oh, I see the way you two go all googly-eyed when he's here. I may not be the brightest crayon in the box, but I know love when I see it."

Whoa, whoa, whoa. Errrt. Pull the emergency brake, bucko. Love? As in L-O-V-E?

"Um, I have no clue what you're—"

August holds up his hands. "Look, I get it. Everything is all new and shiny with him. But baby girl, I've been there." He steps into me and lays a hand on each shoulder. "May not be what you expected, but it doesn't make it any less true."

I toy with my apron strings, dropping my gaze to follow the action. "Can we talk about something else?" I avert my gaze to the table. "What are you making? Maybe I'll help."

Something akin to pity fills his eyes, but I refuse to give it any attention. Instead, I focus on the table. Focus on the ingredients August is cutting for sides, quiche, and frittata. Grab my own knife and join in on the task. Monotonous. Tedious. Something that requires my full attention. And for a small blip of time, I zone out at the prep table with rock music playing from the Bluetooth speaker.

BRAYDON

30 minutes out. Any dinner requests?

I stare down at the screen and smile. The past week and a half with Braydon as my boyfriend—yeah, it still sounds weird— has been interesting. Since we spend time together sporadically, it's been a great way to ease us both into the whole relationship status. For different reasons, neither of us wanted more than sex for years.

Then we met, and the constant pull between us was too hard to ignore.

ALESSANDRA

Catalina's?

BRAYDON

Tostadas?

ALESSANDRA

Yes, please. With rice, black beans, chips, salsa and guac.

BRAYDON

Text me the number and I'll call it in. It'll probably be ready when I get there.

I text him the number to Catalina's Cantina, followed by *drive safe.*

This weekend will be the first true test of our *relationship.* After wrapping up the story and talking with his father, Braydon scheduled some time off. He took tomorrow (Friday), Monday, and Tuesday off, giving him a long weekend. With me. In Lake Lavender.

Once the days were set, he called and let me know he'd be here and all mine for five days. When he mentioned calling the bed-and-breakfast after he got off the phone with me, I told him not to worry about it. Without overthinking, I told him to stay at my apartment. If we were doing this—a romantic relationship—I didn't want to half-ass it. Most couples in a happy, healthy relationship wouldn't sleep apart. And considering the amount of sex we've had, why should we?

After Lucy drops off the goods from the bakery, I set the alarm, lock up, and head upstairs.

The cork pops from the wine bottle when a knock sounds at the door. Setting the bottle and opener on the counter, I amble to the door and peek through the peephole. On the other side, Braydon stands tall with his shoulders back and eyes scanning the ground below. Not necessarily on alert, but still on the lookout for anyone out of place.

A buzzy warmth expands beneath my breastbone at how this man wants to keep me safe. Of course, my friends and family also want me unharmed. But Braydon having this urge to protect me, it isn't the same. His desire for my welfare resonates deeper. Sinks in my bones and bathes me in solace.

Disengaging the lock, I twist the knob and open the door. "Hey, Care Bear. Get in here with that deliciousness." I step aside, let him in, and take the bag while he toes off his shoes.

He empties the bag and sets dinner up at the small dining table. I pour us each a glass of wine and join him. We dig in and don't come up for air until a few bites later. We do a little catching up—I tell him how busy the café has been with people flocking in for the summer festival, and he shares the date of the next issue of Washington's Hidden Gems and how giddy his dad is over the story. The evening is all so... normal. Dinner and conversation and existing in the same space. Something I have never had. Something I am starting to love.

"The festival is this weekend?"

Hand over my mouth, I nod while I finish chewing. "Mm-hmm." I swallow then take a sip of wine. "Saturday, Sunday, and Monday. Some are the same as the centennial event—rides, food, games, and local vendors. Several of the shops on Main will have abbreviated hours to let staff work at and enjoy the festival." Though I expect some of the same fried treats, I anticipate new items such as melon and popsicles and ice cream.

Pushing the beans around his plate with his fork, a slow smile tips the corners of his mouth. "You know we're going, right?" White teeth brighten his smile. "Only makes sense. It's how we met in the first place, just not in the summer."

Insert swoon here.

"I'd love nothing more."

After cleaning up dinner, we curl up on the couch and watch a movie. Midway through, I yawn and Braydon snuggles me closer. I don't make it another five minutes without yawning again. A long, busy workday, good food, wine, and burrowing in the crook of Braydon's arm is the perfect equation for heavy eyes.

Saying nothing, he picks up the remote and powers off the television. He kisses my temple, rises from the couch, and takes our glasses to the kitchen. As if we have done it hundreds of times before, he offers his hand and I slip mine in his. Plant my feet on the floor and stand up. We wander to the bedroom, turning off lights as we go.

The soft glow of the bedside lamp lights the room enough to see as we strip our clothes away—I his and he mine. And for the first time, we crawl into bed without groping and kissing and kneading one another. He lies on his side of the bed and I curl into his side. The soft, slow touches of our fingers the only language we speak as we drift to sleep.

The last thing I remember is Braydon kissing my hair. "Sweet dreams, firecracker."

CHAPTER 28

BRAYDON

Cold sheets greet me as I reach out for Alessandra. Opening my eyes, I close them just as quick when sunlight blinds me temporarily. Hand over my eyes, I slowly open them and separate my fingers until my eyes adjust to the light. Scooting up to a seated position, I stretch my limbs.

As I open my mouth to call out for her, I spot a slip of paper on her pillow. I swipe it up, bring it close, and narrow my eyes to read the note.

Care Bear,
You looked so peaceful, I didn't want to wake you. I'm downstairs. When you're ready for breakfast, text me then come down.
Your firecracker

My cheeks sting as I stare at the last two words. *Your fire-*

Swinging my feet out from under the covers, I finger-comb my hair and reach for my glasses on the nightstand. I slide them on and plant my feet on the floor, stretching more when I stand. Grabbing the throw blanket on the foot of the bed, I wrap it around me as I pad to the entry for my duffel.

Back in the bedroom, I riffle through the duffel and pull out clothes for the day. Tossing the throw back on the bed and my glasses on my clothes, I head for the bathroom and crank the shower faucet. Steam barely has enough time to fill the bathroom before I cut off the water and towel off. I forgo shaving—after all, I am on vacation—and brush my teeth.

Dressed save for my shoes, I hang the towel in the bathroom, fold the throw blanket and lay it back at the foot of the bed, then move my duffel and dirties to the floor on my side of the bed, stashing her note in the bag.

My side of the bed. I don't hate the sound of those words in my head.

I grab my phone from the charger and open the messaging app.

BRAYDON

Up and presentable. Putting on shoes, then I'll be down.

The small gray bubble dances on the screen.

ALESSANDRA

Can't wait to sleep in tomorrow. I'll get your order in then come to the back door.

My naughty side wants to toss out a perverse comment about back doors. For now, I keep it to myself.

BRAYDON

Be down in a minute.

I stow my phone in one back pocket, wallet in the other, and shove my keys in the front. As I sit on the entry bench and tie my shoes, my eyes drift around the space. Not that I haven't seen Alessandra's apartment. Admittedly, most of my time here, I missed seeing the place with the curtains drawn back, sunlight dancing across the hardwood and minimal furniture. In the evening, the apartment has a dark, industrial yet modern vibe. But in the daylight, I notice the softer hues. Cream and soft blue and gray. The occasional pale yellow, baby pink or lavender. Against the brick and sharp lines of black, it works.

After one last look, I rise from the bench and head out the door. At the foot of the stairs, Alessandra stands with one hand on her hip and my favorite smile on her lips. My feet hit the pavement and I wrap my arms around her middle, pressing my lips to hers.

"Morning, firecracker."

Her smile widens. "Morning, Care Bear."

Every time she calls me Care Bear, I want to ask which one. Is there a Nerdy Care Bear? If so, I'd say it is one-hundred-percent me. Knowing her, she would probably call me Funshine Bear or Bedtime Bear. There isn't anything wrong with Funshine Bear. I just don't see myself as being super chipper all the time. And as long as Bedtime Bear is *fun*, I'm cool. But I'll save asking for another day.

"Hungry?" She holds the door open and gestures for me to enter.

I step inside and the place is so different from my last visit. Pans clang against the gas range. The whir of the oven serves as background noise. A slightly sweet smell floats in the air—hints of bread and berries and something I can't quite place. Oddly, it smells like Alessandra and I inhale deeply. A tall black man stands between the range and a stainless steel table, shifting back and forth between cutting fruit and vegetables, cooking food on the range, and slicing a fresh loaf of bread.

"If I wasn't a minute ago, I definitely am now." I take in another lungful of air. "God, it smells incredible back here." My eyes widen. "How the hell do you get anything done? I'd be eating all day."

"Time and control, Care Bear." She takes my hand and walks me closer to the man. "August, I'd like you to meet Braydon. My boyfriend."

At this, his brows shoot to his hairline. His eyes dart between us as a knowing smile lights his face. He wipes a hand on his apron then offers it to me. "August. Nice to meet you, Braydon." He shoots Alessandra a mischievous grin. "I haven't heard nearly enough about you."

"Oh, shush you."

August and I laugh before I add, "Right back atcha. Might need to catch up later."

Before he or I get another word in, her hands are on my chest and shoving me toward the small office just off the kitchen. Laughter spills from my lips as she plops me in the guest chair. She starts shutting the door but leaves it cracked. She pokes her head out and hollers, "The order I placed, just bring it here." August says something I don't hear then laughs. Alessandra gives him a stern look before closing the door.

I really do love it here.

Sitting on the edge of the bed, I watch Alessandra as she gets ready for the evening. Tonight is the first time I have seen her in red. I trust it won't be the last. The color makes her creamy skin pop. Thin straps on her shoulders give me more access to her skin. The bust hugs the curves of her breasts while the skirt flairs enough to disguise what I know to be underneath and stops just above the knee.

I sit awestruck as she leans closer to the bathroom mirror. Draws dark lines on the edge of her lids and coats her lashes with mascara. Even from my spot on the bed, the kohl makes her blues more vibrant. She swaps the mascara tube for lipstick. Cap off, she twists the end, lifts it to her mouth, and slowly paints the rouge over her supple lips.

She better bring the tube in her purse. Not sure how I'll resist kissing it off of her.

As if hearing my thoughts, she caps the lipstick and exits the bathroom with it in her hand. Parting my legs, she steps between them and runs a hand through my hair. My eyes fall shut as I tip my head back slightly and lean into her touch.

"You look handsome."

Her hand drifts from my hair to the line of my jaw to my chin. My arms band around her thighs and tug her closer. Press her breasts to the base of my throat. Gasp as her finger ghosts over my lips. I open my eyes and stare up at her. Stunned at how I get to call this beautiful woman mine.

"No one will look at me with you in the room." I don't say it to discount her compliment. I only speak the truth. And truth be told, Alessandra always outshines every woman, every person in the room.

She drops her lips to mine and hums as my hands trail up the back of her thighs. All too soon, she breaks the kiss. An audible groan crawls up my throat as my frame wilts.

"Much as I'd like to stay in, Care Bear, we should head out. Otherwise, we'll never make it."

Staying in sounds like the perfect night, but I would never steal her time with her friends. Plus, getting to know the people she holds close to her heart is a good idea. One day, her friends may be my friends. Or so I hope.

I release my hold on her and harrumph. "Fine."

As she steps back, she hauls me up and off the bed. "Come on, Care Bear. Time for food and dancing."

And just like that, I can't wait to get her on the dance floor.

I'd been on edge before leaving the apartment. Biting the inside of my cheek as we approached the restaurant. Knee bouncing under the table the first ten minutes after we were seated. But it was all for naught. The past hour and a half with Alessandra's friends have been wonderful. I expected an endless list of questions to be asked. To be judged on whether or not I was good enough for her. To be under serious scrutiny.

But none of that happened.

In a matter of minutes, they accepted me. Shook my hand or gave me a quick hug. Teased Alessandra about it taking forever for her to find someone. The women spilled a little of their history together while the guys joked about more recent events.

Geoff and Mags met in the fall. He says it was love at first sight. She says it was like they'd found each other after being lost for a lifetime. Either way, I love how they look at each other. How when their eyes meet, no one else exists. Their love is the kind I hid from for the past four years. The stomach-flipping, soul-quenching, can't-get-enough love.

And somehow, in a matter of weeks, the idea of having love like that doesn't scare me as it once did.

The others at the table—Lena, Logan, and Owen—share tidbits about themselves, but nothing too deep.

"Ready to settle the check and head upstairs?" Geoff asks the table but looks to Mags for a response.

"That a serious question?" Logan scoffs.

Mags rolls her eyes and subtly shakes her head. "Yes," she answers Geoff then leans in and kisses him chastely.

With his booming laughter and need to insert himself in every aspect of the conversation, Logan is the most outgoing of the group. He has also made it abundantly clear when talking about different women that he prefers singledom and playing the field. I get wanting to stay single. Been there, but probably for different reasons. My urge to hookup was definitely less often than his, but I attest it to my past.

Owen is the shyest in the group. He also gets teased the most because of his innate impulse to work twelve-plus hours a day. Nothing wrong with a strong work ethic, but if I had to sit in my small office at the magazine for more hours than required, I'd lose my sanity.

Lena… I am still trying to get a read on her.

The server sidles up to the table and passes out the check holders. "As always, it's wonderful to see everyone."

Like a stadium wave, each chair at the table slides back once we settle our bills. Logan all but runs through the tables to take the stairs two at a time. I can't help but laugh.

Taking up the rear of the group, her arm hooked with mine, Alessandra and I take our time going up the stairs. On the second floor, I lean in and drop my voice. "Logan is a trip."

Alessandra laughs louder than expected. "Uh, yeah. That's putting it nicely." She turns her gaze my way. "Wait until he's more comfortable with you. He'll probably ask you to be his wingman."

"Seriously?" When she doesn't rebut, my brows tighten. "But we're together."

The whimsical sound of her laughter fills the air. The second it hits my ears, soft flutters erupt beneath my sternum. Months ago, I would've shoved the sensation down and smothered it with sex or solitude. Not anymore. Now, I want to hear her laughter. Want the dizzying sensations. Want her.

"Logan doesn't care." She shakes her head. "He has a one-track mind. Getting someone between the sheets. If he wasn't otherwise a good guy, I'd avoid him."

"He ever hit on you?"

Her brows shoot up as one corner of her mouth slowly kicks up. "You don't need to be worried about Logan. Not when it comes to me or us."

We reach the entrance of the club, show our IDs, then weave our way through the crowd.

"Didn't answer my question," I say on a growl. Whether or not intentional, her evading my question heats my blood. Has me borderline feral. He may be a good guy, but fuck if I'll let him think he has a chance with Alessandra.

No. She is mine.

Her lips on my cheek cool my anger, but only to a low simmer. "Before Mags and Geoff were official, yes, Logan hit on me," she says, and I grind my molars. "Hey." She jerks to a stop, grabs my chin, and forces me to look at her. "You have nothing to worry about. Promise." She chuckles. "Before we met, he saw me in On Tap. Tossed out some cheesy one-liner and I literally laughed in his face."

The last of my anger fizzles out. "You did?"

She laughs as if recalling the memory. "Yeah, I did. Honestly, I have no clue if he remembers me from that night. He was *really* drunk. And he's never said anything since Mags and Geoff brought our two circles together." She shrugs. "I let it go." Her hands frame my face. "Please, don't let it bother you. It went nowhere."

Swallowing, I nod. "I will." I press my lips to hers. "But if he asks me to be his wingman, I'll laugh in his face."

Her hands fall away. She laces her fingers with mine. "Come on. Let's go see where they are." Spinning around, she walks backward, facing me. "Then we're dancing."

CHAPTER 29

ALESSANDRA

Braydon and I danced to three songs before I dragged him off the dance floor and toward the exit. I texted Mags and Lena good night as we made our way out of Black Silk. The entire ride back to my apartment felt frantic. My needy hands on him. His starved hands on me.

I unbuttoned his shirt in the car. He slid his hand under my dress, beneath my panties, and sank two fingers between my thighs as he drove down Main Street.

We barely made it into the apartment with our clothes on. The moment the door closed, I stripped him bare in the foyer, dropped to my knees, and took him in my mouth. The rest of the night was a blur of lips and tongues, teeth and hands, the two of us connected in every way imaginable.

As I stare at him in the faint morning light, I should be exhausted. Should be sore. Shouldn't be thinking about straddling his hips. Definitely not thinking about waking him up with my mouth on his skin. Or rocking my hips over him until he's hard and taking him the moment he is.

I shouldn't, but as my knee hits the mattress and I press my arousal to his cock, I don't regret my decision. Beneath me, his body slowly stirs to life. Lowering myself, I bracket his head with my forearms. Kiss my way up his neck. Suck the sensitive spot beneath his ear.

A low groan rumbles in his chest as his hands come to my hips. "Firecracker," he rasps in my ear.

On the next forward rock of my hips, I graze his tip with my entrance then sink down on him. His fingers bruise my hips while mine dive into his hair. I kiss my way to his mouth, tangle my tongue with his, and pick up my pace as I ride his cock.

Without warning, he sits up. Slides his hands to my ass, rocking me harder against him. Then my back hits the mattress, but only for a breath. He pulls out, flips me on my belly, fists my hips, and hikes my ass in the air. A hand snakes up my spine before drifting back to my tailbone.

"Can never get enough of you, firecracker." His finger drifts over my puckered hole. A whimper slips from my lips when he keeps going, running two fingers through my wet pussy. He inserts the digits and groans. "Patience, firecracker."

He pumps his fingers slower than desirable. I try to push back against him. Try to pick up the pace. In response, he pulls out. Toys with my clit. Rubs his fingers through my folds. But he doesn't give me any more than that.

I open my mouth, ready to beg, but snap it shut when his fingers drift back up. He paints that forbidden place with my arousal but doesn't insert his finger. He goes back and forth, slicking both holes and driving me insane with the action.

"One day, I'll take you here too," he says and presses the tip of a finger in the tight hole.

I moan as adrenaline hits my bloodstream. "Yes."

The mattress shifts under my knees a second before he fills

me with his cock. In unison, we gasp. And then he moves. Presses the palm of his free hand over my spine and fucks me like the world is on fire. His hips piston at breakneck speed while his finger pumps in and out of my ass. My fingers find my clit and rub vicious circles. His hand drifts up my spine, his fingers fisting the hair at the nape of my neck and yanking my head back.

"So fucking beautiful when I fuck you," he growls out and I moan. "Look at you." He leans in and licks up my spine. "Can't get enough. Can you, firecracker?"

I circle my clit then move my hand down. Graze the base of his cock before taking his balls in my hand. "Never." I roll his balls in my hand and he growls.

Skin slapping skin echoes off the walls. Sweat slicks my skin. The smell of him, of us, floats through the air. I peek over my shoulder, meet his heated gaze, and lick my bottom lip before pulling it between my teeth. His hand releases my hair, drifting until he palms my breast and he lifts me up. My back to his front, his hips and fingers slow.

"Kiss me."

I obey, bringing my lips to his. Palming the back of his head, I deepen the kiss. A sting of pain shoots from my nipple as he rolls it between his fingers. My nails dig into his scalp. He frees my nipple, his hand roaming lower. Gasping, I break the kiss as his fingers find my clit and his hips move faster.

"This is mine." His teeth clamp down on my shoulder.

I fist his hair. "Yes."

He nips his way up my neck to my ear. "Say it," he demands.

Fuck. I love this side of him.

"It's yours. *I* am yours."

"Damn right you are." His hips smack mine in a vicious

rhythm. His finger in my ass is deep and curling while the fingers of his other hand circle my clit. "You're close, aren't you, firecracker?"

I tug his hair harder. "Yes," I choke out. My breaths come in labored pants.

"Fucking love how I know." He adds more pressure to my clit. Hits harder each time he bottoms out. "Like you were made for me." He licks from the edge of my shoulder to the sensitive spot beneath my ear. "Come for me, firecracker."

Heat builds at the base of my spine and snakes its way up my body. One more stroke of my clit and I shatter. He pulls his finger from my ass, grips my hip, and pounds me harder.

"All." *Thrust.* "Fucking." *Slap.* "Mine." *Pound.*

His finger leaves my clit. Both hands clutch my hips and bruise them. His whole frame shaking as he comes inside me on a growl. I reach down and fondle his balls, causing his fingers to tighten further.

As he stills behind me, I push off him and spin around, his release dripping down the inside of my thighs. I take his face in my hands and kiss the hell out of him. His arms snake around my waist and he lowers me to the mattress.

"Waking up with you is never a bad day," he whispers against my lips.

"Back atcha, Care Bear."

Heat blankets my skin as the sun shines down from above. Fingers laced with Braydon's, we trek the sidewalk from my apartment to the summer festival. Many of the shops have closed; several with tents at the event. Residents and tourists swarm the park at the heart of Main Street.

A local band plays a rock-bluegrass mix under the gazebo. Cheers erupt as game players win prizes. Temporary carnival rides whir and whistle as they fling riders in circles at high velocity. Children and adults stroll the promenade with flavored shaved ice, sliced fruit or frozen confections. The scent of batter-dipped fried foods catches on the breeze.

I peek up at Braydon behind tinted lenses. "What do you want to do first?"

He presses his lips to mine. "Rides before food."

We ride the roller coaster and pirate ship—which doesn't go upside down, thank god—followed by the Ferris wheel. Much as I love rides, I prefer the kind that doesn't move from town to town. I'd rather drive hours to an amusement park than risk my life. I want to have fun, but not at the expense of my life.

As we exit the Ferris wheel car, I tell Braydon I'm good with not doing any other rides.

"How about a few games before we check out the vendors and food?"

I hook my arm in his. "Sounds perfect."

We toss baseballs at bottles. Braydon looks to the sky and groans when I knock all mine down before him. I dance in victory as the attendant hands me a small stuffed dog. Braydon laughs and wraps his arm around my shoulders.

We skip the goldfish ring toss and step up to the basketball game. I make the first two baskets but miss the last three. Braydon gets all five and sticks his tongue out at me. His reward is a sparkly stuffed unicorn. He hugs it to his chest like it's his new favorite keepsake and I snort-laugh.

"Not nice to laugh, firecracker." He hauls me into his side

and kisses my neck before blowing a raspberry in the same spot.

"I-I'm sorry." I laugh.

"Are you? Not sure I believe you."

I shove him away and work to regain my composure. I lean to the side, look over his shoulder and narrow my eyes a split second before returning to him. "One last game. Then it's food time."

"Lead the way." He shuffles to the side and gestures for me to walk ahead.

The closer we get to the high striker, the more I mentally shake my head. *What the hell am I thinking? How heavy are those mallets? Will I get anywhere near the bell at the top?* Too late to worry about it now.

I step up and the attendant looks at me with a teasing smile on his lips. Immediately, I want to bang the hell out of that bell.

"Two please," I tell him.

Braydon pays the man and we step up to the mallet stand. "Want to go first?" he asks.

I shake my head. "No, you go first. I'll keep your sparkly unicorn safe."

Throwing me my favorite smile of his, he hands over the toy. "Be right back, Princess Periwinkle."

I snort-laugh. "Did you seriously name this stuffed unicorn in the last three minutes?"

He slaps a hand to his chest. "I am her father. Have you not named yours yet?" he asks, mock offended.

I bite the inside of my cheek. Look down at the brown stuffed dog in my arm. Shrug and meet his gaze. "Nope. But if you hit the bell, I'll name it."

"Ooh. Challenge accepted."

Braydon steps up to the plate with the mallet in his hand. Shuffles his feet into a comfortable stance. Swings the mallet a few times before lifting it high, locking both hands in place, and bringing it to the platform with as much force as possible. The metal clapper shoots up the rail but falls short of the bell by inches.

His bottom lip juts out and is downright adorable.

I hold up my hand and pinch my thumb and forefinger together with a tiny gap. "You were so close."

"Wanted to win you the big bear."

I pat his shoulder. "It's okay." I press my lips to his cheek then hand over the stuffed toys. "My turn."

As I step up to the mallet stand, I feel the weight of more than Braydon's eyes on me. The attendant tries to tell me how to hold the mallet and hit the platform. I tune him out.

Here's the thing. I may be small in stature. May not look very muscular to the naked eye. But looks are deceiving. Owning a restaurant, no matter the type, you have to be able to lift heavy boxes and bags. At least once a week, I hoist hundred-plus-pound burlap sacks of coffee beans. Lift twenty-five-pound bags of sugar. The perishable deliveries are more frequent. Even with the lighter weight of milk crates, the repetition of lifting has toned my muscles.

So as I step up to the platform in my sundress, I listen to my body as I swing the mallet. Take a deep breath, raise the mallet up and over my head, then bring it back down with as much oomph as possible.

Thwack.

Ding.

I drop the mallet on the ground, dance like an idiot, and squeal in victory. The attendant stands awestruck while onlookers cheer and clap. Braydon runs up to me, wraps his arms around my middle, toys dangling behind me, and twirls me in circles.

"Holy shit," he says as my feet hit the ground. He takes my mouth with his. "That was so fucking hot."

"Yeah?"

"Hell yeah." He shifts us to the attendant. "Go get your prize, firecracker." His hand smacks my ass.

I end up with a stuffed panda almost too big to hold or carry. Braydon gives me the two smaller toys and takes the panda. We meander through the vendors and food trucks, several people congratulating me as we pass.

Eating a few items, we bag some to take back to the apartment.

"You have fun?" Braydon asks as we exit the park.

"I did. You?"

He nods, hugging me closer to his side before pressing his lips to my crown. "I did."

As we approach the back stairwell for my apartment, a thought flares to life.

Will it always be like this? If Braydon and I stay together, will our life be like this? Carefree. Full of laughter. Insatiable.

I truly hope so.

CHAPTER 30
BRAYDON

L eaving her each time is the hardest damn thing. Not that I have much choice.

Our relationship is far too new for me to suggest something more permanent—like me moving closer. But damn, I would move anywhere for her. In a heartbeat.

And that… is scary as hell.

Begrudgingly, I shove my clothes in my duffel. The same clothes she washed and folded yesterday without me knowing. Ugh. At least she isn't in the room while I pack. At least her intense stare isn't following my every move as I prepare to go.

As the sun pinked the sky, Alessandra dressed and headed out the door. I'd heard the faint *thump, thump, thump* of her footsteps as she'd trekked down the stairs. And then, nothing. I'd tugged her pillow closer. Inhaled her scent on the cotton. Snuggled it against my frame as I drifted back to sleep.

I'd woken with the pillow still in my arms and dreams of

Realization hit me hard in that moment. The exact moment I *knew*, with absolute certainty, I'd fallen in love with her.

"Do I tell her?" I mumble to myself as I shove the last item in my bag.

The zipper buzzes as I close the duffel. I hoist the bag off the bed and sling the strap over my shoulder. The moment reality set in this morning, the moment it dawned on me I love her, everything shifted. Time ticked slower. Nervousness I hadn't felt in weeks came back in full force. And all I did was think, think, think.

Should I tell her how I feel?

I close my eyes and try to picture it. Me confessing how I feel. No matter how many ways I spin the idea in my head, I can't see her reaction.

This—us—is newer than new. How do I know what I feel is love?

The last time I loved a woman, she ripped my heart out and left it to wither. Gabby had said she loved me countless times. Perhaps in her own way, she did. But Gabby's version of love had been so different than mine. Years of her saying those words... "*I love you, babe.*" ...they were all bullshit. A phrase on repeat after saying the first year or two.

In the beginning, before Gabby and I graduated high school, I didn't doubt we loved one another. But college tugged us in different directions. I focused on schoolwork while Gabby partied more and more. When I look back now, I see where the division began. The moment when saying I love you was more out of habit than actual sentiment.

And I don't want that to happen again. Not with Alessandra.

Those three little words want to make themselves heard, but I fear the grand impact they will have if I say them.

After one last look around the apartment, I slip on my shoes and walk out the door. I stow my bag in the car then pull my phone from my pocket.

BRAYDON

Out back with a growling stomach.

The gray dots dance on the screen. My fingers tap the front of my thigh.

ALESSANDRA

Be there in a sec. On the office phone.

BRAYDON

No worries.

I lean against the front of my car and go through emails. Then I open social media and get lost in the abyss of videos.

The door swings open and I glance up to see Alessandra with red blotches on her cheeks. I lock my phone and shove it in my pocket. Push off the car and reach her in four strides. Frame her face and stroke her cheeks with my thumbs.

"What's wrong?"

Her fingers wrap around my forearms and she pulls in a shaky breath. "Come on." She tips her head toward the café. "Let's go inside. Get some food. Then we can talk."

Well that sounds serious, and not the good kind of serious.

"Yeah. Sure."

I wave to Sharon at the prep station as Alessandra leads us into her office, a sad smile on her lips as she regards us. That one look twists my stomach. Has me shutting down the idea of confessing how I feel. Something is wrong and now is not the time to confess feelings and put each other on the spot.

The soft click as the door shuts sounds decibels higher. My

eyes never leave Alessandra as she ambles around the desk and sits in her chair. A thump echoes in the small office as her elbows hit the desk a second before she drops her head in her hands. Passing the guest chair opposite her, I walk around the desk and sidle up to her. Brush my fingers over her temple. Toy with her ponytail. Lean in and drop my lips to her crown.

"Please tell me what's wrong," I whisper against her hair. "You have me worried."

Pans clang in the background. The now familiar ding of the kitchen bell rings before Sharon calls out an order number. Hints of fresh baked goods and maple and bacon waft in the air. But they all fade to the background the longer Alessandra remains silent.

The tips of her fingers dig into her scalp before she sighs and straightens.

"Spoke with Sheriff Blackstone."

I stroke her hair. Massage the back of her neck. Soothe her with small physical reassurance and let her know I am here while I wait for her to say more. Most importantly, I keep my lips sealed and let her speak when she is ready.

She tips her head back and meets my gaze. "She says they'll keep the case open but have reached a dead end." Her eyes fall shut as a heavy sigh deflates her frame. "The café is an isolated incident. No other businesses have been targeted." Veiny, tear-rimmed blues look up at me. "Someone is doing this to *me*, Braydon."

Tears paint her cheeks and she rushes to wipe them away. I squat down and spin the chair so she faces me head-on. Roll her closer and cup her cheek.

"Hey," I whisper and wait until she meets my gaze. "We'll get through this." Another tear falls and I wipe it away with my thumb. "Promise." I lean in and press my lips to hers.

"With the cameras and extra eyes on the property, they'll catch whoever this is."

Her eyes dart between mine as she sniffles, her bottom lip quivering. "Hope you're right. I don't want to lose faith, but I feel it slipping away."

"I have enough for both of us if you need a break." My fingers graze her brow and tuck fallen locks of hair behind her ear. "Let's get something to eat and mull over what to do next weekend."

She plucks a tissue from a nearby box and blots under her eyes. "Yeah, I definitely need sugar and carbs," she says with a laugh.

I rise to my full height and bend to kiss her crown. "Stay here. I'll ask Sharon to make us something."

A hint of a smile perks up the corner of her mouth. "Thanks, Care Bear."

At first, the pet name she'd given me felt weird and childish. But the more she says it, the more endearing I find it. In this moment, with the slight rasp in her voice and the soft way it falls from her lips, the nickname wraps itself around my heart and holds on for dear life.

Without a shadow of a doubt, I love this woman.

"Hate that I have to leave, firecracker."

Fingers laced in mine, she tightens her hold. Silently telling me she hates this as much as I do. Neither of us may be ready to put a voice to the infamous three-word sentiment, but I feel it in the way she doesn't let go, in the slow strokes of her thumb over the length of mine.

I love you.

The words dance on the tip of my tongue. Beg to be said. Don't give a damn it may be too early.

But I bite my tongue. Resist once again. *Not the time.*

"It's only a few days." She inches forward and steps between my legs. Drops my hand and snakes her arms around my waist. Hugs the breath from my lungs and rests her head on my shoulder. "A few more days," she whisper-repeats.

My arms around her tighten as I press my lips to her crown. "Spend some time with Mags and Lena while I'm gone. Have a girls' night in. Weekdays are tougher but don't sit in the office and dwell. It won't solve anything." More than ever, Alessandra needs distractions. Any activity to take her mind off the negative.

Her arms give a quick squeeze then release as she leans back. I sweep the hair off her cheek and tuck it behind her ear.

"I'll text them in a bit."

"I'd stay longer if I didn't have meetings in the city."

Hell, I'd considered calling Dad several times in the past hour to ask if he was okay with me working remotely. But I didn't want to assume Alessandra would be okay with me doing so. Staying in town would be my choice, but my being in her space is her decision to make. I won't take away her right to decide. I don't know if what I want is what she wants.

The corner of her mouth tips up. "I know you would." Her fingers trace the line of my jaw before she presses her lips to mine. "But we both have jobs to do, and yours isn't here."

A pang forms beneath my sternum at her words, at the truth spoken aloud. Less than a hundred miles separate us when I return to the city, but each one of those miles feels like a barrier. Another roadblock to navigate. Another hurdle to jump.

"Wish it was," I mutter

She peers over her shoulder at the back door. "I should get back inside. The lunch rush starts soon."

I reach for her hand and pull her flush against my chest. Drop my lips to hers and kiss her with equal parts strength and tenderness. Let the kiss tell her what my voice keeps at bay.

I love you. I'm here for you. I will do anything for you.

We are breathless when I break the kiss. Speechless when I stroke the apple of her cheek. Lost to the world around us as we soak each other in one last time before I go.

"Drive safe," she rasps out before taking a step back.

Immediately, I miss her warmth. Miss her body close to mine. Miss the way my heart hammers in my chest when she is in my arms.

"Always." My feet drag as I walk to the car door. "Call you when I get home."

Her arms wrap around her middle. "See you Friday." She takes a few steps backward and stops beside the door.

I hop in my SUV, crank the engine, and tug on my seat belt. Throwing the car in reverse, I back out of the space then pop the gear in drive. When I look up, ready to wave goodbye, Alessandra is nowhere to be seen.

I'd stolen quite a bit of her time this morning. Her heading inside before I drive off shouldn't form a knot in my gut. She has several things to do before the next rush and I'd monopolized every precious minute for the past two hours.

Alessandra heading inside before I said one final goodbye shouldn't bother me, but it does. Because that is what happens when one person loves more than the other. They feel the hurt first.

CHAPTER 31

ALESSANDRA

"This doesn't add up."

Willow perks up on the opposite side of the desk. "One of the tills off?"

My brows pinch together as I look up from the figures on the screen. "What?" I shake my head. "No, it's not that." My eyes drop back to the sales numbers over the past week. I narrow my eyes as if squinting will change the figures. "We've been packed every day since the start of the season. Not an empty table for hours at a time."

Willow stops filling out the bank deposit slip. Her gaze hot on my profile. "Yeah, this year is our busiest yet."

I spin the laptop and show her the screen. Lean in and peer around the side. Point to the figures at the bottom—the comparison of this week and the same week last year.

Willow is right, this year has been our busiest yet. But it isn't reflected in the sales, by a lot.

"How the heck are we down? Not possible."

She shoves the deposit aside and hauls the laptop closer

Eyes glued to the screen, she scrolls and clicks with the same fire I feel in my veins.

For an hour, I stared at the figure and the numbers that tally the sum. Sales should have easily been three times what they are. The season hasn't peaked yet, but every day feels busier than the previous. Sharon and August never have a down minute in the kitchen. The front counter has lines out the door for hours at a time. Oftentimes, we have trouble keeping up with taking orders and keeping the tables bussed.

The past two weeks, I considered adding another busser position. Though Caleb was on summer break from college, he still worked fewer hours than the other part-time employees. Same for Roberto. I didn't fault them. After busting tail all semester, time off is a treat.

But if the income isn't there, I can't bring on another employee.

"I'll have to spend more time out of the office and in the dining room." My eyes lose focus as I rack my brain for an explanation. "I've been holed up in here more. Maybe I'm missing something major by not being out there enough."

Willow spins the laptop back in my direction. "This isn't your fault, Lessa. I've been out there when you're not and I haven't noticed anything to explain this."

"Aaahh," I all but yell.

Reaching across the desk, she takes my hand. "We'll figure it out," she says in a staccato. "Even if we have to patrol the dining room all day. Sales aren't bad. They just aren't as great as the foot traffic says they should be." A smile splits her face as she releases my hand. "What you need to do is wrap up the day, go upstairs, and get yourself ready for your man. Won't he be here soon?"

Braydon. He'd been gone three week-long days. Staying

busy makes me miss him less. But damn, I miss him on an unhealthy level.

Nights after work are the worst. Hours of time alone. Hours I could have spent with Mags and Lena, but they'd had other plans in place.

I don't fault them for having a life or prior engagements. As far as they are concerned, everything with me is good. Minus the vandalism, which I haven't mentioned since the cops taped off half the café, nothing cataclysmic has happened. Worrying my friends for no reason is a fool's errand. Yes, they are my business partners, but no good news has come from the sheriff. No sense in riling everyone up.

So instead of sitting in my apartment alone and zoning out in front of the television, I wear myself out in the café. Scrub the tables and chairs with a little more gusto. Sweep and mop and polish the floors like it's never been done. Deep clean the coffee makers and espresso machines until they shine in the light. I ignore the kitchen—August and Sharon would throw a fit if I cleaned the ranges or coolers improperly.

Then each night, I lug myself up the stairs, shower, and fall into bed.

Though I work through the lonely hours, it never fully erases how much I miss Braydon. Tired as I am, sleep doesn't come easy. I toss and turn for hours. Cuddling the pillow he slept on helps, but it isn't the same. And I miss waking up in his arms. I miss staring at his profile for what feels like hours before I finally get up. Oddly enough, I also miss his sporadic, rumbly snores.

Missing him like I do... terrifies me the most.

Seems impossible, but what if Braydon doesn't want me the way I want him? What if he is happy with this whole *see each other on weekends* relationship?

In the beginning, it was ideal. We were both busy, lived an hour's drive apart, and had our reasons for being anti-relationship before us. Easing into this—into there being an us—is the smart move. Hell, a month hadn't passed since we agreed to more than hooking up.

But I want more. What more entails... I have no clue.

"Earth to Lessa." Willow waves a hand in front of my face, a smirk on her lips.

"Yeah. Sorry." I glance at the time on the computer. "He should be here soon." I close the lid to the laptop. "Sure you're good to finish up?"

"Pssh." She waves me off. "Are you kidding?" She stuffs the bank deposit in the bag, seals it, and locks it in the safe. "The minute you're out the door, I'm cranking the radio and singing into the end of the broomstick."

I laugh, picturing her doing just that. Not many people enjoy cleaning, might as well make it fun.

Hinges creak as I roll the chair back from the desk and rise. I grab my purse off the hook near the door and shoulder it. Take a step outside the office and peek over my shoulder.

"Don't have too much fun," I tease.

With a roll of her eyes, she shoos me away. "Quit worrying about me and go. *Have fun.* I'll see you later."

Just as I pick up my fork, my cell phone rings.

"Shit. Sorry." I dig the noisy device from my purse and smile down at the screen before answering. "Hey, Baby A."

Braydon's brows furrow as he mouths, "Baby A?"

I cover the phone speaker and whisper, "My little brother."

Turning my attention to the call, I ask, "What wilderness range are you tromping through now?"

Hearty laughter rings through the line. "You make me sound like a barbarian," Anderson teases. "And I'm not tromping through any. Which is part of the reason I called."

The line falls quiet as I wait for Anderson to continue. My fingers toy with the napkin in my lap as my eyes roam the table. Geoff holds a forkful of parmesan-crusted chicken out for Mags to taste. Logan takes a sip of beer before sawing away at the T-bone steak on his plate. And then I reach Lena... Eyes downcast, she picks through her salad and sorts every ingredient into its own pile. Confused by the sudden shift in her demeanor, I study her. Watch as she stacks cucumber slices, creates a mound of shredded carrots, shuffling slices of chicken away from the veggies.

Has she done this before and I never noticed? No. Not possible I'd miss such a habit.

"Care to elaborate?"

"Uh..." I picture Anderson rubbing the back of his neck, one of his nervous tells. "I'm thirty minutes south of the Oregon-Washington border. Was wondering if I could stay with you."

Anderson and I always got on well as toddlers and teenagers.

When we were school age, most of my friends with siblings got annoyed with their younger or older counterparts. They were too needy or a nuisance or the bully who teased them incessantly.

But Anderson and I had never been the siblings irritated with one another. Some of my classmates thought it odd a brother three years my junior didn't irritate me to death. I shrugged off their comments and snide remarks.

Since the day he came home from the hospital as a newborn, Anderson has been my favorite person. Our bond has always been different than the one I share with Mags and Lena. Not because he is my brother. We simply clicked from the beginning. We understood each other. Gravitated toward similar ideals and ways of living. Though I made permanent roots in Lake Lavender, I envied Anderson's travels. The ability to be his own person. Live life by his rules and desires. To have true freedom.

And maybe the need for freedom is why I never committed to anyone. Never tied myself down in every way. Not until Braydon.

"Always. Everything okay?"

Across the table, Lena stirs all the ingredients back together then tops the salad with dressing. Her focus on her food is so damn *weird* and I am curious as to the cause.

Before I answered the call, Lena and Logan had been reminiscing. Joking about the pie-eating contestants at the summer festival. Laughing about their run from the banquet tables to the dunk tank. Faux gagging over the murky water in the tank. Praising the fact they didn't have to clean up the mess.

Now, she sits silent and has caved in on herself. As if someone scolded her for enjoying her evening.

"Things are good. Just need to be home for a bit."

At the mention of home, the next question slips out. "You talk to Mom and Dad?" I already know the answer.

Joan and Samuel Everett... I have never known two people so fiercely dedicated and loyal. To their marriage. To their children. To their community. To their beliefs. As wonderful as our parents have always been, they never understood Anderson's need to stretch his wings. They never supported his desire to travel, to see the world, to experience different ways of life.

Through their unwillingness to encourage Anderson, a rift has formed in our family. No matter what my brother does, I will always be there to cheer him on. I only wish our parents would do the same. And because they haven't, we have all slowly drifted apart.

"No. And please don't tell them I'm coming."

"I won't. Promise."

A heavy sigh muffles the line. "Thank you."

"Always, Baby A."

"Stopping to eat now. I should be there in a few hours."

Across the table, Lena spears her salad as if committing homicide. She sits a fraction taller but doesn't own an ounce of confidence. After dinner, once we are upstairs, she and I are having an in-depth conversation.

"Take your time. I'm at dinner with friends." Braydon twists in my direction, brows shooting up. I roll my eyes. "Text me when you're close."

"I will. Love you, Ales."

"Love you more, Baby A."

I end the call, silence my phone, and set it on the table rather than stow it in my purse.

Braydon kisses my temple. "So, you have a little brother?"

I pick up my fork and twirl the tines in my pasta. "I do." The creamy pasta hits my tongue and I moan.

Beneath the table, Braydon's fingers wrap around my knee, give a small squeeze, then inch up my thigh and under the fabric of my dress. All thoughts of talking about my brother vanish. I stop chewing. Stop breathing. Force myself not to swallow so I don't choke on my dinner. His ascent stops midthigh and I take a breath. Start to chew the bite in my mouth. Swallow the bite and take a sip of water.

Braydon's arm brushes mine. His breath hot on my ear. "I love when you wear dresses."

I set my glass on the table and pick my fork back up. "Mm, I bet you do." Dresses hadn't been in my attire rotation for some time—dresses aren't ideal when you run a restaurant—but I love wearing them when Braydon is here.

"And if you moan like that again…"

I gather more pasta on my fork, spear a piece of shrimp, and lift the creamy lemon bite to my lips. But my lips don't part. Instead, I twist in my seat—the action causing his hand to inch up my thigh—and smirk.

"Yes?" My legs part an inch. "What will you do?"

His hand on my inner thigh hasn't moved. Not a single twitch of his fingers. To the rest of the group, Braydon appears cool and collected. But I know better. Heat radiates off him. The buzz I always feel when our skin connects hums through my veins.

When it comes to us, I don't put anything past Braydon. If he wants me now, he will find a reason for us both to step away from the table. But I don't think it'd be so simple to explain both of us leaving the table in the middle of dinner. Not unless we had to leave the restaurant.

His scarred brow peeks over his glasses. "Guess you'll have to find out." He turns back to his plate, picks up his fork, and scoops up salmon and rice. He doesn't remove his hand from my lap but sparks a conversation with Geoff about his favorite hiking spots in the area.

One bite after another, I eat my meal without sound effects. I chat with Lena about the boutique and ask if the influx of tourists has been good for business. She brightens and talks at length about the difficulties of keeping the store well stocked. I share my recent find with sales numbers and tell her Willow and I are plotting to figure out why sales aren't reflected in the traffic.

Almost done with dinner, I decide to test Braydon. His hand still rests in the same place. Hasn't moved an inch.

I scoop noodles and shrimp onto my fork, part my lips, and moan louder than necessary as it hits my tongue. No one looks my way, but beneath the table, Braydon's fingers curl into my flesh. The blunt edge of his short nails adds a hint of bite.

But nothing else happens.

Mentally, I smirk and cross my arms. Call him out for being all talk. Later, when we are in the middle of the dance floor upstairs, I will taunt him for not delivering on his promises.

"How was everything this evening?" The server sidles up to the table and starts clearing dishes. "Anyone for dessert?"

Logan and Geoff turn down the offer.

Fingers drift up my inner thigh and I bite the inside of my cheek. Dessert orders sound off around the table, but I don't hear a single one. The tips of Braydon's fingers brush the fabric of my panties.

"What's on the dessert menu?" Braydon asks, his voice level and eyes on the server.

The server starts listing off options while Braydon strokes up and down, again and again, over the damp center of my panties. I do my damnedest to not pant at the table. Do my damnedest to not let on what is happening beneath the oak and cloth.

A finger grazes the edge of my panties, slips underneath, and glides through my folds. I part my legs more. Inhale deeper breaths. Fisting the napkin in my lap.

When the server reaches the end of the list, Braydon turns to look at me. "Want to share the chocolate lava cake?" he asks as his finger dips inside.

I clutch his wrist beneath the table. Swallow past the anxiety of being caught in a crowded restaurant. Lick my lips and smile. "Sounds delicious."

One corner of his mouth kicks up as his fingers glide out. He looks back to the server, expression relaxed. "One chocolate lava cake." Two fingers plunge into my core. "Two forks. Please."

"Yes, sir." The server walks off with empty dishes and our orders.

Conversations spark back to life around the table, oblivious to the constant pump of Braydon's fingers between my thighs. In and out. In and out.

My eyes roll shut as fire and energy and a hunger unrelated to food expand in my chest, in my lower abdomen. I tighten my hold on his wrist, claw at his flesh; a silent plea to stop, but also to continue. He kisses my temple once before his lips hover near my ear.

"Don't make a sound, firecracker." He pumps his fingers faster. Curls them to rub that spot deep inside me no one else hits but him. "So fucking beautiful," he whispers, so only I hear.

I open my eyes, scanning the table and restaurant to see no one paying us any attention. Grip his wrist and the napkin tighter as my orgasm builds. Part my lips and pant, not caring if anyone hears. Heat licks my skin, undoubtedly pinking my neck and cheeks in the dim lighting.

"Almost there, firecracker." His fingers circle my clit once, twice, then dip back in. "Come on my fingers. I want to lick it off when dessert arrives."

The mere thought of him licking my orgasm off his fingers in front of everyone is a turn-on I never expected. And just as the server approaches the table with dessert, I come undone.

Clutch his hand and lock it in place as I drop my chin and catch my breath. Knuckle by knuckle, Braydon removes his fingers with a satisfied smile on his face.

Braydon cuts the lava cake in two with his fork. With his other hand, he dips two fingers in the liquid chocolate and then sticks them between his lips. "So. Damn. Good."

Best dessert of my life, that is for damn sure.

CHAPTER 32

BRAYDON

I didn't expect to finger fuck Alessandra in the middle of the restaurant, but I'd do it again.

Bass vibrates my bones as a thrill hums in my veins. Hands on Alessandra's hips, I grind against the swell of her ass. Move my body with hers as sultry music roars through the club. She weaves a hand up and around my neck, fingers fisting my hair as I open-mouth kiss my way down her neck.

As my arms snake around her waist, she drops hers, spins and drags her hands up my shirt. I open my mouth to say we should leave. Get out of here and go back to her place. After the stunt at the dinner table, I want more than chocolate cake for dessert.

Minus time on the dance floor, our night with her friends—people I one day hope to call *my* friends—is nearing the three-hour mark. No one will fault us if we call it a night.

"Let's get out of here," she says over the music.

A hand trails up her spine then back down before falling away. "Whenever you're ready."

She slips her hand in mine and weaves us through the

crowd. Hugs and handshakes are exchanged when we reach everyone at the couches. I don't miss how Alessandra holds Lena a little longer and whispers something only for her ears.

As they inch apart, Lena holds Alessandra's gaze and nods. A secret among girlfriends I won't ask about or intrude on. Though I kept the observation to myself, Lena's shutdown when Alessandra's brother called was unmistakable. Had I been part of their group longer, maybe I'd know the reason behind the sudden reclusive behavior. Then again, the way Alessandra watched her friend, maybe we were all in the dark when it came to Lena and Alessandra's brother.

My hand on the small of her back, I guide us out of the club and down the stairs. A shiver rolls down her spine as we exit Black Silk. I wrap an arm around her shoulders and hug her to my side, rubbing a hand over her bare arm.

"Forgot my jacket," she chides herself as I open the car door for her.

"Would've been a bother until now. Besides…" I close her door and jog to the driver's side, hopping in. "I'll keep you warm."

I crank the engine, back out of the space, then pull out of the lot. As I lay a hand on her thigh, a chime sounds from her purse. She digs out her phone and taps the screen.

"Anderson messaged. Says he'll be at the apartment in twenty minutes."

"Anderson?" After the call at dinner, I assume Anderson is the brother she so affectionately called *Baby A*.

"Sorry. My brother." She lays a hand over mine. "Got distracted at the table and forgot to mention his name."

Flipping my hand palm up, I weave my fingers with hers. "No apology necessary." I lift her hand to my lips and kiss her knuckles in turn. "Now, tell me about this brother of yours."

I park next to Alessandra's car and dash to her side as she steps out. A beep and flash of my running lights bounce off the wall as I lock the car. Arm looped in mine, she clings to my side and warms her trembling limbs.

"Let's wait for him upstairs," I suggest.

"No, it's fine," she says, a slight chatter to her teeth.

Hauling her front to mine, I swath her in my arms. Rest my cheek on her crown. Rub my hands over her exposed arms and upper back. Blanket her in warmth and press my lips to her hair.

"I love you."

The words fall from my lips with ease, but I don't miss the way her body stiffens. Don't miss that she hasn't taken a breath. Don't miss the way her shiver from moments ago seeps into my skin, my bones. Wouldn't be the first time I said those three words and the receiving party didn't reciprocate. Not that I fault her silence.

Any person brave enough to be vulnerable for someone else is bound to be hurt. Our relationship is young, and it may be too early to profess such sentiments. Wasn't my intention to hand her my heart, at least not this soon. But there is no taking it back. Not that I want to.

When Gabby pulverized my heart four years ago, I swore off love. Swore I would never give another person so much power over me or my heart. Told myself to not get attached, to not develop feelings, to squash any semblance of emotions when it came to women.

Then Alessandra happened.

Her lack of response and rigid frame should set off alarm

bells. Should make my hackles rise and stomach twist. Oddly enough, it does none of the above.

If my relationship with Gabby taught me one thing, it is to expect the unexpected. I may have said the words, but it would be brazen of me to expect them immediately in return.

Delightful as it would be to hear the sentiment returned, I won't force the words from her lips. Every time our lips meet, every small touch and smile she gives only me, every whispered exchange and side glance... I sense it. I see it. I *feel* it. The deep affection she holds for me in her heart.

And for her, I will wait.

Tightening my hold on her, I whisper against her hair, "Don't feel pressured to say it back." Her frame relaxes a fraction. "Wasn't my intention to make you uneasy."

She inches away and tips her head back to meet my eyes. Uncertainty lingers in her blue irises, darkened by the night. Hair sweeps across her cheek and I lift a hand, brush the tips of my finger over her brow, and tuck the strand behind her ear. My thumb strokes the apple of her cheek as her eyes dart between mine.

"Braydon, I—"

"Shh." I drop my lips to hers and she kisses me back. *Thank god.* "Unless the next words out of your mouth are, *I never want to see you again,*" I say, painting the edges of her lips with my fingers, "you don't need to justify how you feel."

Her gaze falls to my lips for one, two, three breaths before meeting my eyes again. In the dimly lit alley, I see much more than expected in her eyes. Fear. Indecision. Guilt. Disbelief. Longing. Something akin to love.

The last one... I cling to it. Let it fill me up and drive me forward.

A flower doesn't suddenly appear from nothing. Doesn't

blossom and expose itself without warmth and support and time. And love is no different.

"I-I'm just not… ready."

I cup her cheeks and press my lips to hers. "Whenever you are, I'll be here."

Before either of us says another word, a camel-colored camper van parks on the opposite side of her car. Alessandra drops her arms and steps out of my hold. A wide smile brightens her face as the door opens and a man with identical hair color to hers steps out.

She dashes around me and slams into him just as the car door closes. He wraps his arms around her waist and lifts her off the ground, swinging her in circles.

"Missed you, Baby A."

He peeks over her shoulder and locks eyes with me. "Missed you too, Ales."

With one look, one action, my lack of concern over her response to my admission does a one-eighty. I am not jealous of her brother. But I am jealous of the instantaneous affection without hesitation.

And jealousy never ends well.

CHAPTER 33

ALESSANDRA

Rolling onto my side, I stretch my arm and discover the sheets beside me cold. I crack my eyes open, give them a moment to adjust to the early morning sunlight peeking through the blinds, and zero in on the vacant pillow.

I bolt upright, the sheet pooling at my waist as I scan the room. "Braydon," I rasp out.

No response.

Did he leave? After his proclamation last night and my inability to tell him how I feel in return, it wouldn't surprise me if he ran. *Please tell me he didn't run.*

I toss the comforter from my legs and swing them off the bed. Rise and tug on my robe. Use the bathroom and brush my teeth before I shuffle for the bedroom door.

Muffled conversation and the low volume of the television hit my ears as I open the door. A sigh of relief caves my shoulders when I hear Braydon speak, his tone serene. Leaning against the frame, I eavesdrop on the quiet exchange between Anderson and Braydon. Anderson talks about his travels throughout the country, and Braydon pops in a question or two when he pauses.

The two men met less than twelve hours ago. Exchanged names, handshakes, and a *see you in the morning* before we went into our respective bedrooms. Dark half-moons under his eyes and a sluggish tempo to his stride, Anderson would crash in minutes. Would sleep through the muffled noises across the hall.

Darkness hadn't blanketed my bedroom until after two this morning. My legs tangled with Braydon's and palm over his heart, sleep came easily with him in my bed. It always did.

I glance back at the clock on my bedside table—8:47a.m.

How long have they been awake? They spoke like old friends that hadn't seen each other in months, not like unfamiliar company.

Deciding I've invaded their hushed moment long enough, I step into the hall and shuffle toward the sound of their voices. Anderson spots me first, stopping midsentence to throw me a toothy smile.

"Morning, sleepyhead."

I run a hand over my hair as I round the couch and plop down between them. "Morning." I reach out and ruffle Anderson's shaggy blond locks. "Looking a bit rugged, brother." My hand cups his cheek. "But I like it."

Throaty laughter fills the room as Anderson hauls me into his chest, hugs me tightly, and rubs his knuckles over my scalp. My fingers dig into his side, along the edge of his rib cage, and wiggle until he shoves me away.

"Okay, okay. You win." He holds his hands up in surrender.

"Missed you, Baby A." I ruffle his hair one last time.

Scooting back, I shimmy into Braydon's lap, twist my head and give him a chaste kiss. "Morning."

His arms band around my waist and hug my back to his front. "Morning, firecracker."

"How long have you been up?"

He rests his chin on my shoulder, his stubble faintly scraping my cheek. "Maybe an hour." He cocoons me in his arms. Shows no sign of discomfort in his display of affection while in front of my brother. "But I wasn't the first up."

I glance across the couch to my brother and catch the momentary downturn of his lips as he watches us.

Far back as I recall, Anderson has always had this shadowy disposition. A cloud looming overhead. The first time I noticed his despondency, he'd been eight. I'd walked from middle school to elementary, so we could go home together. He'd walked out of the double doors, hands fisting his backpack straps, head hung, and shoes scuffing the sidewalk. When he reached me, I asked what was wrong. He'd waved off my concern and said a few of his classmates had teased him about his new haircut but then apologized. I wanted to believe him, but something twisted in my gut. Told me it had nothing to do with hair or other kids.

Five years later, Anderson had weekly appointments with a psychologist. Our parents didn't want him "hopped up on pills" but wanted him to be the "happy boy" from years prior. Obviously, they hadn't been as observant. They hadn't noticed Anderson's joyless smiles or sheltered habits like I did.

Our parents are good people and want to see the light in everyone. A light Anderson feels shame for not having. Their single-mindedness inevitably erected a wall between us— Anderson more so than me—and divided our family.

I love my parents, but not like I love my brother. For

Anderson, I'd fight battles. The day he announced his new job as a travel influencer, I inwardly cheered while my parents grumbled it wasn't a *real* job. After I'd given Anderson the fiercest hug, I'd turned to my parents and told them to be happy for him or shut up. They'd remained tight lipped the first year. When the second year rolled around, Mom appeared more amiable whenever Anderson's name came up. I spoke to Anderson once every four to six weeks. My parents were lucky to hear from him once or twice a year.

Each time Anderson called from the road, I'd heard the lightness in his voice. The peace he'd found by being on hidden highways and in nature. Freedom gifted him something our parents never did... the ability to breathe.

I extend a hand and tap Anderson's knee. "You sleep okay?"

His head tilts left then right before straightening. "Been a while since I've slept anywhere but the van, but it wasn't bad."

"Want to help make breakfast?"

Breakfast could be as easy as calling downstairs and having Sharon whip us up something. Pancakes or eggs or a breakfast sandwich. Anything, it didn't need to be on the menu. But I didn't want to interrupt the kitchen in the café. I also wanted more time with my brother, and making breakfast together was a weekend tradition we had as kids.

His eyes light up and I have my answer before he says, "Absolutely."

I turn and kiss Braydon. "You too." I peel his arms away and rise from his lap. "Three is better than two."

"Uh..." Braydon says on a chuckle. "Might be best to task me something I can't burn."

I reach for his hand and haul him up off the couch. "Done," I say as his chest bumps mine and he drops a kiss on my lips.

"How long will you be home?" I stab a couple blueberries and pieces of pancake then grab the whipped cream in the middle of the table and spray the forkful until all you see is cream. Both men stare at me as I shove the sweet delight in my mouth. "Wha?" I mumble around the bite.

They both shake their head and laugh.

"Not sure," Anderson answers, eyes downcast as he dunks his sausage in maple syrup. "Is that okay?" His shoulders stiffen. He looks up, eyes darting between me and Braydon. "I don't want to intrude."

A loud clang sounds as my fork hits the plate. I reach across the table and take Anderson's hand. "One... you are never a burden or intrusion." I give a quick but strong squeeze of his hand. "Ever." I wait until he nods to continue. "Two... you can stay as long or little as you want. I love having you here, but understand if you need to leave." My other hand reaches for Braydon and he weaves our fingers. "Three... we have a lot to catch up on. When I'm not working nonstop, Braydon and I spend time together."

The corner of Anderson's mouth tips up. "Nice to see you happy, Ales." He pats Braydon's shoulder. "Can tell he's a good guy."

Now I am even more curious about what the two of them talked about before I woke. Neither Braydon nor Anderson is the type to gush over people they hold close. My relationship with Braydon may be new, but in our time together he has never babbled on about other people.

Memories of last night pop in my head. Of the moment when Braydon said he loves me. Of the instantaneous knot in my belly at hearing the words. How my muscles locked up and my rib cage constricted my lungs. More than anything, Braydon's confession made me mentally stumble backward.

Love. It was never a word I'd said to someone other than family or Mags and Lena.

When it comes to Braydon, my feelings run deep. But love? I have no idea if what I feel for him is *love.* I have nothing to compare it to.

The sentiment lingered in the air, the single word heavier than gravity. I'd wanted to tell him I cared deeply for him, but he cut me off before the words left my lips. Probably better that I hadn't said anything. The night may have ended differently had I not been cut off.

"He is a good guy." Warmth spreads beneath my breastbone as I say the words. *Is that love?*

Braydon lifts my hand to his lips and kisses my knuckles. The warmth from seconds ago burns hotter. *Maybe it is love.* Either way, I'm not ready to admit it out loud.

I blink and refocus on Anderson. "Anything you want to do today?"

Lifting the mug to his lips, he sips his tea. "Nothing in particular. Did you have plans?"

"With the Fourth coming up, we didn't plan much this weekend," Braydon says.

Though the Fourth of July celebration has always been a major shindig in Lake Lavender, it feels more monumental this year. With all the festivals recently added to the town's lineup, the events we previously celebrated have been given more attention. There won't just be fireworks over the lake this year. Nope. Mayor Higston wants to close two blocks of Main Street to vehicles and throw a party. Smoked meats, face painting, games, and more. If it is considered summer fun, she plans to add it.

"How about hiking?" I suggest.

The last time I truly hiked was with Anderson. He and I have explored so much in the area, but not every trail. Weeks ago, Braydon mentioned his love for the outdoors. It is one of the main reasons he enjoys traveling for work. Not only did he see new towns, he also got to trek through different forests.

Braydon looks to Anderson, a spark of hope in his amber eyes. Since Braydon and I started dating, we have yet to hike or camp. Most of our time has been spent in the apartment, out with my friends, or clouded by the vandalism.

Shit. Should probably mention all the craziness to Anderson.

Later. I will catch him up later.

"Hiking sounds great." He sets his mug down. "Let me get some stuff from the van and scope out the trail maps. Then we can head out." Anderson grabs the seat of his chair, scoots back and rises with his empty dishes.

The soft click of the front door echoes through the apartment, followed by the *thump, thump, thump* of Anderson's feet as he descends the stairs for his van.

Braydon picks up his mug and downs the last of his coffee. "Your brother is great."

Pride fills my chest. Had Anderson heard Braydon's compliment, he would have reddened and dismissed it.

"He is." I push back on my chair, stand and collect my dishes. "Thank you."

I head for the kitchen as Braydon stands and gathers his own dishes. As I set my plate in the dishwasher, arms band around my middle. Heat blankets my back from shoulder to hip as Braydon snuggles closer. His lips on my neck a beat before the tip of his nose trails the shell of my ear.

Without him saying it, I *feel* the words on the tip of his tongue. *I love you.* But he says nothing. His silence is equal parts relief and hurt.

Badly as I want to hear the words again, to know how much he cares, I also hope the sentiment is forgotten. At least a little longer. Until I figure out what it is *I* feel. What it is *I* want.

Selfish as it is, I need time. Time to mull over my feelings. Time to think without Braydon here. And time to ask advice from people who have known me most or all my life. I just need time… to decide and then tell Braydon. And hopefully, neither of us gets hurt in the end.

CHAPTER 34
BRAYDON

She is pushing me away. All because I opened my mouth too soon.

Damnit.

Late Sunday afternoon, I left Lake Lavender with the tingle of her kiss still fresh on my lips. The weekend was nice. Spending time with and getting to know her brother was a big step. But with each new conversation I'd had with Anderson, Alessandra pulled away a little more.

She'd been quiet, reserved. Traits I hadn't seen from her prior. I chalked it up to her wanting to spend time with her brother.

But her near silence the past three and a half days has my stomach in knots.

I stare down at my phone screen at the message I sent before I left for work this morning. Almost five hours ago. The message she has yet to respond to.

"The café is probably slammed with tourists," I mutter to myself.

Shoving the phone aside, I wrap up the small article I

wrote on Stone Bay, another small town near the state's western coast. After I click save and email it to the editor, I shut down my laptop and stow it in my bag. As I clear the papers from my desk, Dad knocks on the open office door.

"Done for the day?"

With the Fourth landing on Friday this year, Dad opted to close early Thursday and all day Friday and Monday. The staff was more than enthusiastic about having a four-day weekend. Me... I look forward to time with Alessandra and Anderson. With the lack of—or super delayed—response to my texts, I can't say she feels the same in return.

"Yeah. Just sent my story to editing." Hands on the arms of my chair, I rise and shoulder my bag. "One less thing on my plate."

Dad steps into my cramped office, closes the door, and sits in the guest chair.

Guess I'm not leaving yet.

"Mind if I ask you something?" He rests a foot on the opposite knee and leans back.

I drop back to my seat and shrug. "Not at all."

His fingers toy with the lace of his black dress shoes as he sorts through his thoughts. Then irises identical to my own hold my gaze. A somberness in the lines of his face. Slight apprehension in the twitch of his eyes. An heir of uncertainty on his tongue as he rolls his lips between his teeth.

"You don't seem yourself this week." His fingers move to the bottom hem of his slacks. "Everything okay?"

One thing I will never do is lie to my father. As if built into our bond, we both know when the other isn't on the up-and-up. Dad has always been honest when I ask about the past or how he feels. When I was younger, he phrased his answers differently so my adolescent mind could understand.

Now, we throw all the cards on the table. Share without hesitation.

Springs squeak as I lean back in my chair and run a hand through my hair. "I don't know."

Thick brows tug together as his eyes assess. "What has you unsure?"

My hand falls to my lap. I tip my head back and stare at the indentations in the ceiling tiles. Take a deep breath, then another as I count to ten and collect my thoughts. When I reach ten, eyes still on the ceiling, I blurt out, "I told her I love her."

"And?" Dad asks, voice edged with concern.

I level my gaze and exhale a shuddering breath. "And she has been more distant since I opened my mouth."

At this, Dad straightens in his seat and drops his foot to the floor. "Give her time, son. Love is a big step for anyone. We both know love is scary as hell, but maybe the experience is different for her. From what you've told me, neither of you was the relationship type beforehand." He leans forward and rests his forearms on the desk. "Maybe there's a reason she's so guarded. A reason she isn't ready to share yet."

Alessandra and I haven't shared deeper details of our previous relationships. Did someone break her heart too? She'd said her busy workload is why she never did relationships but was there more to it than that? What about before she owned the coffee shop? What held her back then?

"Maybe," I concede.

Dad raps the desk with his knuckles then stands. "Just give her time and the space to be who she is. I gather there's more to it than she's sharing."

I rise from my chair and follow Dad out. "Thanks." I hook

an arm over his shoulder and hug him close. "You always say the right things."

A devious smile tugs up the corners of his mouth. "Storing that line for the future. Just in case."

I roll my eyes. "Whatever, old man. Have a great weekend." I kiss his cheek. "Tell Gretchen and Shawn hi from me and I love them."

"Will do." He pats my shoulder. "Love you, Braydon."

"Love you too, Dad."

CHAPTER 35

ALESSANDRA

"This cannot be happening."

The days surrounding events in Lake Lavender are always busy. Always. This week has been no exception. Well, from a visual standpoint, it hasn't. From a business stance, though, I have more of an idea why sales are down while the café is packed.

Monday morning, I had a meeting with the staff on duty. Not wanting to sit on the couch all day, Anderson came down and offered to help out. During the meeting, I shared minute details of what Willow and I noticed in the sales. I watched the reactions of everyone present and saw wide eyes as I relayed my concerns. Lyndsey, Caleb, and Roberto mentioned seeing fewer tips and more outside cups or packages as they bussed tables.

Since the day the doors for Java and Teas Me opened, bringing in your own cup was encouraged. Not only do we discount orders if customers bring their own cups, but we also thank them. It cuts down costs and causes less waste.

But one thing we never allow is outside food or drinks.

Granted, exceptions are made when children or health issues come into play, but it is a rare occasion. The menu is vast enough to cater to almost everyone, so it has never been an issue.

Then I walked the floor during the Monday rush. Saw crumpled bags from another coffee shop on the outskirts of town as I cleared tables. Tuesday was more of the same and I hated the idea of policing the front door but decided I would on Wednesday.

We still had long lines each day. The same familiar faces smiled back at me as I greeted them and made their favorite beverage. As I wiped tables and sparked conversations. Business was still good but should have been better.

Then Wednesday arrived.

Wednesday had been a shitstorm. The first hour the doors were open, more than a dozen people left because they couldn't come in with food and drinks from another food establishment. Hour two was worse. By hour three, I wanted to scream. Wednesday felt like a nightmare... until today.

This morning, I came downstairs and went about my morning routine. Flipping chairs in the dining room, starting the coffee makers, bringing out the tills, sifting through emails and responding. Everything had been great until I sat down in front of the computer.

Unread emails—267.

On a normal day, my inbox got a couple dozen emails, give or take. The season brought more because of supply orders and invoices, but the inbox never hit triple digits. Especially overnight.

When I opened the folder, the majority of the messages were from Google or Facebook. *Congratulations! You have new reviews for your business.* My gut soured when it should have edged with excitement.

I opened the first email and clicked the link to the review.

If I could give this place negative stars, I would. Owner is a bitch. Told me I wasn't welcome.

Not once had I said no one was welcome here. I had, however, told several people outside food and drinks were not welcome. And this was the result. Hundreds of derogatory reviews for my business on social media and search engines. It would take an act of god to fix this mess. And I didn't have the time or energy to do it.

"How the hell did this happen?" I mumble in my hands for the umpteenth time.

A hand rests on my shoulder. "We'll figure it out, Ales." Anderson kisses the top of my head. "I'm here and I have nothing else to do. Let me help."

Ding. My phone lights up on the desk and I groan. "Shit."

"What?"

I hold up my phone for Anderson to see the notification from Braydon. "He's on his way here and I've barely spoken to him this week." I drop my head to the desk with a loud thump and tinge of pain. "He probably thinks I hate him," I grumble against the grain.

Anderson grabs my shoulders and straightens me in the chair. "You should call him." He gives my shoulders a squeeze. "Let him know things have been crazy here." He releases my shoulders and I whine. Stepping around the desk, he stops next to the door and waits until our eyes meet. "I know he freaked you out with the love bomb drop, but don't push him away, Ales. You care for him. I've heard it in our talks this week. It's okay to not say it back right away, but don't string him along. If you care for him, tell him as much. But also tell him why you're scared."

The backs of my eyes burn as tears well the rims. "I will. Promise."

"Love you, Ales."

"Love you more."

Anderson exits the office and closes the door.

I close my eyes and take a few deep breaths. Squash the emotional overload I have felt this week. Focus on the image of Braydon in my mind's eye and let it relax my muscles. No matter how freaked out I am over the *I love you* moment, Braydon always brings me a level of comfort no one else has.

Unlocking my phone, I open the text message.

BRAYDON

Leaving now. Should be an hour. Is that okay?

I hate that he felt the need to ask if coming is okay. His uncertainty is my fault. I let the madness of the week get between us. My responses to him all week had been clipped. I'd been frustrated with the recent discoveries and I took it out on him.

It isn't fair I made him the scapegoat for my issues. He has no idea what chaos has ensued. My lack of communication probably mucked everything up.

I tap his name at the top of the screen and hit *call*. The call connects after the second ring.

"Hey, firecracker."

"Hi," I choke out, immediately hating how small my voice sounds.

"What's wrong?"

"It's been a shitty week. Sorry I didn't text more or call. It's just—" I cut myself off before I started to cry. Tears have threatened several times this week. Only in the privacy of my shower did I let them fall this morning.

"Did someone tag the building again?" Anger edges his tone.

"No. Something else, I'll explain when you're here." I futz with the string of my apron. "Miss you," I whisper. Part of me wants to add I love him, but I bite my tongue. *Not yet.*

"Miss you too, firecracker." Silence settles over the line for a beat and I know he wants to say the words too. "Want me to grab dinner?"

Anderson made dinner every night since Braydon left and I felt guilty for not returning the favor. I didn't have a culinary degree, but I knew enough to make mouths and stomachs happy.

"Dinner would be wonderful. Anderson will eat whatever you order, he's not picky."

"'Kay. I'll figure something out." He pauses and I hear him suck in a deep breath. "See you soon."

"Soon," I whisper then disconnect the call.

God, I am a mess. When the hell did my life spiral out of control? When did it go from simple and routine to mayhem and dysfunction?

Not sure when the cupid *and* hatred targets got painted on my back, but I need at least one to go away. I need my life to right itself. I need something to give. And I fear the wrong thing will let go first. Because of this war on my life... I am ready to throw the white flag. I am ready to give up.

CHAPTER 36

BRAYDON

One look at my firecracker is all it takes. I exit the car and all but run to her.

Tears well in her eyes as her frame sags forward in defeat. I ignore the food in the car and go to her. Wrap her in my arms and haul her close. The second her cheek rests on my shoulder, her body shakes. She fists my shirt and sobs.

I smooth a hand over her hair and shush her cries. Let her know everything will be alright. At this, she snakes her arms around my middle. Tightens her hold on me and constricts my breathing. I don't complain. Don't tell her to loosen her hold. Don't do anything but hug her harder.

"I got you." I kiss her hair. Rub small circles over her back. "You're safe. I'm here. I won't let anything happen to you."

Minutes pass and neither of us loosens our hold. She cries on my shirt and doesn't say a word. Her fingers curl and unfurl my shirt again and again. All the while, I hold her. Reassure her with touch and whispered words that I have her

The back door opens and Alessandra straightens, swiping at her cheeks. I look up to see Anderson with a forlorn expression as he takes in his sister. Then his eyes meet mine and he shakes his head.

"Been a rough week."

"Tell me about it over dinner," I say, reluctantly stepping away from Alessandra to grab the bags from the car.

Anderson takes the bags of food when I reach for my duffel. "Meet you upstairs." He shifts his gaze. "Didn't lock up yet."

"'Kay."

I follow Alessandra into the café and help her flip off the lights. Weaving my fingers with hers, we exit, lock up, and take the stairs. After we ditch our shoes, I take my duffel to the bedroom. As I round the wall separating the kitchen and dining from the living room, I see my girl with her head in her hands.

Initially, when she was slow to respond to me this week, I thought it was her pushing me away. Now, I see it is much more than her being distant. Something bad happened this week. Whatever it is, my firecracker looks ready to fizzle out. And I will be damned before it happens.

"No way this is a coincidence."

Anderson's brows furrow. "No way *what* is a coincidence?"

Before I left Sunday, I wanted to give Anderson the lowdown on all the weird things that have been happening at Java and Teas Me. The odd social media messages. The spray-painted vandalism with zero traces of who did it. The change in traffic and revenue. But time got away from us and there never seemed like a good time to bring it up.

Now, there are hundreds of horrendous reviews online. Some target specific employees with vile, untrue opinions, while others are juvenile in nature and complain about the taste of the coffee or the art on the walls.

Until this whole debacle came about, she said there had never been such hostility pointed her way or the business. Going from zero to hundreds... Alessandra is being targeted. But why?

I explain all the strange occurrences over the past couple of months. With each one, Anderson's eyes widen further. Alessandra hasn't ignored each occurrence. She dealt with them as they happened. But it is more than that. Each incident taints her business, and her. Each event is a puzzle piece to a much bigger picture.

The issues happened weeks apart, all seemingly unrelated, but they are all connected. I just haven't put the pieces in the right places to figure out who and why. Which domino fell first?

"Ales, he's right. All these mishaps, they're tied together." Anderson sets his fork down and rubs the back of his neck. "But who the hell would do this? I know I haven't been around much, but no one in this town would ever be so callous. We look out for each other here. But this..." He flattens his palms on the table, takes a deep breath and shakes his head. "This is personal. No one goes to such lengths to hurt someone without it being personal."

Eyes downcast, Alessandra dunks a tortilla chip in guacamole over and over. At the center of all this hate, she has to want to pull her hair out. Scream at the top of her lungs. Hit something, hard. She earned the name firecracker for a reason. She is a force to be reckoned with.

With each new incident and the stress it tacks on, Alessandra has become a shell of herself. The light in her eyes just a flicker. The fire in her spirit slowly extinguishing.

And fuck, it makes me angry. Ready to rattle the person at the helm of this torment.

Under the table, I lay my hand over hers. Weave our fingers and pass every ounce of strength—mental and physical —through the connection.

"We'll figure this out, firecracker. No matter what it takes, we'll find out who's doing this."

Beneath my hand, Alessandra stiffens. Then she yanks her hand from mine, shoves the uneaten plate of food to the middle of the table, and tosses her napkin beside it.

"Really?" Her tone is harsh and a contrast to the shaky, sobbing woman I witnessed when I arrived. "I don't see how." The grating of chair legs against the floor has me wincing as she scoots back and stands. "When did you get your detective badge? Hmm?" Planting her hands on her hips, she tips her head back and stares at the ceiling. One, two, three breaths pass before she drops her gaze and audibly exhales. "Thanks for dinner, but I'm no longer hungry."

Her feet assault the floor as she plods off toward the bedroom and out of sight.

She is upset, frustrated, annoyed by the events of the past two months. Can't say I blame her. But her walking off, angry with me as I console her… it hurts.

Yes, she is hurting too. Redirecting the pain elsewhere grants her temporary relief. Lightens the turmoil festering in her bones. Eases the ache in her soul, the one that whispers someone is out to get her. Lifts the shadow clouding her heart, even if just for a fleeting moment, and gives her an inkling of solace.

But damn, it stings to be the target of her pain.

Hands on the edge of the table, I push up to stand. But before I get the chance to step away, a hand wraps around my forearm and locks me in place. My gaze falls to his hold before meeting his eyes.

"If you crowd her, she'll pull away."

True as that may be, if I give her too much space, she may think I don't care. Which is worse? Her thinking I care too much or not enough?

"Yeah." I nod and he releases my arm. "But if I do nothing… I might as well grab my duffel and walk out the door."

For minute-long seconds Anderson studies my expression. Faint lines appear at the corners of his mouth and eyes as he gives me a sad smile. "Be there for her, but give her space too."

I pat his shoulder. "Will do," I say and mirror his smile. "Thanks, man. Glad you're here when I can't be."

With that, I pad across the living room, down the short hall, and slip into the bedroom. The sound of running water filters through the closed bathroom door. Badly as I want to knock and ask if everything is okay, I steer clear of the door and opt to turn down the bed. I light candles and set her current book near her pillow. Pick up the dirty clothes and carry the basket to the washer.

I gift her with solitude but leave small reminders that say I am here and always will be. Whenever she needs me, my arms will be open and ready.

And then I join Anderson on the couch for mindless television and thought-provoking conversation. We have spent less than a week around each other, but Anderson feels like a friend I have known my entire life. With similar interests and viewpoints on life, our talks flow effortlessly.

Maybe having him here while the madness ensues is kismet. Perfect timing. The extra support Alessandra needs and the buffer to stop me from overstepping.

After the whole *I love you* drop, I'd be an idiot to not notice the crack dividing us. The timing of my confession sucks, but I refuse to take it back. The emotional wall I erected when Gabby left? Alessandra knocked it to the ground. Every rule I instituted to protect myself from heartache again, Alessandra tore in two.

Falling in love with Alessandra had been effortless. Like taking my next breath. And without saying as much, I know she reciprocates the sentiment.

But if the twinge in my gut is any indication of what is to come, I may lose her. Not because she doesn't love me. The exact opposite, actually.

Maybe with Anderson at my side, I stand a chance. Maybe with him here, she will open up and let me in.

If I lose her... I doubt anything will bring me back from that darkness.

CHAPTER 37

ALESSANDRA

*B*oom. Pop. Fizzle.

The sky explodes in color. People nearby ooh and aah at the sparkling display over the lake. Eyes heavenward, residents and tourists sit on blankets and point out their favorite fireworks as they light the night sky. A musty, sulfuric smell wafts in the breeze alongside the mouth-watering smell of grilled burgers and hot dogs. Children laugh as they dance with sparklers, writing their names in the air with the glowing sticks.

Braydon tightens his arms around my waist. Scoots closer, crushing his front to my back. Nuzzling my neck before taking a deep breath. Rests his chin on my shoulder and hums in contentment.

I all but *hear* his I love you.

And for some unknown reason, his swell of affection has me itchy. Ready to jump up and run away. Not because I feel nothing for him. But because I feel more than I thought possible.

Loving someone, loving him, scares me more than

anything. Loving him and possibly losing him keeps me from uttering the three-word phrase back.

"Fireworks are never this brilliant in the city," he whispers, breath hot on my ear.

I twist, and my lips graze his. Soft and warm and inviting. "Light pollution," I blurt louder than necessary. "Sorry," I say at a lower volume. "When the town does fireworks, the mayor cuts all the lamppost lights in the immediate area." Turning back to face the lake, I lay my head on his shoulder. "Less light pollution makes the show ten times better."

"Agreed."

His lips skim the curve of my neck. Imprint my skin with a kiss. Then another. And another until he reaches the spot just beneath my ear that makes my knees wobbly. His fingers knead my flesh with newfound softness. His legs bracket mine, adding a layer of security and privacy as his fingers dip beneath the bottom hem of my shirt.

My eyes dart around the crowd. "Braydon…" My voice breathy and unrecognizable. "We're surrounded by hundreds of people."

He sucks my earlobe between his lips while fingers trace the waistband of my shorts. "And no one is paying us any attention."

Turned on as I am at the idea of Braydon doing naughty things to me in the middle of a crowded park beneath the fireworks, I lay my hand over his and stop him. What if the person responsible for all the harassment is here and they snap pictures?

The negative social media commentary had been a nuisance. An additional, unplanned expense was spurred by the exterior vandalism. The drop in sales due to an overabundance of out-of-towners clogging the café was more a shock than anything.

But the countless nasty reviews online… had been the peak of the roller coaster. The moment when I no longer held back the tears. The moment I hit freak-out mode. As per usual, I bottled most of it up. Released a hint of frustration or a dash of irritation when everything got to be too much. Didn't happen often, but when it did, I took it out on the wrong people.

Last thing I need right now are photos online of me and Braydon making out in the park with children nearby. Whoever is behind this will surely stir the shit pot with "unsavory" photos. I see the commentary now.

Pervert.

Public indecency.

Having sex in public with children ten feet away.

My stomach flips and I swallow past the bile rising in my throat.

"Braydon." I shake my head, push his hand away, and sit taller. "No. Not here. Not with everyone so close."

He scoots back and I shiver at the loss of his warmth. I hug my legs to my chest and drop my forehead to my knees. Tears sting the backs of my eyes and I will them to go away, but they don't. A hand rubs small circles between my shoulder blades, but no other part of him touches or consoles me.

"Sorry, firecracker," he mutters just before another *boom, pop, fizzle* steals the silence.

I can't do this.

His hand stops and I suck in a breath.

"What?"

Shit. Did I say that out loud? *Shit, shit, shit.*

When I don't respond after a moment, he pulls his hand away. The summer night air turns frigid as I work up the courage to sit up and say something. Anything. The longer I remain silent, the longer I shut him out, the longer I don't let him help... it's a setup for disaster, for the end.

And I am not ready for this to be the end of us. But I also don't know how to explain the cacophony in my head. The confusion of how I feel. The desire to *tell* him how I feel—love shadowed by fear. Either way, I need to say something.

Just tell him what you meant. That dealing with this lunatic has you batty.

I lift my head from my knees, swallow past the panic-induced lump in my throat, and open my mouth to confess to Braydon. But he isn't there.

My eyes scan the shadowed sea of faces, but none belong to him. "Maybe he went to get water," I mutter, not an ounce of conviction in my voice.

When the fireworks end, the spectators fold up blankets and collapse chairs. They shoulder totes and carry sleeping children to cars. Fetch coolers and toss trash in nearby bins. All the while, I sit here alone, hoping to see him in the thinning crowd.

But he isn't here. He left. He got up and walked away. All because I couldn't engage with him. All because I opened my mouth and said the wrong damn thing in a weak moment.

"Damnit."

I pull my phone from my back pocket, unlock it, and open the messaging app. Clicking on our text history, I type a quick message and hit send.

ALESSANDRA

Where are you?

The bubble pops up and dances across the screen.

BRAYDON

In the apartment. Packing.

Packing? He's leaving.

I bolt up, gather the blanket under my arm, and dash for home.

He can't leave. Not like this. Not because of a misunderstanding.

How many times have I stopped myself from telling Braydon I love him because I feared losing him? More than I have fingers to count.

He said I didn't need to say the words yet. To say them when I felt ready. That he would wait. But this—him walking away and abandoning me while I search for the right words— is the worst type of pain. Like a punch to the solar plexus with spiked brass knuckles.

I'd said *I can't do this*, but I wasn't talking about him or us. I meant I couldn't get frisky in the park with half the town nearby.

I jog down the alley, two buildings away, when I see him bound down the stairs, duffel slung over his shoulder.

"Braydon. Wait," I yell, winded.

He jerks to a stop beside his driver's side door, chest heaving, back to me. "Now you want to talk? Now you can *do this*?" Venom and heartache lace his words, and guilt gnaws at my heart.

I wrap my fingers around his forearm and he flinches, but I don't let go. *Stab and twist.* "I didn't mean us when I said that earlier."

"Should've known." He shakes his head. "Since the day I opened my mouth and told you I loved you, you've been pulling away. Shutting me out." His hands ball into fists.

"Fuck!" he yells, his voice bouncing off the buildings in the alley.

"It's not because you said you love me," I whisper.

He spins around and drops his duffel with a heavy thud. "No?"

I shake my head incrementally. "No."

"Then why?"

Eyes locked on his, my fingers toy with the hem of my shirt. *Tell him the truth. Tell him you love him too.*

"I'm scared." The words are next to inaudible as they leave my lips. "Scared of whoever is doing this." I wave a hand toward the building. "Scared of this." I gesture to his bag and car as tears blur my vision. "Everything feels out of my control. Life. Work. Love." I break eye contact as the first tear falls.

Fuck. I don't want to cry. Not anymore. Not because some random person is messing with my life. Ruining every good thing I have. I won't give them the power.

Braydon clasps my chin with his thumb and finger, bringing my eyes back to his. "Love?" The single-worded question faint on his lips.

Another tear escapes. "You know I do." I nibble at my lower lip. Try to hide the quiver of my chin. "But saying it… I've never…" I press the heel of my palm to my breastbone. "You walked away from me tonight. Rather than giving me time to process, to say the right words, you got up and abandoned me." Tears paint parallel lines down my cheeks as my arms band around my middle. "That hurt me, Braydon. *You* hurt me." I swipe the tears from my cheeks. "Losing you"—I laugh without humor—"is what scares me most."

Strong arms capture and haul me close. Smother me

against his chest. Shush me as the dam bursts and soaks his shirt with my tears.

"Sorry I walked off. It was juvenile and shitty." He hugs me tighter. "I love you so damn much it hurts," he whispers against my crown. "And when you said you couldn't do this, it was a knife to the heart." Warm lips kiss my hair. "Every time we kissed, every time we touched, I felt loved. But I don't have the greatest track record with intuition."

I inch back and look up to meet his eyes. Swallowing, I dig deep and drag my bravery to the surface. "I do love you."

His entire frame melts and molds to mine. He lifts a hand and brushes away stray locks stuck to my cheek. "Thank god." And then he crushes my lips with his.

CHAPTER 38
BRAYDON

Every minute of our free time over the long weekend was spent in the apartment after Alessandra confessed her feelings. Movies and takeout and hours on the couch in pajamas. I'd never had a better weekend with her.

When she had to work, Anderson and I hiked the lakeside trails. We cooked dinner and he laughed at my inability to cut vegetables with any type of skill. We talked work and favorite places we visited as well as bucket-list trips. There wasn't much Anderson hadn't seen, but it'd be nice to travel with him and Alessandra.

"Why can't you stay?" Alessandra sticks out her bottom lip as she drapes her arms over my shoulders and hauls me in for a kiss.

"Believe me, I don't want to go, firecracker." I fist her hips and drag her body flush with mine. "Maybe I need to talk with Dad about working remotely."

"Mmm. I like this idea."

I love that she likes the idea.

The office I occupy in Washington's Hidden Gems is more of a catchall than a necessity. Not as if I own the magazine and have meetings with shareholders. The meetings I attend are more brainstorming sessions on where to go next—all of which can be done via conference call or video chat. The only people to go in my office are me when I need a space to write and Dad when he wants to talk with me about a story or plan a get-together.

My best writing is done outside the cramped office. If I ask Dad to let me work remotely, he will grant me the privilege. If it will bring me happiness, his answer will be a swift yes.

Years back, we talked at length about the future of the magazine and my position in the company. From the start, Dad wanted the magazine to stay in the family. To never sell to a bigger name, regardless of the financial temptation. Upon retirement, his original plan was to pass the reins to me, to make me CEO. I declined. Honored as I am that he holds me in such high esteem, I'd rather explore and write stories than remain rooted in an office all day, staring at financial and sales goals.

Shawn is the better candidate to pass the company on to when the time comes. He has the more analytical mind. Loves numbers and marketing and people-pleasing. He is goal oriented and ambitious and eager to make our parents happy.

Once I hit the road, I will call Dad. Ask to have dinner tonight with the family. Toss out the idea of working remotely as we sit around the table and share a meal. Dad may not be keen on the idea, but he knows cramped quarters, clunky desks, and fluorescent bulbs make me twitchy. He knows my love for the wilderness, the sun heating my skin, the crisp air in my lungs.

The idea may not thrill him, but he will agree to it.

I kiss her forehead, the tip of her nose, her lips. "Call you tonight." My lips find hers again and I moan as she deepens the kiss. "Love you, firecracker."

She presses her forehead to mine. "Love you, Care Bear."

Heat radiates from the center of my chest and warms me toe to top. *I love those words on her lips.* May have taken a slap of reality for her to confess, but knowing they didn't come easily makes them that much sweeter.

Reluctantly, I release her hips and step back. Open the car door and slip behind the wheel. Crank the engine and blast the air conditioning. Throw the car in reverse and wave as I back away.

This weekend may have ended much differently had she not caught me before I got to my car Friday night.

In twenty seconds, both our lives would have changed. Me driving away angrily while she cried over holding back how she felt. I would have been devastated. Fat, furious tears blurring my vision as I left her behind. Destroyed in a matter of minutes as I swore off love and women for good.

But she did catch me. She did stop me and say the words I had silently begged to hear.

And now, everything is different. Better. Whole.

Alessandra loves me, and I can't wait to see where we go from here.

CHAPTER 39

ALESSANDRA

The numbers on the page blur as my eyes cross.

My elbows thump on the desk, a wince stretching my lips as I drop my head in my hands. Though summer sales are better than any previous year, I hate how much the shop missed out on because imbeciles with a grudge clogged the café. Horrendous reviews aside—which I already contacted Google and Facebook about—I choose to see the positive in this whole fiasco.

Good always outshine the bad.

Ding. Bzzz.

I shuffle the papers on my desk in search of my phone. Tap the screen when I find it. "Holy crap," I mutter, noticing it is after nine.

BRAYDON

Dad voted yes and smiled like a loon.

Laughing, I type out my response and hit send.

> **ALESSANDRA**
> Don't know your dad, but I like him.

The piercing sound of glass shattering jolts me in place. My fingers tighten around my phone as I rise from the desk and tiptoe toward the cracked office door. *Whoosh, whoosh, whoosh.* My pulse thrums violently in my ears. I pause at the door and type out a quick message.

> **ALESSANDRA**
> Heard glass break in the next room.

His response is immediate.

> **BRAYDON**
> Still in the café?

> **ALESSANDRA**
> Yes. In the office.

> **BRAYDON**
> Alone?

> **ALESSANDRA**
> A is upstairs.

> **BRAYDON**
> Stay put.

Shoes crunch glass while muffled voices float through the air. A splintering bang fills the silence and I flinch. Quietly, I close the office door and lock it. Tiptoe back to my desk and duck behind it. Pull up the keypad on my phone and dial 911. Press the speaker to my ear and make myself small on the floor. My phone buzzes in my hand as the call connects.

A raspy feminine voice states, "9-1-1. You're on a recorded line. Please state your emergency."

"Hi. This is Alessandra Everett," I whisper into the line. "I own Java and Teas Me on Main Street. Someone has broken in and I'm locked in the office off the kitchen. I don't think they know I'm here."

Fingers tap a keyboard on the other end of the line. "Are you safe where you are? Is there another exit point?"

"I locked the doorknob. There's no other exit."

The clanging of pans hitting the floors echoes just outside the office. A hint of propane, lighter fluid, and burning papers hits my nose.

Oh god.

"I smell fire," I whisper-shout into the phone.

More furious typing on the other end. "Officers are en route, as well as fire and rescue. Stay where you are."

Stay where I am? If I don't get out of this office, I will burn alive.

Shouts and sharp cracks boom from outside the office. Anderson screams my name before another crack ripples the air. Then another. Loud shrieking sounds a second before water sprays down from the ceiling. I reach on top of the desk, grab my laptop, and hug it to my chest. Thank goodness I back everything to the cloud.

Plugging the other ear with my finger, I tell the operator, "My brother is fighting them, I think."

"Stay in the office, ma'am. Officers just arrived."

Just as the words hit my ears, new voices join the mix and boom over the wail of the fire alarm. "Lake Lavender police. On your knees."

At this, I rise from my spot on the floor and dash for the door. "They're here," I tell the operator. "Thank you." I unlock the door, whip it open, and cough as a cloud of smoke smacks me in the face.

"Stay safe. I'll inform the officers you're coming out."

The call disconnects and I tuck my phone in my pocket. I lift the collar of my shirt and mask my nose and mouth. The earsplitting sound of the fire alarm quiets, but the water continues to shower the entirety of the shop.

"Anderson? Hello?"

"Ms. Everett?" a muffled voice calls out.

"I'm here." I shuffle toward the dining room and the sound of whoever spoke. "My brother is in here too."

A man decked in bright-yellow fire gear comes into view, a shielded mask with a respirator on his face. "We have him outside. Come with me." He offers his hand and I take it.

As we rush from the kitchen, several firefighters bolt past us. With each step forward, the smoke clears. With each step forward, I take in the disaster zone that is my business. Splintered chairs. Shattered glass. Pricey machinery on the floor and in pieces. Slits cut diagonally in the canvases on the wall. Vulgar words spray-painted on the walls and floors. My entire life in a pile of ash and rubble.

The second I step outside, Anderson is there. He hugs the breath from my lungs, mumbling words of reassurance in my ear as he steers me away from the building.

Down the sidewalk and in front of my business neighbor, three young men sit on the curb, hands cuffed behind their backs. Heads down, two stare at the ground with downturned lips. The third narrows his eyes at me and curls his upper lip.

None of them look familiar, not that I know every resident in Lake Lavender. Maybe they are rowdy teens who didn't want to come on vacation with their parents. But why vandalize and burn a store? Seems a bit harsh.

Anderson guides me to the ambulance. "Let's get you looked at."

"I'm fine, A. Damp and cold, but otherwise okay."

"No arguments. You weren't in the thick of the fire, but you still inhaled smoke. At least sit with the oxygen tube for a few minutes."

I open my mouth to decline but slam it shut and nod when I take in the worry lines on his face.

The paramedic drapes a blanket over my shoulders and secures an oxygen tube under my nose. While she checks my vitals, I dig my phone from my pocket and open my messages.

BRAYDON

Called Anderson. He's coming.

BRAYDON

Leaving the city now. Be there ASAP.
Love you.

Damn, I must have scared the hell out of him. Had our roles been reversed, I would be in full panic mode. I have no clue where he lives in the city. The thought of not reaching him in time has my blood pressure spiking.

ALESSANDRA

Got out safely. Thanks for calling A. Love you too.

Just as the message delivers, my phone rings. Braydon's name flashes on the screen.

"Hey," I answer.

"Fuck am I happy to hear your voice."

"Right back atcha."

"Are you okay? What happened?"

I inhale a lungful of the cool oxygen. "I'm good. More

shaken up than anything." The three guys on the sidewalk flash in my mind. "Some guys broke in and destroyed the café. Set something on fire in the kitchen."

"Shit." The rev of his car engine purrs on the other end.

"Please slow down. I'm okay." I shudder at the idea of how much worse it could have been. What if I hadn't been down-stairs? Half the building would have burned to ash before Anderson or I knew what was happening. "Don't need you getting in an accident on the way."

"Could have fucking lost you," he mumbles.

"But you didn't." I pull the tube from my nose. "Drive carefully. No doubt we'll still be right where we are when you arrive."

"I love you, firecracker." His words warm my bones and kick-start my pulse.

"I love you too, Care Bear. See you soon."

CHAPTER 40

BRAYDON

S oot and foam coat every surface of the kitchen. Burned wood, rubber, grease, and an unpleasant chemical smell linger in the air. Much of the kitchen is charred from the fire, but the emergency system kicked on early enough to douse the worst of the flames.

Firefighters deemed it safe for us to sleep on the second floor but suggested we leave windows open for ventilation. After police and rescue left the scene, we climbed the stairs on wobbly legs and crashed face-first onto the bed. When my eyes cracked four hours later, the sheets beside me were cold. Alessandra nowhere in sight.

I'd found her on the couch, knees to her chest, blanket wrapped around her form. Without a word, I'd padded across the room, taken a seat next to her, and pulled her into my arms. We stayed like that until Anderson came out an hour later.

After a healthy dose of coffee, Alessandra called each employee and passed on the news of the break-in and fire. Asked them to come in for their shift, but instead of serving customers, they would help with cleanup. If the equipment was salvageable, they'd make a plan for a makeshift café until the shop was fully operational again.

Now… it is aftermath time.

Broom in hand, I sweep glass shards and fractured pieces of window framing. Anderson separates the dining furniture into sections—intact, damaged, and broken beyond repair. Alessandra picks up and inspects the machinery behind the service counter. Checks the fridges and bakery cases. Pauses every few minutes to hang her head or wipe tears off her cheeks.

An hour and three loaded trash bags into cleanup, several employees and members of their family step through the front door. Their gasps and tears say more than any words.

"Brought goodies from Sweet Spot." August holds up two brown bags.

Anderson points to the undamaged tables. "Those are safe to use."

After a quick break to snack and catch up, we all get to work. August and Sharon go to the kitchen and curse the mess as they step in. Piece by piece, we do our best to restore Java and Teas Me.

As the minutes tick by, more people show up. Fellow shop owners along Main. Friends and family. Residents and tourists. With each person that appears, another set of hands pitches in. Cleans or delivers food and drinks. Just past noon, someone shows up with a grill and coolers full of burgers, hot dogs, and drinks. Another person with buns and condiments and sides.

I have seen nothing like it. Community. People coming together when help is needed more than ever.

We pause to sit on the patio and eat. Burgers and fresh fruit and macaroni salad. Quiet conversations about work and summer vacations and what else we should tackle before we call it a day. As I rise to toss our trash in the garbage can, a police cruiser parks in front of the storefront.

"Be right back," I say, giving Alessandra's shoulder a quick squeeze.

I jog inside, toss our paper plates in the bin, and dash back out. Two officers stand on the opposite side of the patio rail, talking to Alessandra, her fingers twisting in front of her waist.

"Once we rattled off charges and the length of time they'd spend behind bars, the boys cooperated without resistance," the female officer says.

"And?" Alessandra wraps her arms around her middle.

"And a woman—Myrtle Payne—paid the boys to do everything. Spray paint the exterior. The mass of unpaying customers. The online reviews. And the destruction that happened last night."

"What about the outlandish commentary on social media?" I ask.

The second officer meets my gaze. "Now that we have a name and contact information for her, we'll find out if she's the one responsible for the comments." He rests his hand on the butt of his gun. "More than likely, it is her."

"What happens next?" Anderson pipes up.

"Next, we find this Myrtle Payne and bring her in for questioning. With the boys' written confessions and a long list of damages—physically and financially—to your business, I imagine she'll lawyer up and it'll take time before everything is resolved."

Alessandra wilts and I wrap an arm around her shoulders. Let her lean on me for support while she takes this all in.

The female officer pulls out her phone and taps on the screen before turning it to face us. "Does this woman look familiar at all? The boys told us they met her in a chatroom. This is her profile image."

We lean in and look at the image on her phone. Something about her is familiar. I ignore the color of her hair and narrow in on the shape of her face. The lines around her eyes. The plumpness of her cheeks. The dimple in her chin. Beside me, Alessandra shakes her head. I turn my gaze to her as recognition sets in.

"It's been months, and she doesn't look the same in this picture, but isn't that the woman your barista spilled coffee on the day I returned?"

Alessandra inches closer. Scrutinizes the image harder. Then she straightens, her eyes wide as she sees the similarities. She slaps a hand to her mouth.

"That *is* her." She shakes her head in disbelief. "Oh my god." A tear falls down her cheek and she wipes it away. "She did all this over an accident?" She turns her gaze down the sidewalk as more tears fall.

I pull her to my chest and wrap her in my arms. The officer stows her phone and gives a sad smile.

"We'll be in touch, Ms. Everett. In the meantime, let us know if there's anything we can do to help."

With that, the officers back away from the patio, get in the cruiser and drive off.

The crowd of helpers goes back inside and continues with the cleanup. Alessandra and I remain on the patio, wrapped up in each other and silent as we digest the truth behind the damage over the past two-plus months. No words could convey the shock I feel after learning who is behind this. All this anger and violence over a barely noticeable drop of coffee on her shirt. Some people must have nothing better to do with their life besides making others miserable.

But Myrtle Payne won't be causing any more problems. And I hope they throw the book at her for all the hurt and damage she caused.

"So glad you're here." Alessandra fists my shirt and rests her head on my shoulder. "Don't know what I'd do without you."

I kiss her crown and rub a hand up and down her spine. "Nowhere else I'd rather be." I cup the back of her neck as she tips her head back, her blues on my ambers. "Love you, firecracker."

She pushes up on her toes and presses her lips to mine. "Love you too, Care Bear."

EPILOGUE

ALESSANDRA

Six months later

J ust as life develops a layer of normalcy, something new pops up. At least this change is a good thing.

Since the night of the break-in and fire at the café, Braydon and I haven't spent a night apart. His dad had insisted he take two weeks off the help me and the Java and Teas Me family clean up. Get as much of the town's beloved coffee shop in order so we could open our plywood-covered doors and serve the people of Lake Lavender.

To say the town showed up would be an understatement.

Not only did countless townspeople volunteer to clean and rebuild, but they also held fundraisers and delivered lunch and lent a shoulder or an ear. In all my years in this small town, I never experienced this level of love.

The first weekend post-incident, Braydon's family came to town. They slipped on gloves and worked right beside us during the day. In the evening, they took us to dinner. Chatted about anything other than the mayhem and occupied our thoughts with good news. Before they packed up and drove home, Braydon's father pulled me aside.

"*Lovely to finally meet you, Alessandra. Wish it would have been under better circumstances.*" His eyes dart over my shoulder, a gentle smile on his lips and tenderness in his eyes. "*I've never known my son to love someone the way he does you.*" He pulls me in for a hug and sighs. "*Thank you.*" His hold on me tightens then relaxes as he steps back. "*It's wonderful to see him smile, really smile, for the first time in years.*"

Before Edward Harris walked away, he handed me an envelope. Insisted I take it and not open it until they were gone. The moment their taillights vanished on Main Street, I tore open the envelope and gasped. Tucked inside was a note and a check… for ten thousand dollars.

> *Alessandra,*
>
> *This won't cover all the repairs, but it will help get you up and running. Please accept this gift from the Harris family. And don't you dare try to pay us back. We love everything about your shop and the town. We love how happy you make Braydon. Let us know if you need more helping hands.*
>
> *See you soon,*
> *Edward + Gretchen*

I held the check for a week. Left it in the envelope, hidden in the pocket of my warmest jacket—something I wouldn't don for months. The check sat ignored for days as we repainted walls, replaced furniture, and watched as new windows were installed.

Then Edward called Braydon. Mentioned the check not clearing his account. Before the end of the day, I walked into Lake Lavender Savings and Loan to make a deposit. Though he said not to pay him back, I will find a way. Because his money opened the Java and Teas Me doors sooner than anticipated.

Edward Harris says I don't owe him anything. I disagree. Not only did he give new life to my business, he also gave me Braydon.

"That one ready?" Braydon asks as I fold the box flaps.

"Yep." I tap the cardboard. I pick up the black marker and write *Habitat for Humanity—kitchen* on the top.

Sidling up to me, he presses his lips to my temple before lifting the box from the counter. "I'll take it to the car." And then he is out the door.

My eyes scan the empty open cabinets of the kitchen, the bare countertops, the naked walls. Not that the surfaces were crowded to begin with. Most of the dishes and some of the appliances are being donated to charity. A few appliances and all of the art are coming home with us to *our* apartment in Lake Lavender.

For six months, Braydon and I have effortlessly coexisted in the same space. Every other weekend, we drove to his apartment in the city and gathered more of his belongings. By the time we talked about officially moving in together, more than half his clothes had occupied my closet. His favorite brown-and-blue stoneware mug sat on the kitchen counter next to the coffee maker. His juniper-colored throw draped over my cream-colored chunky knit blanket. And his super firm, natural latex pillow replaced the previous pillow of mine he'd used.

Some may say it is too soon for us to move in together. Dating for eight months before making the leap. Though we unofficially lived together six of those eight months, this step sealed the deal. Screamed serious in every possible way.

And I have never been more ready.

The door swings open. Braydon greets me with a smile and the stomp of his boots, a light dusting of snow on his beanie. "One final walk-through before we lock up?"

"I'll start in the kitchen."

After we inspect every empty inch of his apartment in the city, he locks the door and sighs. "I loved living in the hub of Seattle, but I won't miss it."

"No?" I ask as we descend the stairs and I slip on my gloves.

He shakes his head. "This apartment served me well over the years. It was close to work and gave me a place to eat, bathe, and sleep. But it never felt like *home*."

"And now?"

His fingers weave through mine as we walk toward the complex's office to turn in his keys. As we reach the door, he stops and spins me to face him.

"Now I know where I belong and who is home."

"*Who?*"

He cups my cheek and lowers his lips to hover over mine. "You. Wherever you are, that is my home."

I fist his jacket, close the space between us, and press my lips to his. "Love you, Care Bear."

"Love you more, firecracker."

"Good." I rub my gloved hands together. "Now get me inside before I freeze to death."

He yanks the door open, hands over the keys, and says goodbye. And as we drive away, I can't help but wonder what adventure life will take us on next. So long as Braydon is at my side, it will be worth every minute of the ride.

EVERY THOUGHT TAKEN
LAKE LAVENDER SERIES—BOOK THREE

Every Thought Taken is the third and final book in the Lake Lavender series!

As young children, an unshakable friendship brought them together. As teens, they discovered an undeniable love. Then life pulled them in different directions—into darkness and light—and slowly ripped them apart. Years later, he returns home in the hopes of a second chance with his first love and to conquer the demons of his past.

EVERY THOUGHT TAKEN TROPES
💕 Childhood friends to lovers
🏔 Small town Washington
🌼 Grumpy-Sunshine
💜 First love
🕐 Second chance
👀 Mental health awareness
🌙 Secret relationship
🏔 Best friend's brother / Sister's best friend

🚗 One that got away

⏳ Slow burn

Get ready for Every Thought Taken, book three in the Lake Lavender series!

NOTE Every Thought Taken will have trigger warnings for depression, self-harm, bullying, death of a parent (off page), and discussion of attempted rape (act off page). Please take these into consideration before reading.

While you wait, check out Depths Awakened—book one—or start the Bay Area Duet Series with Through the Lens, book one in the Click Duet, a best friends to lovers, second chance romance!

MORE BY PERSEPHONE

Depths Awakened

A small town romance which captivates you from the start. Mags and Geoff are two broken souls who have sworn off love. Vowed to never lose anyone else. But their undeniable attraction brings them together and refuses to let go.

Every Thought Taken

As young children, an unshakable friendship brought them together. As teens, they discovered an undeniable love. Then life pulled them in different directions–into darkness and light–and slowly ripped them apart. Years later, he returns home in the hopes of a second chance with his first love and to conquer the demons of his past.

Distorted Devotion

Free-spirited Sarah lives life to the fullest. When a new love interest enters her life, she starts receiving strange gifts and letters. She doesn't want to relinquish her freedom or new love, but fears the consequences.

Transcendental

A musician in search of his muse and a woman grieving the loss of her husband. Two weeks at an exclusive retreat and their connection rivals all others. Until she leaves early without notice. But he refuses to give up until he finds her again.

The Click Duet

High school sweethearts torn apart. When fate gives them a second chance, one doesn't trust they won't be hurt again. Through the Lens

(Click Duet #1) and Time Exposure (Click Duet #2) is an angsty, second chance, friends to lovers romance with all the feels.

The Artist Duet

A tortured hero with the biggest heart and a charismatic heroine with the patience of a saint. Previous heartache has him fighting his desire to be more than friends with her. But she is everywhere, and he can't help but give in. The Artist Duet is an angsty, friends to lovers slow burn.

Penny

Everything familiar falls apart when her boss announces the sale of the tattoo shop, and that the new owner is on his way. When the bell over the door jingles and a familiar face appears, confusion and old feelings surface. He isn't just her brother's best friend and the guy she crushed on for most of her life… he is also her new boss.

Broken Sky

Their eyes meet across the bar, but she looks away first. Does her best to give him zero attention. But when he crowds her on the dancefloor, she can't deny the instant chemistry. After one night together, he marks her as his. Unfortunately, another woman thinks he belongs to her.

Ink Veins

Persephone Autumn's debut poetry collection, Ink Veins, explores topics of depression, love, and self-discovery with a raw, unfiltered voice.

THANK YOU

Thank you so much for reading **One Night Forsaken**, book two in the **Lake Lavender Series**. If you wouldn't mind taking a moment to leave a review on the retailer site where you made your purchase, Goodreads and/or BookBub, it would mean the world to me.

Reviews help other readers find and enjoy the book as well.

Much love,
    Persephone

PLAYLIST

Here are some of the songs from the **One Night Forsaken** playlist. You can find and listen to the entire playlist on Spotify!

Still Don't Know My Name | Labrinth
Losin Control | Russ
Doing It Wrong | Drake
Living U | 6LACK
The Loudest Silence | Maurice Moore
Stay With Me | Angus & Julia Stone

CONNECT WITH PERSEPHONE

Connect with Persephone
www.persephoneautumn.com

Subscribe to Persephone's newsletter
www.persephoneautumn.com/newsletter

Join Persephone's reader's group
Persephone's Playground

Follow Persephone online

instagram.com/persephoneautumn

facebook.com/persephoneautumnwrites

tiktok.com/@persephoneautumn

bookbub.com/authors/persephone-autumn

goodreads.com/persephoneautumn

amazon.com/author/persephoneautumn

pinterest.com/persephoneautumn

ACKNOWLEDGMENTS

To my family... Thank you for your endless support and cheering me on through this author journey!

Ellie and Rosa at My Brother's Editor! Your expertise is invaluable. Thank you for making my manuscript better than it was before I sent it to you. Just when I think I have things figured out, you prove me wrong 😊 Fuck commas!

Abi of Pink Elephant Designs! I am so fucking in love with all the covers you made for this series! You took my fumbled ideas and made something brilliant and stunning. Thank you so much for your talent and expertise 🤭

Bloggers!! I would be nowhere without you! Thank you for reading my words, creating magical edits and videos, and promoting my books all over the internet. YOU ROCK!!

ARC readers! If this is the first book of mine you've read, thank you for taking a chance on me. Those that've read me before, I love you more than words! Thank you for reading my books and supporting me. Your reviews are GOLD! Without you, I wouldn't be where I am. Complete gratitude!

Author peeps... I love you! This business is rough and exhausting, but I love how we lean on and support each other.

To belong to a community where every person wants everyone to thrive and succeed… I love it and you!

Readers are the best humans! Thank you to each and every one of you for reading my words. For choosing one of my books, thank you times a million. If I could hug you all, my tentacle arms would squeeze you tight.

ABOUT THE AUTHOR

USA Today Bestselling Author Persephone Autumn lives in Florida with her wife, crazy dog, and two lover-boy cats. A proud mom with a cuckoo grandpup. An ethnic food enthusiast who has fun discovering ways to vegan-ize her favorite non-vegan foods. If given the opportunity, she would intentionally get lost in nature.

For years, Persephone did some form of writing; mostly journaling or poetry. After pairing her poetry with images and posting them online, she began the journey of writing her first novel.

She mainly writes romance and poetry, but on occasion dips her toes in other works. Look for her non-romance publications under P. Autumn.

Ingram Content Group UK Ltd.
Milton Keynes UK
UKHW011826160323
418676UK00004B/289